W9-BIM-825

The Best of Sports Illustrated: 1

The Best of Sports Illustrated: 1

by The Editors of Sports Illustrated

A Sports Illustrated Book
Little, Brown and Company — Boston – Toronto

COPYRIGHT © 1971, 1972, 1973 BY TIME INC.

ALL RIGHTS RESERVED. NO PART OF THIS BOOK MAY BE REPRODUCED IN ANY FORM OR BY ANY ELECTRONIC OR MECHANICAL MEANS INCLUDING INFORMATION STORAGE AND RETRIEVAL SYSTEMS WITHOUT PERMISSION IN WRITING, FROM THE PUBLISHER, EXCEPT BY A REVIEWER WHO MAY QUOTE BRIEF PASSAGES IN A REVIEW.

FIRST EDITION

T04/73

The following material is reprinted from *Sports Illustrated* with the kind permission of the authors, agents and publishers acknowledged:
"The Original Little Old Lady in Tennis Shoes" by Melvin Maddocks.
"Pop, Pop, Hit Those People" by Don DeLillo. An excerpt from the book *End Zone* (Houghton Mifflin Company). Copyright © 1972 by Don DeLillo.
"Gospel of False Prophets" by Bil Gilbert.
"Concentrate on the Chrysanthemums" and "There Have Been Shootings in the Night" by Kenny Moore.
"In a World of Windmills" by Pat Jordan. Copyright © 1972 by Pat Jordan. Reprinted by permission of The Sterling Lord Agency, Inc.

"Running Scarred" by Tex Maule. An excerpt from the book *Running Scarred* (Saturday Review Press). Copyright © 1972 by Hamilton B. Maule.

Sports Illustrated Books
are published by
Little, Brown and Company
in association with
Sports Illustrated Magazine

Library of Congress Cataloging in Publication Data
Main entry under title:

The Best of Sports illustrated.

"A Sports illustrated book."
1. Sports stories. I. Sports illustrated (Chicago)
GV191.B42   796'.08   72-13768
ISBN 0-316-80758-3

Published simultaneously in Canada by Little, Brown & Company (Canada) Limited

PRINTED IN THE UNITED STATES OF AMERICA

PREFACE

Every year *Sports Illustrated* prints approximately 600 stories and 2,000 illustrations. Some of the very best of those published in 1972 are in this book. There are a few articles written under the deadlines and imperatives of immediate news, others that were composed at a more leisurely pace. The same is true of the illustrations, for the magazine is a combination of features, usually topical, and news reports which are as distinguished, authoritative and colorful as they can be made.

Sports *Illustrated* goes well beyond the confines of the typical sports page or TV commentary. It links sports to society, and tells us about ourselves through the things we are fondest of doing or watching. Americans by the millions have recognized this, which is why SI has been called the biggest magazine publishing success since the Second World War.

ACKNOWLEDGMENTS

Editorial supervision and coordination by Ken Rudeen, Senior Editor of *Sports Illustrated*.

Special thanks are due to Andre Laguerre, managing editor, Ray Cave, Pat Ryan, Nancy Kirkland, George Bloodgood and Sharon Savage for their assistance in the publication of this book.

CONTENTS

ILLUSTRATIONS

UP, UP, UP AND AWAY

John Underwood

RICH CLARKSON

What one small foot can do to a great big pro football team is dramatized in the following account of the sport's longest game. It all came down to which team had the best foreign-born, soccer-style placekicker.

Somehow it would — must, surely, on Christmas Day — come to this. That the longest game in the history of American professional football would be decided by the smallest player on the field. That he would not be American-born at all, but a Cypriot, with an accent. That he would be a painter of neckties for profit, and uninhibited in his high good humor. A teller of outrageous jokes on himself, agreeable and gregarious. And cuddly. The people of Kansas City would see him in there in the shadow of his Miami teammates and wonder, what is a Garo Yepremian? Did the Dolphins get him for Christmas? And the answer would be that the Dolphins got him two years ago from Detroit, where he was hiding out in his basement painting ties, ashamed to show his balding head after being cut by the Lions. The Lions considered him a clown. And at 6:24 p.m. CST on Christmas Day the Dolphins gave him to the Kansas City Chiefs. Right between the uprights.

The record will show that 82 minutes and 40 seconds after it began, the American Conference playoff between Miami and Kansas City was decided in Miami's favor, 27–24, on a perfect 37-yard field goal off the left instep of little Garo's size-seven soccer boot. When it happened, Miami Quarterback Bob Griese laughed out loud. He was standing on the sidelines, not watching the ball but the holder, Karl Noonan, and when Noonan raised his hands in triumph, Griese laughed, giddy in the final release of tension and fatigue. The game had gone five quarters-plus to sudden death (or sudden victory, as Pollyanna Curt Gowdy insisted on calling it on the TV), from a slug-colored unseasonably warm Missouri afternoon through nightfall. It had been played both crisply and sloppily, with consummate skill and heartbreaking error. It had been dull and heavy, and then exquisitely exciting. And it went down ultimately to a lightning bolt and a laugh.

At the top, what it would seem to have proved beyond the elevation of the Dolphins to the AFC's best bet for the Super Bowl is that Miami's foreign-born placekicker was better than Kansas City's foreign-born placekicker, Jan Stenerud of Norway. Stenerud missed his chance to win it, Yepremian did not. As a result, Yepremian was at the center of a vortex of hilarity in the Dolphin dressing room, while Stenerud sat alone in his cubicle at the end of the world and said his failure was "unbearable." Yepremian said he felt bad for Jan, "but I feel good for me" because he had been disconsolate when Stenerud made the Pro Bowl and he, Garo Yepremian, the No. 1 scorer in all of pro football, did not.

What the record will not show, however, and what few of the 50,374 in Municipal Stadium appreciated, was another extraordinary contribution Yepremian made to Kansas City's downfall. Some background is in order. Yepremian is 5′ 8″. He weights 170 pounds. Mostly from the kneecap down. When 260-pound blockers come his way, Garo has been known to sprint resolutely in the opposite direction. "I must protect them from my magnificent body," he says, but it is his life he is anxious to protect. It is unheard of for him to make a tackle. The Miami coach, Don Shula, does not really require it. Against Kansas City, Garo remained under no obligation. But with a minute and a half to play in the fourth quarter, he took a swipe at Ed Podolak that made it possible for Curtis Johnson to save the Dolphins. Miami, rallying for the third time, had made the score 24–24 on Griese's five-yard pass to Marv Fleming, and Yepremian kicked off. Podolak, who had an exceptional day (349 yards rushing, receiving and returning kicks), took the ball on his goal line, broke through the first wave of Miami tacklers and was suddenly at midfield and in the clear. Clear in a relative sense. Yepremian was still hanging around. He did not make contact with Podolak, but he did make the attempt and was, briefly, in the way. Having to veer off, even slightly, cost Podolak a vital step or two. From behind and the opposite side, Cornerback Johnson angled in hard, running Podolak out of bounds at the Miami 22. Four plays later, with 35 seconds to go in regulation time, Stenerud pushed his 32-yard field goal attempt to the right — "the worst thing that ever happened to me." Stenerud also missed a 29-yarder in the second quarter and had a 42-yard attempt blocked in the first overtime period.

But to get back to Bob Griese. Although he completed 20 passes for 263 yards (seven for 140 to the incomparable Paul Warfield), and attacked in a skilled, surgical manner the bewildering scaffolds of zone and man-to-man coverage and irregular line splits Kansas City threw at him, what moves grown men like Larry Csonka and Shula to rhapsodize about Griese is a near-hidden thing. It is obscured partly because Griese himself does not reveal much of Griese — he is notorious for lingering in the shower till postgame interrogation has petered out — and partly because, in his cool self-confident way, he does not seem to require ego trips every game day to enjoy being a quarterback. The fact is that he would rather *not* throw 45 passes a game, as he did in 1969 the last time Miami played — and lost to — Kansas City. His best games this year, as he led the conference in passing, were those in which he threw fewer than 20 times. "He enjoys working within the system, being able to take advantage of an offense," says Shula. "He gets a kick out of calling the right play."

But what made Griese extra special this day was what had come before it, and what he had overcome. For four weeks he has been bothered by a very sore left shoulder, damaged against the Bears. For public consumption, he minimized the damage, and still does. Unable to lead properly when he threw and unable to follow through with his customary snap, his passing suffered. He threw behind receivers, he threw interceptions. Miami lost to New England and Baltimore. Even in a winning effort against Green Bay in the last regular-season game, Griese was not altogether right. The week of that game a friend unthinkingly clapped his shoulder and Griese recoiled in pain. But no one outside the Dolphin circle knew how much the injury was affecting him.

Griese's first pass against the Chiefs was underthrown. He had an indifferent first quarter. But then it began to come. Down 10–0, he found Warfield, in his inimitable fashion, out there bewildering the Chiefs' Emmitt Thomas. By the third quarter Griese was as sharp as ever. On the drive to tie the score at 17–17 he hit on four straight passes. To tie it again at 24–24 he hit on six out of seven to four different receivers.

For the most part, Kansas City successfully shut off Miami's big-back ground attack. The front four read well and clogged things up, and the linebacking was brutal. "It's one thing to run against a grizzly bear," said Csonka of Middle Linebacker Willie Lanier, "but when he's a *smart* grizzly bear. . . ." So Griese threw more than he had intended, and his protection held up well. Three times he was hit hard, twice after passes, once on a scrambling run, and though he was slow getting up, it did not take him long to recover. He said the pain "jabbed him a little," but went away quickly. Griese not only threw a greater variety of passes than Lenny Dawson, the veteran Chief quarterback, he was also more effective because he was getting the ball to his favorite receiver, Warfield, whereas Dawson, inhibited by a swarming, deep-containing Miami zone, could not get to *his* favorite, Otis Taylor. Taylor caught only three passes for 12 yards.

But in the end the call that Griese used to beat Kansas City was not a pass at all, but a run. A "Csonka special," he said later. "Zonk likes it, and we hadn't used it, and it seemed like the right time." Miami had possession on its 35 in the second overtime. Jim Kiick had just run for five yards. The call was "roll right, trap left." A misdirection play, against the flow. Kiick and Griese flow to the right, Csonka takes a step up, then comes back against the grain. Doug Crusan cleared out the defensive end, and Csonka followed Tackle Norm Evans and Guard Larry Little into the hole. "I got hold of Larry's pants," said Csonka. "He's faster than I am, and I had to hold on to keep up."

Csonka was to the Kansas City 36 before Safety Jim Kearney dragged him down. Griese now worked the ball carefully down to the 30 and into the middle of the field, and Shula ushered in Yepremian and Noonan. "You gave me beautiful position," Garo told Griese afterward. "Perfect. I knew if it was less than 50 yards I would make it." And, of course, he did.

"I knew we would win because last night I was very good at cards," Yepremian said. "I say, 'When I win at cards, we win.' " No team should be considered complete without a Garo Yepremian.

"And now," said the littlest Dolphin of them all, "I am hoping Baltimore will win, so we can play them again and show them some sunshine."

The next day, in the dreary mud and rain of Cleveland, Yepremian's sunshine dream came true, for the Colts simply smothered the Browns 20–3.

Reviewing the Dolphins' astonishing progress before their game, Shula had said, "This team, hard as it has worked, deserves to go farther than the Chiefs." Now, to go farther, the Dolphins do not have to go far — in fact, around the corner to the Orange Bowl to meet an opponent they know like a neighbor, one they love to hate.

The Colts won convincingly, John Unitas consuming time and sapping confidence with his probing passes (13 for 21 and 143 yards) and loosing Running Backs Don Nottingham, who was in for injured Norm Bulaich, and Tom Matte to punish Cleveland with body blows.

The Baltimore defense — those friendly undertakers Bubba Smith, Mike Curtis, Ted Hendricks, *et al.* — intercepted three passes, blocked two field goals, dropped Quarterback Bill Nelsen four times and generally made a dark day in Cleveland that much darker for the Browns. By this time the Dolphins were home in Miami, watching on TV, and Unitas gave them a refresher course on what he is all about. On the second Colt possession, following the first of Bubba's blocked field goals, Unitas took his team 93 yards in 17 plays. The drive ate up eight minutes before Nottingham, who gained 92 yards in 23 carries overall, plowed across from the one.

After the first of two Rick Volk interceptions, Nottingham darted seven yards for the second Baltimore touchdown, and two Jim O'Brien field goals wound up the scoring for the Colts.

Curtis had said before the game, "We're just pure team. When it's all over, and if we played well, you're not able to pick out any one man and say he's responsible."

Yepremian aside for the moment, the same could be said for the Dolphins, and on Sunday two pure teams ought to produce pure mayhem. In the past two years they've played four times, and each has won twice. Heck, the game won't be just for the AFC title, it's for the championship of the block.

6

AN UGLY AFFAIR IN MINNEAPOLIS

William F. Reed

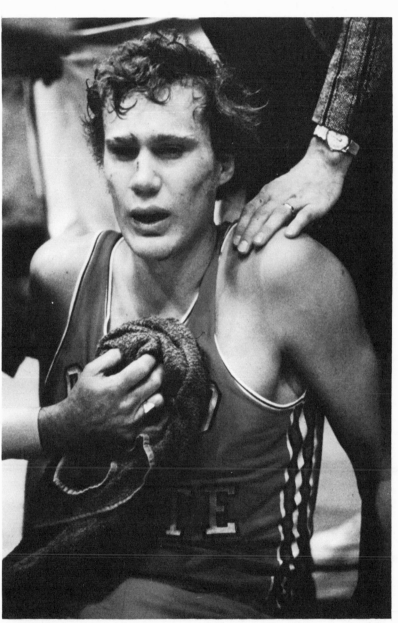

HEINZ KLUETMEIER

Few SI stories have been greeted by votes of approval
so firm or protests so strident as this report on a Big 10
encounter that began as a basketball game
and in the end resembled a mass mugging.

He had been wheeled out of Minnesota's Williams Arena on a long stretcher, bleeding and numb. At the university hospital he had spent an hour in the emergency room, where they patched him up as well as possible, then admitted him for the night. Now, on the day after the riot, only hours after he had become the victim of what the governor of Ohio called a "public mugging," Luke Witte was a mess. His right eye was completely covered with a white patch. His left ear was swollen and colored purple. An angry red scab was on his left cheek. His lower lip was swollen and a large, flesh-colored Band-Aid covered the stitched-up gash on his chin. When he got on the plane that was to take him away from Minneapolis, a stewardess looked at him, smiled a stewardess' smile and asked, "Oh, did something happen to you?"

"Yeah," said Witte, managing an answering smile from under his bandages, scabs and stitches, "I had an accident."

Accident, indeed. What happened to Witte last week and others on Ohio State's basketball team can only be described as assault and battery. The attackers were the players and fans of the University of Minnesota, an emotional lot who apparently would not stomach the idea of losing to the Buckeyes in their Big Ten showdown. So, with 36 seconds left and Ohio State holding a 50–44 lead, they rioted. For a scary, improbable interval of one minute and 35 seconds, they came swinging and kicking at the Buckeyes from all sides of the floor. Witte, Ohio State's talented seven-foot blond center, took his most serious blows when he was on the floor, writhing in pain and completely defenseless. It was an ugly, cowardly display of violence, and, when it was over, when the police and officials had finally restored order, the fans had the audacity to boo Witte as he was helped, bleeding and semiconscious, from the floor.

The final 36 seconds were not played, for fear that the Gophers and their fans would rage out of control. Later, when Paul Giel, Minnesota's new athletic director, visited the Ohio State locker room, he found Fred Taylor, the Buckeye's coach, pale and quivering with rage and indignation.

"I knew it would be emotional," said Giel, apologetically, "but I had no idea it would be like this."

"It was bush," answered Taylor. "I've never seen anything like it. But what do you expect from a bush outfit?"

Specifically, Taylor was referring to young Bill Musselman, Minnesota's new coach, and the basketball program he brought with him from — of all places — Ohio. At Ashland College, Musselman built a reputation for showmanship, stingy defense and winning records. It was a reputation that was not always admired by a professor of philosophy who followed his teams there, Dr.

Wayne W. Witte, father of Luke. Asked to comment on the brawl, the elder Witte said, "I'm not surprised. Musselman's intent seems to be to win at any cost. His players are brutalized and animalized to achieve that goal."

Musselman inherited a sagging program at Minnesota this season. The Gophers had not won a Big Ten title outright since 1919 (they shared one in 1937) and student interest was low. He was the fifth Minnesota coach in five years. Nevertheless, when the selection committee asked him how long it would take to turn Minnesota into a winner, Musselman said, "We'll win right off. I don't believe in rebuilding years."

He does believe in big, strong teams. Soon after he arrived in Minneapolis, Musselman picked up two junior college transfers — Ron Behagen (6' 9") and Bob Nix (6' 3"). Together with another JC transfer, Clyde Turner (6' 8") and Jim Brewer (6' 8"), Corky Taylor (6' 9") and Keith Young (6' 5"), already at Minnesota, they instantly comprised the most intimidating team in the conference. All except Nix were blacks who had learned the game on city playgrounds. The only question was how they would get along with Musselman, known always as a strict disciplinarian. "Discipline is the most important thing in life," says Musselman.

Next to winning, of course. To help achieve what Musselman considered a winning environment, inspirational slogans were painted by an assistant coach on the walls of Minnesota's locker room in maroon and gold. Over the door to the players' shower is this message, the pith of the Musselman philosophy: "Defeat is worse than death because you have to live with defeat."

The fans loved the team, they loved Musselman and they especially loved the Gophers' fancy pregame Globetrotters' warmup routines. By January, when the Big Ten part of the schedule opened, the team was ready. Minnesota knocked off four straight foes, while Ohio State had three conference wins heading into last week's showdown.

The tension and emotion began to build early. When the Buckeyes came on the floor, they were booed. Then came the Gophers with their Barnum & Bailey act. While their ball handling, passing and dribbling tricks — all done to the loud, steady beat of heavy rock music played over the P.A. system — are entertaining, they also are designed to hype up the team and the crowd. Musselman says, "It motivates my players."

In retrospect, that seems an understatement. By the end of the warmups, and long before the start of the game, the Gophers and the 17,775 fans were motivated to the point of frenzy. Later, after Musselman's "disciplined" team had come unglued, Ohio State Athletic Director J. Edward Weaver pointed to the warmups as the underlying cause of the riot.

As a whole, the game was rough and nerve-racking, but also cleanly played and well-officiated. The only incident of any sort before the slaughter came when the teams were going to their dressing rooms at halftime. As Nix passed in front of Witte, his left arm raised in a clenched-fist salute, the Buckeye center tried to shove the fist out of his way with an elbow and in the attempt clipped Nix lightly on the jaw. Later, Musselman claimed that was the incident that incited his players. "Our kids were really upset at halftime," he said.

With 11:41 remaining in the final period, Minnesota took a 32–30 lead on a jump shot by Taylor, replacing Behagen who had fouled out two minutes earlier. But then Ohio State scored 10 straight points to go in front 40–32. Try as they might, the Gophers could never get any closer than five points. As defeat became more and more apparent, the crowd began to turn ugly. At one point, the officials stopped the game because of various debris — peanut sacks, peanuts, pennies, Coke cups — that was splattering the floor. When it was announced that any more throwing would result in a technical foul against Minnesota, there were boos — and more debris. Still, the players seemed under control.

Then it happened. With the Buckeyes ahead 50–44, Witte was driving in for what promised to be an easy layup. Instead, Minnesota's Turner cut in front of Witte and clobbered him. Almost instantaneously Taylor got Witte with a sweeping overhand right hook on the ear. The crowd cheered, then booed when it was Turner who was called for a flagrant foul and ejected from the game. As Witte rolled over and slowly got up on all fours, Taylor walked up and extended his right hand in what seemed to be a gentlemanly gesture. But when Witte was almost to his feet, Taylor abruptly pulled him forward and drove his right knee into Witte's groin. The big center crashed back to the floor. Then the arena erupted in a swirl of flying fists. Later Taylor claimed, through Musselman, that Witte triggered the incident by spitting at him. But an inspection of slow-motion films does not reveal the spitting.

"I wouldn't have done it in the first place," said Witte. "And even if I wanted to, I couldn't have because I was down too low."

When Ohio State Guard Dave Merchant moved in on a retreating Taylor, Jim Brewer hit Merchant with a combination of punches and then, along with Turner, chased him down the sideline. Meanwhile, Behagen rushed from his seat on the bench to where Witte was lying helpless and viciously stomped the Ohio State player's neck and face.

Fred Taylor pulled off Behagen who, according to Taylor, screamed, "Let me go, man, let me go." Dave Winfield, who recently joined the Gopher varsity, joined the fray, too, dodging to mid-court where some Minnesota reserves were trying to wrestle Ohio State substitute Mark Wagar to the floor. Winfield leaped on top of Wagar when he was down and hit him five times with his right fist on the face and head. When the stunned Wagar managed to slip away, a fan pushed him to the floor and another caught him on the chin with a hard punch from the side.

As the riot increased in tempo, with fans now flooding the playing area, only one cop was anywhere to be seen. By the time others arrived and began pulling people apart, the damage was done. Witte and Wagar lay near each other, so dazed that neither could remember anything when questioned later. "I went blank after I was hit with the knee," said Witte. "The next thing I knew, I was in the emergency room at the hospital." Wagar got up and helped Witte off the court but does not recall doing it.

The next day, as everyone was trying to sort out the facts, Ohio State's Benny Allison, a black sophomore guard, introduced the theory that it had all been mainly a case of Minnesota blacks against Ohio State whites. Allison said: "It was a racial thing. You will remember that Wardell [Jackson] and I were right out there in the middle of it, just like everybody else, but nobody swung on us. They just passed us up and went for the other guys. Sometimes things like that happen."

It was left to Wayne Duke, commissioner of the Big Ten and a spectator at the game, to fix the blame. He stayed in Minneapolis to view films and talk with Musselman, Behagen and Taylor, among others, then two days later announced that Taylor and Behagen would be suspended for the rest of the season.

The penalty in a way was assessed by both Duke and Minnesota. Before his announcement, the commissioner received a 10 p.m. phone call from Giel informing him that the university had decided to suspend the two players indefinitely. The next morning the Minnesota Athletic Senate said the suspension would last at least until Feb. 15, but by that time Duke had determined on his stiffer penalty. He also cleared up a few points. The investigation, he said, turned up "no evidence" of racial overtones. As to the Buckeyes' part in the affair, he was satisfied that only in the Witte-Nix incident "were charges of excessive physical contact against Ohio State's players at all justified." He said, too, that "the game was under the control of the officials until the final 36 seconds." His interview with Corky Taylor, Duke said, "did not substantiate the charge of spitting" — Taylor amended earlier remarks to say that he *thought* Witte was going to spit at him — and Duke concluded that the riot was "precipitated" by Taylor's "unsportsmanlike act."

But Duke also left at least two questions hanging. To what extent did Musselman and his program contribute to an atmosphere conducive to violence? And why wasn't Winfield also suspended? Many people, particularly Ohioans, felt that the penalties imposed were not commensurate with the seriousness of acts that Duke himself termed "unprecedented" and "unacceptable in our society." In what was easily his most thought-provoking comment of the day, Duke said, "As you look back at it, isn't it terrible to say 'we were fortunate'?"

Fights always have been a deplorable part of college basketball, a game that thrives on emotion and contact. Lately, though, the brawls have developed in number and intensity to the point where thoughtful basketball people are concerned about the sport's direction. Millions saw the recent donnybrook between South Carolina and Marquette on TV. That was sobering enough, but

Ohio State–Minnesota was different — and far worse. Instead of a fight erupting from blows struck in the heat of competition, this was a cold, brutal attack, governed by the law of the jungle. It could be considered the inevitable result of the malaise that afflicts the sport these days, a stunning example of responsibility abdicated by a coach, the players he recruited and taught and the fans who followed them. Musselman made no attempt to stop the fight and showed no remorse afterwards. As Fred Taylor said, "There's more at stake here than basketball games."

Taylor and his team moved on to Ann Arbor for a game with Michigan at the end of last week. Playing without Witte or Wagar, the Buckeyes were beaten by the Wolverines 88–78 for their first league loss in five games. (On the same day, Minnesota, minus Behagen and Taylor, to whom the Gophers dedicated the game, won 61–50 over Iowa and thus tied Michigan for the Big Ten lead with a 5-1 record.) Ohio State was called for 32 fouls to Michigan's 18 and afterward Taylor said, "What happened at Minnesota had an indirect effect on what happened here. . . . The officials were afraid that the crowd would come out of the stands again."

By week's end, Luke Witte's face was beginning to heal. "I still have some headaches," he said, "but I am feeling better all the time." He was lucky, maybe, but the sport he wants to play again was not looking so good.

ALL-AMERICA, ALL THE WAY

Frank Deford

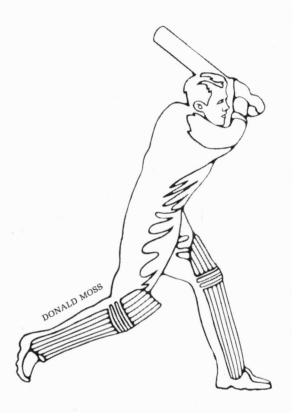

DONALD MOSS

As near a saint as an athlete could be when he was Army's all-everything, he is Major Pete Dawkins now, and Frank Deford finds him eloquently at war both with extremist critics of the military and some troglodytes within.

He was in New York to attend a board meeting of the YMCA, and he was standing there, of all perfect places, under the Biltmore clock. There have been so many rowdy, bumptious years of change since he was an All-America, boy and halfback, but he was instantly recognizable. He does not look older; and, of course, the way things are in his line of work, his hair is not that much longer these days.

There is real comfort to be had waking up one fine, polluted, polarized morning and discovering that there still is a Biltmore clock and a YMCA and a Pete Dawkins. These things actually have survived. Perhaps each morning one last hero should be assigned to stand under the Biltmore clock so we can hear the ticks from the good old times, when peace and prosperity were both lit up at this end of the tunnel and the only shaggy-haired perverts were the four who were making noise in a Liverpool cellar.

Used to triggering such reveries, Dawkins suddenly dropped his smile and spoke almost plaintively. "Do me one thing," he said. "Just one thing. Don't treat me like just another piece of nostalgia. You know, I don't live in the '50s anymore, either."

The trouble with Pete Dawkins, All-America, is that despite his protests he is locked into time. In a professional era when great athletes are ongoing household names from puberty to pension, Dawkins' career seems to have lasted only somewhat longer than a half-time show and hardly as long as a twi-night doubleheader. So much of him was jammed into that glorious Eisenhower autumn of '58 that, like Conway Twitty, much of him must always remain there.

The other youthful stars of that year — Aaron, Unitas, Palmer, Shoe-maker, Robertson and West — still ride shotgun across the sports pages. And those athletic eminences of '58 who have left the scene — Russell and Mantle, for instance — did not retire before spending the prescribed number of seasons as "aging veterans." Of course, they all took home a lot of money. Dawkins' trophy was his calendar year.

He was the very essence of that time, a period that prized humility, respect and clean-cutness from a silent generation. By now we have forgotten that those well-rounded, level-headed scholar-jocks who succeeded Dawkins — men such as Jerry Lucas, Terry Baker and Bill Bradley — were pale imitations of the original Joe Renaissance. There was nothing Dawkins was not, that dreamy senior year of his.

He was appointed First Captain of the Corps and elected class president.

He was a Star Man, 10th in a class of 499, and accepted as a Rhodes scholar. He was captain of the football team, everyone's All-America, the nation's leading scorer and winner of the Heisman and Maxwell trophies.

It was written, first facetiously but gradually at face value, that it was unfortunate that Cadet Dawkins and General MacArthur could not have matriculated at the same time at the Academy since MacArthur would have made such a serviceable adjutant for Dawkins. There were so many New Testament metaphors applied to the young man that, it was reported, he grew sensitive at the sacrilege. After all, he was a former acolyte, a member of the cadet choir, and he collected the offering.

Dawkins could play six musical instruments, he was the highest-scoring collegiate hockey defenseman in the East, he had constructed his own hi-fi (as he had previously built his own Soapbox Derby vehicles) and he went about industriously lifting rocks when he had no quick access to his body-building weights. He was modest, had a sense of humor and made out all right with the honeys, too. Moreover, breathless journalists informed America that Dawkins was actually given to such State U. vernacular as "no sweat."

All accounts of Dawkins began by reporting how he had "conquered polio." He had, in fact, suffered a spot of the disease as a child, which had left him with a slight curvature of the spine, but the implication usually was that he had burst forth from a sideline iron lung midway through the Navy game.

In the Academy yearbook, his classmates wrote a truly incredible encomium, a reverent tribute that began simply: "We have stood in awe of this man." And ended: "We were not completely sagacious, but we knew a great leader, a great friend, a great man." It was left for Colonel Red Blaik, the coach, to say aloud what everyone else was whispering, that Cadet Dawkins was destined to be chief of staff of the United States Army.

And, oh yes, perhaps more than all these things, this too: at that time, 1958, professional soldiers were not popularly dismissed as blackguards. Soldiers were even generally considered to be quite respectable people.

Major Pete Dawkins, at home in faded blue jeans and boots, listening to the music of his friend Kris Kristofferson: "When I was studying at Princeton [at the Woodrow Wilson School, 1968-70], that was the most heated time of the war. People were very suspicious of me, of anyone military, though after a while some people would condescend to say: 'You know, you're really not like those soldiers.' That was supposed to be a big compliment. I'd reply: 'But don't you see, I am a soldier? I am what I am.' Nobody wanted to hear that. Nobody wanted to believe that it was their stereotype that was wrong. I didn't fit the popular stereotype, therefore I was out of place.

"Then one day during that same period at Princeton, somebody came up to me and said: 'You know, looking back, I think of you as the Bob Dylan of the '50s.' That's the greatest compliment I ever received."

Last January Dawkins' orders to return to Vietnam were pulled, and he was assigned to SAMVA, the office of the Special Assistant for the Modern Volunteer Army. SAMVA appears to be both a think tank and a lobby. On the one hand, it must make the new Army attractive for volunteers. On the other, it must convince the old Army (which is still the only Army) that modernization is not necessarily a sign of frailty, that the Republic will be safe even if doors are put on soldiers' toilet stalls.

Dawkins, if the truth be known, is not overly optimistic, but he tries. As soon as he settled himself at SAMVA, he wrote a couple of memos. The subject was hair, that is to say, the length of hair. "I simply maintained that we could not win over the hair issue," Dawkins says. As a reward for his interest he was taken along to a high-level briefing on the subject that General Westmoreland was conducting. Before Dawkins knew it, Westy had him up before the gathering posing as the military hair model. As Colonel Blaik predicted, the kid was really going places.

In the upper echelons of the Pentagon, some of the old soldiers still wax rhapsodic about the halcyon war years when any man in Army issue with a dandy regulation whiffle cut would be set upon by all available women, beside themselves at the very sight. It came as some surprise to a number of officers that a) this was no longer the case, and b) it had nothing to do with Communism.

Symbolically, nothing speaks more directly of declining military prestige than hair. At the time when Pete Dawkins entered the Army, the whole nation aped the military haircut, just as the whole nation — and not just the American Legion and defense contractors — cared deeply about the outcome of the Army-Navy football game. Now a military haircut is a source of shame. The PXs do a thriving wig business, and many of the most dedicated career men try to assuage their social embarrassment by letting their hair sprout some on top. Unfortunately, that only makes the wearer appear as if he had submitted to one of those two-bit Depression bowl cuts. Many of the most outstanding officers in the Pentagon look like members of *Our Gang*.

"You know," Dawkins began tentatively at another of the hair hearings, "it's not just the new recruits who want long hair like everyone else. It's my wife, for instance, and a lot of the wives of my friends, of good officers, who want to know why we can't have longer hair."

A bull general rose, horrified at this clear endorsement of henpeckery. "By God," he thundered, "do you mean, Major, that now the Army should be run by what a bunch of women want?"

Dawkins bowed his head, believing he had been defeated, but happily another general took a stand in his defense. "You know," he said, "the Army's in a lot of trouble these days, but it's nothing like the mess we could be in if all the women turn against us."

So the battle for longer hair turned; but how much longer? The debate raged. This long and that long, how long for hygiene, and how long for discipline; so long for white people, and so long for black people, and what about sideburns vis-à-vis ears, which is all the more complicated because hardly anyone is familiar with precise ear terminology except for lobes. (At West Point it is decreed that for Duty, Honor, Country sideburns must terminate at the top of the tragus, which sounds like something you should not be talking about in polite company.)

At the Pentagon the hair dilemma remained unresolved until Major Dawkins devised a strategy. His maneuver may not go down in tactics textbooks along with Jackson's Valley Campaign, but it was a bold stroke just the same. Major Dawkins suggested, "Let's not say how long the hair has to be. Let's just take pictures showing how long." Stunningly, the Dawkins Arrangement was accepted, giving him the honor of fathering the only visual — rather than verbal — regulation in the history of the U.S. Army.

"We must make changes in the Army, if only because everything is changing," Dawkins says. "Too many people in the Army still think that if we can just hold the line, be the last bastion of traditional America, that the country will come to its senses, get its hair cut and form up again around the Army." He shook his head at this hypothesis.

"You know, to much of the military, Vince Lombardi remains the greatest contemporary civilian hero. I believe that he was so genuine that his teams experienced a contagion for winning that overrode the exceptional demands that he placed on players. But I also believe that his methods — arbitrary and imposed — have become anachronistic. But Army people don't want to believe that. It is like, if you were a theologian, trying to apply things to the present that Reinhold Niebuhr said years ago. Possibly, Niebuhr and Lombardi would have had new approaches for this time. It is wrong to assume that their attitudes were ever intended to be pertinent today. Understand, I am not critical of the way Lombardi operated: I am critical of those who continue to hold this model reverently. I know Lombardi's methods will not succeed in the Army today, and I suspect they would have even less of a chance of succeeding in football.

"Kids demand room for expression in sports as much as in anything else. It may sound frivolous, but I don't believe that enough significance has been attached to the popularity of Frisbee. Think of it: it's the ultimate of its kind, a complete free form. There aren't any rules unless you make them up. The fact that so many people everywhere are devoted to such an unstructured sporting expression says something, I think."

In a poll of the 1971 Army football team to determine the players' sporting idol, Dick Butkus was the overwhelming choice.

Captain Dawkins, in 1966, while he was in Vietnam: "This is the big stadium. This is the varsity."

Pete and Judi Dawkins, and their children, Sean, 7, and Noel, 4, live a half-hour's commute from the Pentagon in one of those developments that has streets named for chic colleges. Their house is on Vassar. The Heisman Trophy is in the living room. Until this past year his parents kept it, but now Dawkins feels enough time has elapsed for the sculpture to become a period piece, so he has taken it on. Sean Dawkins has only one observation about it. "Nice carving," he says. Maybe somewhere a developer is naming streets after Heisman Trophy winners.

Most career servicemen move so regularly that they invariably rent housing. The Dawkinses have bought their home, however, because Judi Dawkins comes from the Washington area, and she and the children will stay there when the major is shipped back to the Far East for a year. "It is not just that Pete has to go, like any other husband off on a long business trip," Mrs. Dawkins said. "It is that he might always be away from us." She means that he might be killed.

Dawkins was first posted to Vietnam in 1965. "We found out in '63 that Pete would have to go two years later," Mrs. Dawkins says, "but that didn't bother me at all, because of course I was perfectly sure that the war would be over by then, by 1965." She shrugs, smiling at the innocence of the time, not the irony.

Though the children are too young to know much, or care, about their father's profession, the Dawkinses have experienced something of the alienation the war has brought to many American families. Dawkins has an older brother Dale, who is an automobile executive; he also has a younger sister Sue, who is a full 10 years his junior, and an even younger brother Mike, now 18.

Mike was only five when Pete had his 1958, and he would toddle about in a sweater with a big, proud Army "A." But as Mike and his sister grew and the war wore on, they more often came to look upon their older brothers not as model successes but as the personification of the military-industrial complex, infiltrating their very family.

"One effect of the tragedy of Vietnam," Dawkins says, "was that the Army was profoundly baffled by the attitudes developing toward it. We didn't understand why we were blamed. The vast majority of soldiers, of lifers, viewed the war with no joy. Just a sense of responsibility.

"Guys picked up and left their families simply because events had occurred and their duty was advanced. Somehow, because of the nation's frustration, the attitudes of these men, our soldiers, were perverted to mean that most of them were opportunistic and self-seeking. Good God, would you want a military that shrank from combat when combat presented itself?"

The 20 men of SAMVA are assigned to the C-Ring of the Pentagon, an area where everyone uses the word "synthesis" profusely. The offices of SAMVA are well lighted; that much can be said for them. Three posters serve as the only decoration. One is an *Easy Rider* photo with Dennis Hopper providing a naughty hand signal. Another, over Dawkins' desk, is by Ben Shahn and carries the message:

YOU HAVE NOT CONVERTED A MAN BECAUSE YOU HAVE SILENCED HIM.

The third poster features a model posing as a t.t.u. soldier — a t.t.u. soldier is a tough, thoughtful, unarmed soldier — which is about the only breed of that cat the public will accept nowadays. Around SAMVA, only "synthesis" is heard more often than "tough, thoughtful, unarmed."

Dawkins, having spent much of his career studying at Oxford and Princeton, teaching at West Point and on policy assignments in Saigon and Washington, is, obviously, very much a living, breathing t.t.u. soldier. He did win an array of impressive medals for his courage in Vietnam, but he does not wear them as a rule, limiting himself to the most austere ornamentation and, of course, his West Point ring. Other officers know Academy graduates as "ring knockers."

The higher up Dawkins moves (and his promotion to lieutenant colonel has been approved), the more scrutiny he will receive. Already, old-line lifers, in from another bivouac, grumble about Dawkins' pantywaist desk tours, and an Iowa Congressman once rose on the floor of the House to protest that the Government was paying for Dawkins' fancy book learning.

Nevertheless, Dawkins is escorted by two totems as he ascends the hierarchy, and one is his football reputation — or, anyway, his overall cadet fame that was founded on the playing fields. In a business that treasures tradition, Dawkins is tradition on the hoof. Moreover, his celebrity gives him a potential outside the military that translates to leverage within. Says Major Josiah Bunting, a close friend who is a novelist and a history professor at West Point: "If ever a time comes when Pete is faced with compromising his principles, he can always say, 'O.K., I'll go be a Senator instead.' Now how can they handle that?"

In fact, most people wonder why he bothers to keep tilling the feudal Army soil. Says Kris Kristofferson, the songwriter, who was also a Rhodes scholar and a combat helicopter pilot: "It used to bewilder me why someone with Pete's intelligence and charisma would stay in the Army. I have such tremendous respect for him. But he sold me. Look at it this way: it's great just to have someone like Pete Dawkins in the military."

Dawkins' biggest edge, however, comes from his contemporaries who have stayed in the service and continue to hold him in awe. Fort Leavenworth, Kansas sits in the middle of the country, and, in the insular manner of most Army posts, in the middle of nowhere as well; the denizens refer to "the outside world." Leavenworth is a large post, and it can be an important one, too, a crucial station for rank-conscious young officers.

A lanky career major, Ranger and Airborne and bowl-cut, drew on his cigarette. "Sure, you find it here at Leavenworth, you find it anywhere in the Army," he said. "There is always a certain amount of resentment about Dawkins — you know, the glory boy. It comes especially from guys like myself who didn't go to the Point. Everybody knows he did only one tour of Vietnam, but that he got special attention from the press. He's on the 5% [early promotion] list, but he hasn't had to get all his tickets punched, like everybody else. But you see, every time this comes up, there's always somebody around who was with Dawkins at the Point or somewhere, and they say, 'Hey listen, he's special, he really is, and the Army would be crazy to make him go through the same garbage as everybody else.' "

The major put out his cigarette on his boot and intently field-stripped it. "You know," he said after a while, "that's a helluva thing when you think about it, when you realize that kind of talk comes from his rivals, so to speak."

Jonathan Swift, in *Gulliver's Travels*: "A soldier is a Yahoo hired to kill in cold blood as many of his own species, who have never offended him, as possibly he can."

Dawkins, stuck in rush-hour traffic near the Pentagon: "The military is never so evil as some would have it, nor so gallant as others. If you do believe that we live in a world where we can abdicate forces, then yes, obviously, the Army is a caricature. But if you read the tea leaves of history, one is obliged to believe that we cannot possibly get by without a competent military force, that we cannot achieve decisions other than in consonance with a military reality."

Defense Attorney Barney Greenwald in Herman Wouk's *The Caine Mutiny*: "See, while I was studying law 'n' old Keefer here was writing his play for the Theatre Guild, and Willie here was on the playing fields of Princeton, all that time these birds we call regulars — these stuffy, stupid Prussians in the Navy and the Army — were manning guns. . . . Of course, we figured in those days, only fools go into armed service. Bad pay, no millionaire future, and you can't call your mind or body your own. Not for sensitive intellectuals . . . [but] a lot of them are sharper boys than any of us, don't kid yourself, best men I've ever seen, you can't be good in the Army or Navy unless you're goddamn good."

Dawkins at 33 is a trim 6′ 2″ with large sloping shoulders. He moves with purpose at all times at what may be described as an organized lope. Tennis is his sport now although he began playing it just two years ago. He took up skiing a while back and was winning slalom races before the snows were gone. If anything, he took longer to master football than any other game. Baseball was his best high school sport. He scored 19 runs in his first cricket game, he made the West Point hockey varsity shortly after he picked up a stick and he earned his Oxford blue in rugby only eight weeks after he first saw a scrum.

In football, though, Dawkins was nothing special in prep school, a weak-passing left-handed plebe quarterback and a fifth-string sophomore halfback.

He was a starter as a junior but merely the other halfback; Bob Anderson was the All-America. It was as if they were saving 1958 for Dawkins. He started off with four touchdowns in the opener, Army never lost, and all along Dawkins drew an inordinate amount of publicity because of the Lonely End formation. Colonel Blaik, nobody's fool when it came to destiny, just upped and quit after 25 years of coaching following that season.

West Point makes it especially easy for Dawkins to haunt Saturday afternoons. There is still a ring dance in the fall at the Academy, a formal, no less, with corsages. The lettermen wear dated little malt-shop zipper jackets with those big fuzzy A's on them — no sweat. Pep rallies are fervent large productions, and football players are treated with deference by their classmates. The Academy chaplain, the Rev. James Ford, thinks it's helpful to hire former football stars as preaching assistants.

"It's important to have a winning attitude," says Colonel William Schuder, the director of athletics who was First Captain of the Corps in 1947, a classmate of Davis and Blanchard. "It's one of the things that encourages a young man to try the Army as a career. You can't have an Army with a losing image."

In support of this widespread notion, bad news has no place at West Point, and, like PDA (public display of affection), simply is not tolerated on the premises. When the superintendent was removed last year to face trial for having concealed war atrocities, the cadets were ordered to go mill under his window as a spontaneous warm tribute. When the football team went 1-9-1 in 1970, the Academy yearbook declared: "It can truthfully be said that bad breaks prevented us from enjoying another successful season." It can also truthfully be said that this is the same rationale which gave us fanciful body counts all these years, too.

The first of Dawkins' classmates to die in Vietnam fell in January 1963, when the present plebes were in the fourth grade. It has been that long that the funeral barrages have been cracking above the Hudson, and almost that long that the Army has wrestled with its soul and the Academy has fought to preserve the middle word — Honor — in the motto it venerates. "It's particularly hard to be an artist as a soldier," Dawkins says, "and if you do have pride, life is trying to be an artist in your job. But being a soldier must always be a derivative value. There is no absolute value in performing the soldier's manifest task: that is, killing. A soldier's life can only draw value from the society that gives it meaning, by preserving those qualities that society believes are worth preserving. The Army must always gain a sense in itself that derives from the public."

When Dawkins first set out to be a soldier in the summer of '55, that sense was easy to behold. A military man, the absolute t.t.u. soldier, sat in the White House, presiding over the nation's massive deterrent. The star-spangled heroisms of Iwo Jima and The Bulge were only a decade past, and the soupy words from the general the civilian had fired had hardly left the top of the Hit Parade: *Old Soldiers Never Die.* It was so easy to want to be a young soldier then.

"You must remember those times," Dawkins says. "I was so ripe for it all. I was obnoxiously headstrong. I'd show them. I was just 17. I had guys in my plebe class who were 21. I never would have taken that crap they threw at us if I had been 21. But everything up at the Point was right for me the summer when I was 17."

No one at the Academy likes to believe that the supply of quality plebes may have diminished in these times less congenial to military evangelism. "We still get those typical red-blooded American kids who have wanted to come here since they were eight or ten years old," says Brigadier General John Jannarone, the academic dean. Obviously, the general does not mean it exactly this way, but implicit in that assertion, one often voiced, is the fact that the U.S. Military Academy is largely inhabited by young men who have not been moved by the events of the 1960s. Certainly, to see Dawkins return to a football game is not so much to watch him come back to West Point but to watch him come back to 1958.

In the huge mess hall the air is feverish with glory be. Nothing seems forced; it is for real. The occasion: Army plays Rutgers tomorrow. That Rutgers has not been a gridiron juggernaut since it won the lidlifter in stocking caps a century ago is of small moment. Army is meeting *somebody* in football.

The band plays rugged martial music, interspersed with lively modern pop. As the meal nears an end, some cadets, as if suddenly infested with demons, climb on their chairs, take off their jackets and wave them like banners, around and around over their heads. This is a tradition.

Other cadets sit backward on their chairs and bounce them about, yelling like banshees, as if they were astride cavalry stock. In one wing of the hall, masters of the art start hurling cakes 30 feet into the air. It is announced that Army has this day defeated Rutgers in 150-pound football, and the hall explodes with cheers that, surely, could not have been rendered any louder or with more pride on the day the word came in that both Gettysburg and Vicksburg were won.

Dawkins, his chest ablaze with ribbons, marches out of the hall, looking self-conscious, as the cadets give him the once-over. "He's still top priority around here," says Bob Antwerp, First Captain of the Corps. There are not many celebrities, never mind heroes, left in the U.S. Army of 1971.

Outside, in the chill winter air, cheerleaders are setting up a rally on a balcony of Washington Hall. The cadets begin to gather below in the courtyard. A cheerleader offers a rocket cheer as something of a benediction, then cries: "We got a super guest star here tonight."

The cheerleaders proceed next with a skit, which ends in a jousting match between the Scarlet Knight of Rutgers ("Hey, youse guys, I'm from Rutgers, New Joisey") and a Black Knight of the Hudson — who is, however, carefully identified as a janitor, not a cadet. This dramatic device is employed so that the Scarlet Knight can win the joust and gain rights to the beautiful Rapunzel without shaming the corps. But, alas, the Scarlet Knight is incapable of climbing up to the buxom lady's lair, which sets the stage for the guest star.

General George C. Marshall: "I have a secret and dangerous mission. Send me a West Point football player."

Cheerleader: "So who could be more worthy of this fair damsel than ST. PETER DAWKINS!?!?!?!"

On cue, from the back of the courtyard, there is a tragus-shattering roar, and the beam from an unmuffled mighty motorcycle begins to lurch about. On the cycle, dressed in a silver lamé helmet, large yellow sunglasses, fatigues and boots, is a cadet obviously playing (broadly, to the crowd) the role of the largely mythical St. Peter Dawkins. The chopper caroms about the crowd, at last finds a path to the stage and zooms toward it.

It screeches to a halt at a ladder, and the Dawkins character leaps toward the balcony stage, with, suddenly, the strains of *Jesus Christ Superstar* swelling to crescendo. On the balcony he removes his helmet and glasses and fatigue jacket, revealing a red, white, and blue, stars-and-stripes Captain America shirt underneath. He also reveals one more thing: that the actor playing the part of St. Peter Dawkins is none other than Major Peter Dawkins.

To the throaty cries of, "Give me some skin," Dawkins smiles brazenly and pulls off his shirt, to stand there, bare-chested in the freezing night. This is another tradition, and Dawkins decides to take it one step further. "O.K., we'll find out the ones who really have spirit," he howls into the microphone. "Everybody, take off your shirts."

In the bitter cold, only a few at first comply. Even for cadets with winning attitudes, there are, after all, some discernible differences between Rutgers and Notre Dame, especially as they relate to creature comforts. But Dawkins keeps after them with the oldtime religion. "The thing that this corps has got to do for the football team is take off their shirts together." In the face of this logic, more in the crowd strip, clutching their biceps and jumping about to stir up circulation.

At last, when only a few misfits remain clothed, Dawkins rears back with a zealot's patter. "One way, one corps, together, always!" he cries with a frightening fervor, ravishing the crowd with frenzy. If, on that balcony, it had not been just Pete Dawkins carrying on but Patton himself firing off his handguns, Sergeant York turkey-gobbling, U.S. Grant taking a Breathalyzer test and Nathan Hale being executed half a dozen times, the audience could not have responded more wildly.

In bedlam, the cadets pile onto each other's frozen shoulders, waving their undershirts and shouting, "Go Rabble!" There is so much shirt waving that, in the spotlight beam, lint particles fall like a heavy snowstorm. The cadets settle down to listen, chattering and slapping at their goose pimples, as Dawkins assures them how special they are and how vital their cheers will be in determining the outcome of the game.

A few days later a visitor made the idle comment to an Army lineman named Jay Kimmitt that the rally had been "quite a scene." Kimmitt, otherwise a most cordial young man, suddenly became testy and on edge. "I wouldn't call it a scene, sir," he snapped. And, well, this much we do know: Army beat hell out of Rutgers.

MacArthur was talking of games and wars when he expressed his homily, adapted from Wellington. It is displayed in a prominent place in the gym, as if to prove that sports have a solid vocational tie-in with battles and are thus deserving of the taxpayers' largesse: "Upon the fields of friendly strife are sown the seeds that, upon other fields, on other days, will bear the fruits of victory."

Dawkins may have been a better soldier in Vietnam for having played football. Bill Carpenter may have had the courage to call napalm down near himself because he had learned, as the Lonely End, how to stand out there naked and vulnerable and still make the right moves and judgments. Maybe these things do count. Don Holleder, another West Point All-America of that period, was killed in Vietnam, and someone once said that Holleder and a couple of journalists were the only *names* ever to be killed in that war.

Imagine that: *names*. This is not a MacArthur time anymore; certainly not so much as it is a McLuhan time. Dawkins' roommate used to tell him: "You're the figment of a sportswriter's imagination," and Dawkins, laughing, reveals that the press "homogenized me." No matter, really: he is close enough to being what he has been portrayed as. Besides, it is not significant in his case whether or not he learned to react or think fast when midway between the sideline stripes. What is important is that Dawkins was ordained a celebrity for his part in the friendly strife.

One military expert blithely writes that Dawkins is "the most highly regarded young officer in the Army, the surest bet there is for chief of staff in the 1980s," and surely Dawkins would have reached this estate had he never played a down of football. But he profits that he did, and when he did — and not just like some other Whizzer White or Jack Kemp or Vinegar Bend Mizell. Sporting successes certainly helped those men demonstrably because they gained exposure in the stadiums; but exposure is just the stuff of TV spots these days.

Dawkins is defined in quite different terms. As the Army has fallen to its low ebb, it has come to mean a great deal to many people that Pete Dawkins ran wild as the leaves changed above Michie Stadium that autumn of his, 1958 — and that he is still there on the team. At the age of 33, damned if he isn't a symbol.

A colonel's wife, sitting across the crowded living room from Dawkins, was on the defense about the Army for no good reason, except perhaps that she has become accustomed to that stance. "Only the bad, that's all you ever hear," she exclaimed. "Is that fair?" She suddenly thrust out her hand and pointed toward Dawkins. "Why do people think he stays in after all that has happened? He could do anything on the outside. Anything. Doesn't that mean something that Pete Dawkins stays in the Army? They all remember him.

"Good God, at least they still remember Pete Dawkins, don't they?"

TRIVIA

Ron Fimrite

In the world of the trivialist, big is little and little, big.
Fimrite, a fast man with an insignificance himself,
visits the biggest little men of all, hears a small tale or two,
and warns the tyro not to trifle.

It is opening time at the Templebar in San Francisco and Mel Corvin is positioned near the kitchen, a squat, imperious figure in a dark suit of impeccable 1952 cut. Sipping coffee soundlessly, he has the wary aspect of an aging gunfighter steeling himself for the inevitable challenge. This is an image Corvin encourages, for he wishes it known that he is "trying my damnedest to phase myself out of this game." He has as much chance of achieving serenity in his time as Wild Bill Hickok had in his, and Corvin knows it. His reputation, alas, precedes him.

"It's getting so I can't walk into a place without somebody nailing me with, 'I got one for you,' " he says.

But this is merely a pose, for Corvin is not as discomfited by the prospect of somebody having one for him as he lets on. He is, after all, a trivia player, a man who welcomes — nay, embraces — challenge. And he knows further that there are only a handful of competitors in his town with the necessary grasp of arcana to extend him. Let them, then, have one for him.

If they should demand of him the batting order of the 1936 New York Yankees (a question so easy Corvin does not think it qualifies as trivia), let them

---

1. Since the NFL draft began, two Notre Dame quarterbacks have been the No. 1 pick. Who were they?

---

try Crosetti, Rolfe, DiMaggio, Gehrig, Dickey, Powell, Lazzeri and Selkirk. If they require the actress who played Humphrey Bogart's long-suffering mother in *Dead End*, give them Marjorie Main. And if they should ask for the opening sequence of the old radio show *Grand Central Station*, he will re-create the sound of a speeding locomotive and then breathlessly announce in a voice hauntingly familiar:

"As a bullet seeks its target, shining rails in every part of our great country are aimed at Grand Central Station, heart of the nation's greatest city. Drawn by the magnetic force, the fantastic metropolis, day and night great trains rush toward the Hudson River, sweep down its eastern bank for 140 miles, flash briefly past the long, red row of tenement houses south of 125th

2. What was the name of the silent film in which John Barrymore played Captain Ahab?

Street, dive with a roar into the 2½-mile tunnel which burrows beneath the glitter and swank of Park Avenue and then . . . Grand Central Station . . . crossroads of a million private lives."

That should hold them. But probably not for long. Indeed, while Corvin and his fellow trivialists are involved in no formal competition, they are seldom off duty. Somebody always has one for them. They are, in fact, part of a subculture group composed of persons of a certain age whose minds are hopelessly cluttered with the detritus of the Depression '30s and the warring '40s. They are, as one of their number, Tom Dunn of Albuquerque, suggests, "Forty-year-old kids singing the Jack Armstrong song." While civilization quavered before economic disaster and military threat, these kids — now, roughly, between 35 and 50 — found enormous pleasure and, as it develops, lasting satisfaction out of Little Orphan Annie, Duke Mantee, Albie Booth, Ossie Bluege, Tonto and Margot Lane.

Trivia players are not to be confused with the current clutch of stowaways on the nostalgia bandwagon; the best of them have been playing the trivia game in earnest for at least 20 years, or from the time they were far enough along to look back. They are obviously in the vanguard of the backward movement.

"I'd almost burned out nostalgia on the air before it became popular," says Dunn, who occasionally livens his morning show on Albuquerque radio station KOB with excerpts from old serials and Orson Welles' *War of the Worlds*.

Trivia players regard the Johnny-come-latelies to old times with undisguised contempt. Likening the new nostalgia crowd to their distinguished company is a bit like comparing *No, No, Nanette* with *A la Recherche du Temps Perdu*. It is a question of sophistication.

A further distinction should also be made between trivia players and those who may be defined as collectors — librarianish sorts who squirrel away old magazines, pulps and baseball guides, often for resale at propitious moments. Although they are not necessarily averse to such exotica, trivia players are primarily attached to the more obvious sources of entertainment — sports, movies and radio. It is the little parts of the big things that entice them. Then, too, they are verbal people not given to rummaging in secondhand bookstores for first editions of *Detective Comics* or *Human Torch*. They are, in a sense, our oral historians.

The expression "Well, that was before my time" is totally alien to the trivia player, who will admit to nothing being before his time. As a child, he was fully as fascinated with the '20s or the '90s as he was with his own decade. He was as familiar with the exploits of T. Truxton Hare or Bugs Raymond as with those of Bruno Banducci or Bobo Newsom. But he is truest to his own period, a time when the big leagues were little and the movies were big, when

3. What Major League baseball player wore the name of his hometown on the back of his uniform?

radio fed the imagination, not satiated it, as television is inclined now to do.

"When we grew up," said singer Mel Tormé, a top trivia player, "the figures on the movie screen were all 25 to 50 times bigger than life. Now we look at TV, and they're all smaller than life — little guys and girls only seven inches high. At that size they just don't seem very important."

Tormé plays the game with such Hollywood chums as Mickey Rooney and Donald O'Connor, who have the melancholy distinction of being trivia figures in their own right. But most trivia enthusiasts are not celebrities. Many may be found in a neighborhood tavern, reciting ancient box scores and flawlessly identifying second leads and faces in the crowd in the old movie on the television screen back of the bar.

"How much d'ya wanna bet that's Rochelle Hudson . . . ?"

The omniscient Corvin is a San Francisco publicist who recently favored New York with his expertise while serving as an advance man for the Roller Derby. "I killed them in P J Clarke's," he modestly acknowledges.

Trivialist Rod Belcher of Seattle, tall and red-haired, is the public information officer for the Washington Department of Highways. He is also a former radio announcer who in 1950 broadcast San Francisco 49er games under the

4. In 1950 the American League season leader in stolen bases had just 15, the fewest in major league history. Who was he?

pseudonym Rod Hughes — a deception made necessary by his sponsor's aversion to the word "belcher" when used in connection with his product, which happened to be beer. Belcher is the composer of *Go, Go, You Pilots!*, the fight

---

5. What actor played the role of the escaped prisoner who hid in the rolltop desk in the first screen version of "The Front Page?"

---

song of the now-defunct American League franchise in Seattle. "We sang *Go, Go*," said Belcher, "and they went. But the record has become a collector's item. Sales have never been better."

Trivia player Bob Hanson of Atlanta is a genial "independent insurance adjuster" who writes mocking crank letters to racist politicians and carries a business card identifying him as a purveyor of "land, whiskey, manure, nails, flyswatters, racing forms and bongos." Hanson's reputation as a trivialist is such that he is frequently called upon — usually at odd hours — to settle arguments of a familiar nature. It is Hanson, answering his bedroom phone, who will inform reveling friends downtown that Ken Maynard's horse was named Tarzan, not Topper, which, of course, was Hopalong Cassidy's steed.

Most trivia players have jobs of some sort. The New York advertising industry has a surfeit of them, and so have most newspaper offices. Other players follow even more respectable trades. Dr. James Loutzenhiser of Kansas City is a psychiatrist; Charles Moylan Jr. sits on the Baltimore City Supreme Bench; Elston Brooks is a theater critic for the Fort Worth *Star-Telegram*; E. Walker Chapman of Honolulu is the assistant general manager of the Royal Development Co., Ltd.; and Christy Schaller of Carson City, Nevada is the executive administrator to Nevada Governor Mike O'Callaghan.

This is not to suggest, however, that trivia players are necessarily men of searching intellect, despite Tormé's steadfast and self-serving assertion that "one has to have a certain erudition, a certain intellectual level, to play trivia."

Corvin, surely one of the best of the breed, has no intellectual pretensions. He is as unfamiliar with, say, Bertrand Russell's scholarship as the British philosopher-mathematician-pacifist was with Corvin's. Still, you ask yourself, could the co-author of the *Principia Mathematica* have recited the passenger manifest of the airplane hijacked to Shangri-La in *Lost Horizon*? Corvin can, and in a trice — Ronald Colman, John Howard, Edward Everett Horton, Thomas Mitchell and Isabel Jewell. Easy.

Despite their obvious advantages, trivia players are seldom intellectual bullies, unlike so many other scholars. Some weeks ago, Corvin found himself in a bar in Piedmont, across the bay from San Francisco. Seated next to him

6. Who was the first man to coach two Heisman Trophy winners?

was a gentleman who informed him that he resided in the nearby community of Martinez.

"Oh, Joe DiMaggio's hometown," said Corvin, making what for him passes as casual conversation.

"Joe DiMaggio," said the Martinez man levelly, "was born in San Francisco."

"I'm sorry, sir," said Corvin. "Joltin' Joe, the Yankee Clipper, he with the lifetime batting average of .325, was born on November 25, 1914 — I believe it was in the early afternoon — in Martinez — I'll think of the hospital in a minute."

"Wanna bet a hundred bucks on it?" the Martinez man inquired.

"Look, I don't want to take your money," said Corvin charitably. "Let's just say that if I'm wrong on any of these particulars, you win and I owe you a buck. If I'm right on all of them, you owe me a buck. Let the bartender be the judge."

Since this was an establishment frequented by sporting types whose arguments often require arbitration, the necessary reference material was available. Corvin, of course, was right on all counts.

"Buy this man a drink," the Martinez man instructed the barkeep. "He just saved me $99."

7. Who broke Dizzy Dean's toe with a line drive in the 1937 All-Star Game? Which toe? Which foot?

A patron in a Tacoma, Washington tavern was not nearly so fortunate following an encounter with Belcher some years ago. Identifying himself as a Notre Dame graduate, the man noisily lamented that his alma mater had never played in a postseason bowl game (this predated the recent Cotton Bowl meetings with Texas). It was an observation guaranteed to bruise the delicate sensibilities of a trivia player of Belcher's stripe.

"Surely, my good man," he addressed the Fighting Irishman, "you forget the 1925 Rose Bowl meeting with Stanford, won, you must recall, by your old school 27–10. Elmer Layden, you will now obviously remember, scored three touchdowns that day, two on pass interceptions. Ernie Nevers, playing with both ankles injured, was a hero in defeat for Stanford. This, it must be clear to

---

8. The major league season record for most doubles is 67. Who holds it?

---

you now, was the Notre Dame team of the Four Horsemen and Seven Mules. I won't even trouble you with the Horsemen, who must be as familiar to you as your own children, but just to refresh your memory, the Mules were Adam Walsh, naturally, at center, Kizer and Weibel, the guards. . . ."

"Hold on, buddy," the old grad interrupted, "I went to Notre Dame and I can tell you. . . ."

"Miller and Bach, the tackles, and Hunsinger and Collins, the ends."

"Yeah, but that game was played during the regular season. I've got $200 that says you're wrong."

Though offended by such abysmal ignorance, Belcher remained a man of scruples, and to take this blowhard's money was beneath his dignity. He merely smiled condescendingly and strode out the front door. Belcher's wife Dorothy had overheard the conversation, however, and though she hadn't the foggiest notion if Notre Dame had played in the 1925 Rose Bowl or if, in fact, the school had even fielded a team that year, she did know her husband and she also knew the Belchers were then slightly on their uppers. "I'm his wife," she blurted out, thinking of mouths to feed at home. "I'll take that bet." To Belcher's ultimate surprise, his household was $200 richer the next day.

---

9. What actress faced life as Portia in the radio soap opera and at the same time played Belle in "Lorenzo Jones?"

Trivia players normally wager only sparingly, and rarely with outsiders. When a game is going — and one can start at any moment — they prefer to

---

10. What was the original title of the Rodgers & Hart song "Blue Moon" when the melody was first used in the film "Manhattan Melodrama?"

---

keep it among themselves. And since the pace is so swift, there is little time for money to change hands. Besides, betting would add an unwelcome note of venality to what is, essentially, a social occasion. Competition and companionship are reward enough, and some of the greatest games have been played only for laughs.

On one memorable day, for example, Belcher and Corvin clashed — for the first time — on Corvin's home turf, the Templebar. This was as close as trivia will ever come to a Super Bowl. Belcher recalls how the match developed:

"I was in San Francisco for a couple of days, and a friend got hold of me and said, 'There's somebody you just have to meet.' So we went into this place,

---

11. In "One Man's Family," who played the part of Teddy?

---

and there was this guy at the end of the bar, near the kitchen. It was Corvin. Well, we started slowly enough, just casual conversation. Then we got going. I hit him with my Stanford teams — the Vow Boys and the boys before the Vow

---

12. Who was the catcher for the 1934 Cardinals' Gas House Gang?

Boys. And he came back with Cal's Thunder Teams. We went all through big-league baseball, the movies and radio. I think we finally got down to the biggest stars at Presidio Junior High School. The guy's just amazing."

There are few remaining witnesses to this Game of the Decade, however, because a normal person can endure a first-rate trivia game for no more than a few minutes before he feels the need for fresh air. And trivia players, for their part, can tolerate only so many "I don't see how you guys can remember all that stuff" remarks. Two or more trivia players in one room will invariably ruin any social gathering. No one, after all, can keep up with them when

13. In "Uncle Tom's Cabin," Eliza crossed a frozen river. What river was it?

they are at full throttle, and this is the sort of exclusivity that breeds cliquishness.

"Just when are those two going to stop it? Captain Midnight, indeed!"

No one, not newly published authors, not converts to militant feminism, not returning vacationers, can clear a room faster than two trivia players at the top of their form. Hostesses who have experienced such debacles have been known to grow faint at the first strains of "Wave the flag for Hudson High, boys. . . ."

Trivia players are often bewildered by these expressions of dread or hostility. Proud as they are of their own considerable gifts, they find it difficult to understand why more people are not like them. They see the ranks of the culturally deprived swollen daily by those who think of Bill Shakespeare as an Elizabethan playwright, not a Notre Dame halfback.

Astonished that so few of his listeners knew the words to the Little Orphan Annie song — "Who's that little chatterbox? The one with curly auburn locks?" — Dunn once cried out in anguish, "Where were all those people?"

Trivia player Hanson stoutly insists the best questions are those that merely revive dormant memories. He hopes fervently to elicit responses like, "Oh sure, I knew it all the time." They are usually long in coming. Hanson and Dunn are democratic trivia players, however, convinced that most people of the right age and background could perform as capably as they if only they put their minds to it. Others, notably Corvin, consider this approach demeaning and tend to move farther and farther out. Take, for example, Corvin's position on Heisman Trophies.

"Anyone can name all the Heisman Trophy winners," he says. "A real trivia player knows who finished second and third in the voting."

Corvin regards 1946 as such a vintage Heisman year that he can name the first four finishers — Glenn Davis, Charley Trippi, Johnny Lujack and Doc Blanchard. He also knows who compiled the best three-year performance as a

Heisman vote-getter — Glenn Davis, who finished second in 1944, second again in 1945 and first in 1946. And the player with the next best Heisman record — Doak Walker, who was third (1947), first (1948) and third (1949).

Belcher's specialty — or hangup, if you will — is nicknames, or rather the given names of persons best known by their nicknames. The unwary will thus be confronted with Hack (Lewis) Wilson, Dixie (Fred) Walker, Jo-Jo (Joyner) White, Tuffy (Alphonse) Leemans or Arky (Joseph Floyd) Vaughan. And Belcher has disarmed many opponents by asking for the real name of Bronko Nagurski. The answer, he is always pleased to say, is Bronko. Belcher may further require a fellow player to give him the name and the academic affiliation of the loutish football player played by Dick Foran in *The Petrified Forest*. The answer, Boze Hertzlinger of Nevada Tech, is one that seldom is remembered, even by the most nimble trivialists.

---

14. Who were the two quarterbacks with the initials Y.A.T. who played football in Yankee Stadium?

The Petrified Forest is, however, a major trivia movie, as are all those in which the characters are isolated for a period of time in either a single room or a vehicle — the airplane, maybe, in *Lost Horizon,* the stagecoach in the original *Stagecoach*. A fairly simple trivia question has always been: What actor was in both the airplane and the stagecoach? The answer, as everyone knows, is Thomas Mitchell.

Animals, particularly horses and dogs, are among the trivia player's best friends. Tormé and Hanson are particularly sound in this field. Here, of course, it is considered bad form to identify just the star's animal. The only

---

15. Who were the 12 Angry Men?

---

horses worth knowing are those ridden either by a sidekick — Smiley Burnette's Ringeye — or a girl friend — Dale Evans' Buttermilk. "Get um up, Scout" is definitely for beginners.

Sidekicks, foils, bad guys and losers are trivia people. Elisha Cook Jr. is of infinitely greater worth than, say, John Carroll or James Craig. Since bigness holds little interest for him, the trivia player tends to overlook the great names of his era.

Joe DiMaggio, for example, is not a trivia person; Vince is. Don Ameche, telephone and all, is not; Jim is. Groucho, Harpo and Chico Marx are not; Zeppo and Gummo are. Judy Garland is not, neither is Deanna Durbin; Gloria Jean is. Tommy Harmon is not; Nile Kinnick is. Abbott and Costello are not; Wheeler and Woolsey are. Eddie (Rochester) Anderson is not; Mantan Moreland is. Even W. C. Fields is not truly a trivia person; his foil, Franklin Pangborn, definitely is.

The Yankees were easily the premier team of the trivia era, an honor worth automatic disqualification in the Trivia Major League. The ideal trivia team is the American League champion Detroit Tigers of 1934-35 — and for

---

16. The actress Margo is remembered for her role in "Lost Horizon," but in what film did she make her debut and who was her leading man in that movie?

---

no logical reason, save that they arrived in between the great Yankee teams and that their starting lineup, when read aloud, had a certain enchanting euphony: Gehringer, Greenberg, Goslin, Owen, Rowe, Rogell, Cochrane, White, Fox. Nickname freak Belcher is especially fond of this team, as well he should be of one fielding a Goose, a Freck, a Schoolboy, a Jo-Jo, a Black Mike, a Mechanical Man and, ultimately a Flea.

The Flea happens to be the protagonist of one of Belcher's favorite trivia questions: What was the Detroit Tigers' starting lineup in the third game of the 1935 World Series? The Tiger lineup, unlike so many today, was fairly rigid then, making it an easy mark for even average trivia players. But in the '35 Series, something awful happened to it. Hank Greenberg played in only the first two games, then retired as the result of a broken wrist. So, Belcher will inquire, who played first base from the third game on? And, for that matter, who was on third? The answer is that Freck (Marv) Owen moved from third to first and little Flea (Herman) Clifton replaced him at third. It was a rare lineup change for the Tigers, and it gave Flea Clifton trivia immortality. The poor man played only 87 major league games in his career, and were it not for trivia players like Belcher he would forever remain in obscurity. The zinger part of the question is, of course, what did the Flea hit in that Series? The answer is .000 — zero for 16.

Flea-type questions are always aggravating, and so are those in which the obvious answer is never correct. On a purely elementary — or low

17. Only one man in modern Major League history ever stole six bases in one game, and he did it twice in less than two weeks. Who was he?

trivia — level, a favorite in this genre is: Who played Frankenstein in the original 1931 movie? A careless thinker would speedily say Boris Karloff. And he would be wrong, for Karloff played the monster. Colin Clive was Dr. Frankenstein.

Then, too, there is the multiple-layer or double-zinger question, favored by Corvin and other obscurantists. Here the player is taunted into an increas-

18. What actor played the Brazilian leading man in "Flying Down to Rio?"

ingly false sense of security. Corvin, for example, might casually inquire, "What was the name of the Green Hornet's car?" When told that it was, as we all know, the Black Beauty, Corvin will then ask, "Where did the Hornet park it?" This is a step up, but a reasonably adept trivia player will answer, "In an adjoining building." Now the zinger: "And what kind of a building was it?" Even the best trivia players have foundered on this. Was it a warehouse? An underground garage? Yankee Stadium? The maddening answer is: "Supposedly abandoned."

The Hornet is a marvelous trivia person, lending himself to endless queries. With the Hornet, a trivia player can deliver an entire biography before he shoots the zinger. Here's an example: Besides the fact they both wore masks, used special weapons (the gas gun and silver bullets), had super modes of transportation (the Black Beauty and Silver), employed sidekicks who spoke broken English (Kato and Tonto), what else did the Green Hornet and the Lone Ranger have in common? The answer: They were related. Britt Reid, the Green Hornet, was the grandnephew of John Reid, the Lone Ranger.

A classic Corvin double-zinger goes like this: Zinger (1) — Who are the four players who have hit four home runs in one game since 1949? That's easy: Gil Hodges, Joe Adcock, Rocky Colavito and Willie Mays. Zinger (2) — What one player was either a teammate or an opponent of the hitter on each occa-

---

19. In the seventh game of the 1946 Series, Enos Slaughter, who was on first base, scored on a hit to left center field. Who hit the ball?

---

sion? The answer, which separates trivia men from trivia boys, is Billy Loes, a teammate of Hodges on the 1950 Dodgers and of Mays on the 1961 Giants and Adcock's foe as a Dodger in 1954 and Colavito's as an Oriole in 1959.

Perhaps the Black Beauty of all trivia questions was posed during a lull between the first and second games of the last World Series by Roger Angell, the *New Yorker* magazine writer and editor:

"You will quite naturally recall the 1949 James Cagney movie *White Heat*," Angell began, innocently enough.

"To be sure."

"Then you remember, of course, that Cagney in the film had something of a mother fixation?"

"Yes, crazy about the old girl."

"And that during a scene in the prison mess hall he noticed some new cons at his table who looked familiar?"

"I can see them now."

"And that Cagney thinks they may have news from the outside about mom?"

"Right on."

"So he turns to the con next to him and says, does he not? 'Ask them: how's mom? Pass it on.' "

"Indubitably."

"And when the word reaches one of the new men, he turns and says something like, 'Mom's dead. Pass it on.' "

"That's it exactly."

"Fine. Now my question is: Who was the third guy to pass it on?"

"Holy moley! Jeepers creepers!"

"No, Jim Thorpe."

Why, that's it! The old athlete was then down to accepting bit parts, and if you look closely at that scene you will see his familiar flat features. Third? Who can say? But he was, indeed, passing word of mom's untimely demise on.

This is the sort of trivia question that warms the soul, joining as it does Corvinian obfuscation with the Hanson recognition principle. One experiences a sense of community with the questioner, and that is really what trivia is all about. Trivia players are forever in search of kindred spirits and shared pleasures. And they are sadly aware that their numbers are not likely to increase. "We are," as Belcher has said "of a forgotten persuasion."

This is really the first, the last and eventually the lost trivia generation. The circumstances that spawned the trivia players can never be re-created. Depression youngsters, particularly those in small towns and cities, enjoyed pretty much the same things. They went to movies — all day on Saturday — they listened nightly to the radio and they lavished uncommon devotion on those flawless heroes of the gridiron and diamond who never smoked, drank, took dope or chased girls. "There was a time," said Dunn, "when it all seemed to fit."

There is too much now, too many things to do and see. Television, even with its *Howdy Doody* revival, is not a proper trivia instrument. The programs haven't the staying power, and there are simply too many of them. Trivia players saw the world through a smaller focus. There were 16 major league baseball teams, not 24 — can anyone recite the starting lineup of the 1971 Milwaukee Brewers? Who, in fact, are they? Professional football was a piddling enterprise in the trivia player's youth. Now the sun rises and sets upon it. There were more movies then, but they were shorter and simpler. You *knew* the actors. The entire communications industry virtually exploded into being in the trivia years, and the trivia players were then able to keep up with it. Nobody can maintain that pace now.

Not long ago a trivia player was recalling for the amusement of some basically non-trivia companions what he half-seriously considered to be the best day of his life.

"It was the summer of 1938, and I was just 7," he said. "But think of it: all in one day I tasted my first marble-fudge ice cream, bought the copy of *Action Comics* that introduced Superman and, to top it all off, was mistaken for Bobby Breen on a Greyhound bus. That is what I call living!"

His friends regarded him quizzically. "I've eaten marble-fudge," said one. "And everybody knows Superman. But just who in the name of heaven is Bobby Breen?"

The trivia player was staggered. Are there grown-up people in this world who have not heard of Bobby Breen, the prototypical boy soprano? Am I, he thought, that isolated from the normal course of events? Am I that old?

But he finally comforted himself with the knowledge that somewhere, maybe down at the Templebar, there would be someone who would think of

Bobby Breen as an old and treasured friend. Perhaps they would hoist one in the little fellow's memory. And maybe, if the mood was upon them, they would lift up their voices in trembling falsetto and sing:

"Oh, there's a rainbow on the river, the skies are clearing . . ."

Trivia players have *that* going for them.

Answers

1. Frank (Boley) Dancewicz in 1946 and Paul Hornung, the bonus pick in 1957
2. *The Sea Beast*
3. Pitcher Bill Voiselle, who came from Ninety Six, S.C.
4. Dominic DiMaggio
5. George E. Stone
6. Ducky Pond of Yale. His Heisman winners were Larry Kelley and Clint Frank
7. Earl Averill, the Cleveland Indian outfielder. Big toe. Left foot
8. Earl Webb of the Boston Red Sox
9. Lucille Wall
10. *The Bad in Every Man*
11. Winifred Wolfe
12. Bill DeLancey
13. Ohio River
14. Y. A. Tittle, Young Arnold Tucker
15. Henry Fonda, Lee J. Cobb, Ed Begley, Jack Warden, Martin Balsam, George Voskovec, Robert Webber, Jack Klugman, Edward Binns, E. G. Marshall, Joseph Sweeney, John Fiedler
16. *Crime Without Passion,* Claude Rains
17. Eddie Collins
18. Raul Roulien
19. Harry Walker

RUNNING SCARRED

SAUL LAMBERT

Tex Maule

Tex Maule, that man of dauntless pro football prophecies,
came out of a massive heart attack with a stop-watch in his hand
and jogging shoes on his feet
as he fought to regain his once-robust health.

Two days after my 51st birthday I had a massive heart attack. I did not know what it was at first. I was drinking coffee with my wife in the dining area of our Manhattan apartment when I broke out in sweat and felt so nauseated I could not finish the coffee. I had been up until four in the morning and now it was eight, and I thought the nausea and the sweat were probably the result of a night of hard work, drinking, smoking, tension and very little sleep. After a few minutes I felt better, and I dressed and packed, preparing to catch a plane to Montreal, where I was to cover a heavyweight championship fight.

Dorothy suggested postponing the trip for a day, but I told her I really was feeling much better. I had not missed a day's work because of illness in over 10 years. I reached the door and was just turning to say goodby when I began sweating again, and the nausea came back so strongly I had to clench my teeth to keep from vomiting. My legs felt weak and trembly. I put the bag down and leaned against the door to keep from falling.

"You look terrible," my wife said. "What's wrong?"

"I'll be all right in a minute," I said. "I'm just tired."

I walked back into the living room and sat down on the couch, and she sat by me, watching anxiously. I smiled at her and tried to light a cigarette, but my hands were shaking so badly that it seemed a long time before I got it lit. I still had no pain of any kind. The cigarette tasted like burning sulphur and made my nausea worse, so I put it out and took three or four deep breaths. This made me feel a little better. My face was wet and the sweat was trickling down my sides. I stood up and took off my topcoat.

I had taken only five or six steps when the pain in my chest started. It was not severe at first, more of a dull ache, but the nausea and the weakness grew with it, and I sat down on the couch again.

The pain now stretched across my chest from armpit to armpit. It was becoming crushing, as though my chest was being mashed down by a giant kneeling on me, growing heavier and heavier. I could no longer breathe deeply. I realized that I was panting, taking shallow breaths like a tired puppy, and for the first time I wondered if I was having a heart attack.

From some medical article read long before, I remembered that the fingernails of a person having a heart attack turn blue, and I held up my hand and looked at my fingertips. The nails were bluish.

I stood up gently and began to walk toward the bedroom and said, "Honey, I think you better call Marty."

Dr. Martin Fisher, our family doctor, also happens to be a heart specialist. By the time he arrived, my daughter, who was then 18, was up, and she and my wife were doing their best to help and growing more and more frightened. Strangely, I never felt afraid; I think I was more irritated with myself than anything else and apprehensive about not being able to make the trip.

Marty felt my pulse, listened to my chest, took my blood pressure and electrocardiogram and gave me a shot. He told Dorothy to call the Flower & Fifth Avenue Hospitals and get an ambulance.

I began feeling embarrassed at being so much trouble, and when the ambulance attendant came into the room with a stretcher I tried to get up and into it myself. I think the first time I realized how serious the situation had become was when Marty stopped me. "Don't move," he said. "Lie as still as you can. They will do all the work."

Once I had been lifted onto the rolling stretcher, Marty tucked a blanket around me. I felt relieved when he did; I knew we would be going down in the elevator from the 11th floor and was not anxious for my neighbors to see me bare-chested. It is undignified enough to be hauled out of your apartment on a stretcher without being exposed as well.

We ran into a problem getting on the elevator. I suppose the builders of the apartment house in which I live — a 20-story affair on the East Side — never thought any of the 300-odd apartment dwellers would have to be removed in this fashion. The elevators are not wide enough or long enough to take a stretcher.

The attendants worked that out by folding the stretcher in the middle, where it is hinged, and I rode down bent slightly at the waist and knees. The elevator operator, an old friend, looked at me sadly and seemed on the point of saying something, but I think he, like most people, was intimidated by serious and sudden illness.

They loaded me into the back of the ambulance, and we left for the hospital with the siren howling. The shot was taking effect, and I was breathing easier. The pain in my chest had died down until it was only a reminder of what it had been.

I remember it was a sparklingly bright, sunshiny day. I looked out the window as the ambulance went through the crowded streets and saw healthy people on their way to work — or wherever they were going — and I felt no sense of sorrow or envy. If I was going to die, at least I was a long way down the road. I had done a lot of things in 51 years. I tried, drowsily, to think of those things, and none came back to me very clearly, but all seemed, in retrospect, in an ambulance making its way up Park Avenue on that bright March morning, good.

I was five weeks in the hospital (10 days of that in intensive care) and another month recuperating in bed at home. As the days wore on, I realized I was no longer the robust man I had always thought myself to be. All my life I had been an athlete, stronger than most, almost sinfully free of illness, conscious of the fact that in most physical confrontations the odds in my favor would usually be better than even.

While recuperating I had, for lack of anything more exciting to do, grown a beard, which I trimmed into a Vandyke. One morning, watching myself as I clipped the beard, I tried to assess the face in the mirror as if it belonged to a stranger — a clearly impossible thing to do.

But I had enough objectivity to realize that it was a face that looked years older than the one I had shaved that morning when I was preparing to leave for Canada. There were wrinkles not evident then and my hair had turned whiter. The beard didn't help. It had come in almost pure white.

I suppose the most accurate description of the clinic Dr. Paul Niehans operated in Vevey, Switzerland would be a rejuvenation center. The handsome hospital in which he treated people who came to him in search of youth was called Clinique Générale la Prairie. (It is still open, though Dr. Niehans died at the age of 89 in 1971.)

When I arrived I was given the most thorough physical examination I had ever had. The tests, according to the attending physicians, were to determine just where I needed help. I also was assured that Dr. Niehans' cellular therapy was perfectly safe for me to take. The treatment is not legal in the United States, since it has not been proved effective to the satisfaction of the American Medical Association. But Dr. Niehans had been using his method to relieve the symptoms of old age and to regenerate failing organs for some 40 years. Rumored to be among his patients were Charles Chaplin, who became a father in his early 70s, and Spain's General Franco. Great numbers of long-in-the-tooth entertainers and movie stars had visited the clinic near Lake Geneva, and while most did not boast publicly of having been there, these people admitted their debt to Dr. Niehans rather freely in private.

The treatment itself was simple enough. The exhaustive examination indicated what cellular therapy one needed, and then the patient received a series of shots designed to stimulate those areas of the body. Niehans used injections made up of cell soups from the appropriate organs of unborn lambs. The cells supposedly pepped up the tired ones in the body and promoted renewed vigor. The effect was delayed. In a small booklet the clinic issued to patients after a week of rest and seclusion, Dr. Niehans explained that any benefits would not be felt for at least 3½ months.

One also received a card that read as follows:

"TO MY PATIENTS!
Your organism has been given precious cells, which start to work after 3½ months. I beg you not to damage them in any way! Therefore:
NO X rays without protecting the rest of the body,
NO short-wave treatment, no ultra-violet rays,

NO very hot hair dryers,
NO bath-cures in radio-active thermal stations,
NO sun-baths, no Turkish baths, no sauna baths, no diathermy,
NO poisons, such as nicotine, concentrated alcohols,
NO drugs (if possible) and no hormones.
These instructions are for your whole life long.

[Signed] Prof. Niehans"

My examination revealed that I not only had a bad heart, but that there were some 10 other areas in which my body was not operating at full speed. I was told the bad news the night before I received the shots. I was considerably disturbed until I learned by checking with others being treated that 11 malfunctioning organs was about par for the course.

At 10 the next morning a doctor accompanied by a nurse and a rolling table loaded with cell cultures and hypodermics, each about the size of a knitting needle, walked into my well-appointed room and cheerfully asked me to turn over on my stomach.

When I had, the nurse bared my bottom and the doctor zapped me 11 times. Then he patted me on the shoulder and advised me to lie on my stomach for the next 30 minutes, advice that was hardly necessary. I stayed in the hospital for seven days and was not allowed to take a walk until the fifth day. This, it was explained, was to give the delicate unborn lamb cells a chance to survive and do their work.

If the treatment did nothing else, it helped me quit smoking. When I drove away from Vevey, considerably poorer but rested, I was off cigarettes and felt much better than I had in quite a while.

One of the temporary restrictions placed on me when I left the clinic was on exercise. "You may walk," the attending physician said, "but no strenuous exercise of any kind. These new cells are very delicate. I would suggest you wait at least three months before you do anything more than stroll." The electrocardiogram that had been taken at the clinic showed the damage of my heart attack, but the doctors felt that after the three-month waiting period, mild exercise would not be harmful. Indeed, it might be advisable and my heart, presumably strengthened by unborn lamb cells, should be better able to accommodate the heavier load.

I had taken the lamb-cell shots on June 3. On Sept. 1 I began a careful program that included a little jogging. Meanwhile, I had set out on my annual trip to the professional football training camps. As directed, I carefully avoided X rays, shortwaves, ultraviolet rays, bath cures in radioactive thermal stations, sunbaths, Turkish baths, sauna baths, diathermy, drugs and hormones. Hair dryers were no problem, but poisons were not so easy, especially "concentrated alcohols."

Since, for one reason or another, I spend quite a bit of time in bars talking to sportswriters, publicity men, club owners and retired football players, I found it very difficult to avoid concentrated alcohol. For two months I drank plain soda. Plain soda is fine when mixed with Scotch, which dampens its tendency toward excessive effervescence. Taken without a mixer, it tends to inflate the drinker until he burbles constantly, like a sleepy volcano. After two months on plain soda, I figured the unborn lamb cells had grown up enough for a beer or two. Beer is not concentrated alcohol, anyway.

So I changed from soda to beer, but beer is a tough tipple to stick with through a long night, especially after a protracted afternoon. I gained about 20 pounds coddling the lamb cells before I decided they were old enough for an occasional vodka and tonic or Scotch and water. Just a glass once in awhile.

At first, each time I sipped a Scotch or a vodka, I could sense the cells curdling. I felt very good, even with the sizable paunch I had acquired, but my physical euphoria was diminished by the guilt I felt for what I was doing to my lamb chips. For a week or so I had a nagging concern about the cells. Then I stopped worrying about them.

By the time I returned from visiting all the NFL clubs I was host to several million alcoholic lamb cells. And several weeks later, when I was back writing stories under deadlines, I began smoking again. I borrowed a cigarette, thinking that I would just smoke one to demonstrate to myself how little I really needed a cigarette. I was right. I just smoked that one that day, but the way was open again. I knew I had lost the battle when I bought a pack. When you walk up to the counter and buy a pack, you're dead. Dead. A peculiarly appropriate word to use.

Well, at this point I was full of dying lamb cells, I was drinking and smoking again and, because of my experiment with beer and all I had eaten while I was off cigarettes, I was 45 pounds overweight.

I was in San Francisco to do a story on why the 49ers always look wonderful and play something less than that. I found while interviewing Lou Spadia, who was then president of the club, that he ran every day, as much as three miles. And I decided it was time to do something about myself. I had read *Aerobics,* a book on running by Dr. Kenneth Cooper, the physical director for the U.S. Air Force. For the next three years it was my manual. I worked out my running schedule by it, improved with it and, in effect, lived by it.

I knew that Dr. Cooper's test for fitness is to discover how far you can go — running, walking, crawling or any combination of the three — in 12 minutes. I decided I would take the test while Spadia was doing his daily three miles on the track at the University of California at Santa Barbara, where the 49ers were in preseason training.

I borrowed gear from the equipment manager; sweat suit, cleated lowcuts and the rest. Before we went out I weighed myself — 215 flabby pounds. As we walked to the track, Spadia told me about his own conversion to running.

He had joined the 49ers many years before, when the club was organized by Tony and Vic Morabito, two San Francisco trucking magnates. Both were to die of heart attacks.

"I hadn't thought much about my heart until Vic died," Spadia said. "But when you lose two close friends in a few years, you begin to wonder about yourself, so I had a thorough checkup. My heart was O.K., but I was overweight, I didn't exercise and I smoked entirely too much. The doctor suggested that I quit smoking, start walking and lose weight."

That had been two years before. On the morning we ran together, Spadia was trim and fit looking. He appeared years younger than his 40-odd, and when he began to run, I found out quickly enough that he was a century younger than I. "I'll go the first half mile with you, then slow down," I said confidently. "I don't want to work too hard at first. I figure it'll take me a couple of months or so to work up to two miles."

The track at Santa Barbara is the conventional quartermile oval. We started running in the middle of the home straight, and by the time we had reached the end of the first turn I was finished. I had run something less than 200 yards and was gasping desperately for breath. When your heart and lungs are as far out of condition as mine were, it is impossible to draw a deep enough breath. I sucked in air, but I hit a barrier in my chest. I could not inhale nearly enough. I stopped running and walked around the track, then started at a gentle jog again.

I quit that day after an inglorious half mile, most of which I negotiated at a slow, wind-broken walk. Spadia ran some two miles during the time I walked, rested, trotted a few steps and rested again. As we went back to the gym to shower and change, I asked him how long it had taken him to run so easily.

"A year," he said. "At least a year. You have to take it easy. But if you stick to it, it's worth it. I had my annual checkup last week. I always ask Doc to check my heart especially, so he takes not only the regular electrocardiogram with the gear on my arm, but he tests the blood pressure in my legs, too. He said I had the best circulation and blood pressure in my legs he had seen in a long time, even in patients younger by 10 years."

The next morning my legs were dreadfully sore, but I went out to the track again. This time I decided I would see just how fit I was by taking Dr. Cooper's test — going as far as I could go in 12 minutes. The test is based on the amount of oxygen your body can use during an all-out effort; the fitter you are, the more oxygen you can utilize and the farther and faster you can go. Dr. Cooper had reduced the complicated testing technique of the laboratory to a simple physical test.

At my age then — this was now two years after my heart attack and I was 53 — any distance under eight-tenths of a mile meant that I was in very poor condition. To qualify as being in excellent condition I would have to run a mile and a half or more.

When we reached the track Spadia went off at his steady, easy pace while I waited and watched the sweep hand of my wristwatch. I started my test as it passed zero, running much slower than I had the day before, determined to at least exceed eight-tenths of a mile. The next category above very poor is poor, and I was willing to settle for that.

The going was no easier than it had been before, and it was made more painful because my legs ached after a few strides. I ran about 50 steps, then slowed to a walk, already puffing. I decided I would try to do the whole thing at the Boy Scout pace — 50 steps trotting, 50 walking. Spadia passed me early on, finishing his first lap. Only four minutes into the testing time, I was laboring heavily and began to run 25 steps and walk 75. Three minutes later I settled for a brisk walk. When the 12 minutes had passed, I had managed to cover only a few yards more than half a mile.

I stood under a hot shower for a long time, trying to ease the ache in my legs. I had blisters on both feet and was desperately tired. I could not imagine ever being able to run as far as a mile. I looked down at the volley-ball-sized potbelly I had accumulated in the last two years and looked at Spadia; his stomach was flat. I asked him if he had had trouble breathing at first. "Sure," he said. "I wasn't any better than you. I guess no one is."

The next day I returned to Los Angeles. It was desperately hot, and I stayed at the Beverly Hills Hotel. I went off as soon as I had registered and visited a sporting goods store, where I bought shorts, a sweat suit and a pair of running shoes. The shoes turned out to be much too heavy, but at the time I thought they gave me a rather professional look.

Late in the afternoon I put on my gear and walked across Sunset Boulevard for a run in the small park opposite the hotel. The equipment did not make much difference, my legs were still sore and my breath short. If anything, I went slower than I had the day before. But I felt better in running gear.

Old ladies sitting on park benches eyed me doubtfully as I slogged along at a fast walk or a minimal jog, but I paid them no attention. I was too concerned with catching my breath. I was acutely aware of my heart. I had read of the pain that exercise can cause a damaged heart, and I monitored mine second by second, ready to stop at the first twinge. I had no twinges, even though my breathing was short and labored. I have never had a twinge running, although my chest felt tight and constricted often enough.

I realize, looking back, that I was extraordinarily fortunate. I violated the cardinal rule of exercise for postcardiac patients by beginning without my doctor's clearance. I survived, but I cannot say too strongly that no one should begin the way I did. Ever.

If there is a more difficult place in the world for joggers than New York City, I would be hard put to name it. You can run outdoors on the streets if you do not mind getting up at six in the morning to avoid the fumes of the traffic and

From the basketball courts of America to the playing fields — and battlegrounds — of Munich, it was a tumultuous year. Wherever the action was, there was a SPORTS ILLUSTRATED photographer (or two or three), and after each event there began a second contest, this one against time, to get pictures into print. The photographs on the following pages were composed in the heat of the struggle and processed by SI with an orderly urgency that by now has become routine.

A giant among giants, the Kentucky Colonels'
Artis Gilmore starts off at 7' 2" but goes quite
a bit higher to block a shot by New York Nets.

a clash of titans, 7' Wilt Chamberlain of Los
ngeles and 7' 4" Kareem Abdul-Jabbar of Milwaukee,
ilt wins — and leads the Lakers to the NBA title.

Hurrying toward the Super Bowl, the Dallas Cowboys' scrambling quarterback, Roger Staubach (left), wrecked San Francisco, while tiny Garo Yepremian (right) kicked Miami past Kansas City in the climactic moment of pro football's longest game, his 37-yard field goal defeating the Chiefs 27–24 after 82 minutes, 40 seconds of play. But when they got to the Super Bowl, Dolphins big and little could not stop a Cowboy stampede named Duane Thomas (below).

Jack Nicklaus lifts his putter and his caddy a triumphant digit to confirm Jack's fourth Masters Tournament victory, and when he won the U.S. Open there was talk of a Nicklaus Grand Slam. Then in the British Open Jack met another golfing Super American — or Super Mex, as he is sometimes called — and with a magical 30-foot chip shot on the next to last hole Lee Trevino (left) slew the slam. Meanwhile, in the gloaming of a fabulous career, Arnold Palmer was grimacing over many a missed putt, as here in the U.S. Open, but Arnie was still making plenty of money and drawing his usual Army of true believers.

Watery winners of the year included unlimited hydroplane driver Bill Sterett Jr., bouncing decibels off the
Capitol on the way to an astonishing upset of favored Bill Muncey in the President's Cup race on the Potomac;
(right) uppity little "Condor," a freshwater yacht out of Chicago, skimming along behind her chesty spinnaker
in the decisive Miami-Nassau race of the SORC series to beat the fanciest goldplaters at sea.

As baseball warmed up, Dick Allen charmed Chicago with more than juggling feats; ultimately he was the American League's leading home run hitter and RBI man. In Pittsburgh, Willie Stargell and the immortal Roberto Clemente swung ferocious bats.

The pursuit of speed sprouted wings on Indianapolis 500 cars, hustled Riva Ridge home in the Kentucky Derby and pulled Jim Ryun through the tape in the U.S. Olympic trials. Then came his Munich catastrophe.

Hockey! Sometimes it seems violence is the goal, as in this Stanley Cup tableau — one of the most evocative sports pictures of any year. It's a blueshirted New York Ranger against a gap-toothed Boston Bruin in a set-to at the boards, and though the Bruins got the worst of this encounter in Boston Garden they eventually won the cup. That came as no particular surprise. What astonished all North America was the subsequent

Canada-Russia series — first, that Canada's NHL pros should consent to play the Russian "amateurs" at all, and, second, that the Russians should prove to be so fit, fast and fiery that the Canadians were able to win the eight-game series only by the skin of their teeth, 4–3–1. Here Boston superstar Phil Esposito menaces the Russians' marvelous goalie, Vladislav Tretiak.

In sport, triumph and tragedy usually mean no more than sweet victory and bitter defeat, but the Olympic Games at Munich were violated by a true tragedy of terrible dimensions. Before the Arab terrorists struck, however, the greatest individual triumph in Olympic history had been completed by America's Mark Spitz: seven swimming gold medals. There were, of course, many other treats — and some sour courses — on the

vast Olympic table. On the opposite page, the tiny Russian gymnast Olga Korbut leaps enchantingly, America's 400-meter gold medalist, Vince Matthews, yawns during the playing of the national anthem (for which he was sent home), the mountainous U.S. bronze medal wrestler, Chris Taylor, gets a bear hug, and Frank Shorter finishes fifth in the 10,000 meters before setting off on the marathon — the first American ever to win it.

And though the flags dipped to half-staff for
the Israeli dead, the Games went on. Diver
Micki King flips, Dave Wottle grimaces beneath
his cap as he wins the 800 meters, and deliriously
jubilant Russians break out the vodka after
handing the U.S. its first Olympic defeat
in basketball — amid we-wuz-robbed cries by
the Americans over the officials' ludicrous mishandling
of the game's chaotic last seconds.

Autumn brought the gaudy Oakland A's into a World Series they were not supposed to win, but did, and college freshmen, newly eligible to play varsity football, into the limelight. At left, Freshman Archie Griffin gets a bit more than three yards and a cloud of dust for Ohio State. Above, Joe Rudi makes that improbable catch in Game Two of the World Series. Below, Johnny Bench, Cincinnati's (and the National League's) most valuable player, tags out pinch runner Blue Moon Odom to end Game Five.

the jeers of the populace. You can run in Central Park, but the pollution there is as bad as on the roads and the people no kinder. Or you can run indoors at one of the YMCAs.

I picked the West Side Y for a number of reasons, the principal one being that several other SI staffers work out there. I was not anxious to demonstrate my turtle pace and deplorable condition to friends, but it is much easier to run in company than alone.

The indoor track is a balcony over the basketball court. Most indoor YMCA tracks are built the same way, although this is one of the better, with a good composition surface and banked turns, so your feet and legs are not punished as severely as on the hardwood tracks you find elsewhere.

I soon discovered another of the advantages of training there. In my running outfit I looked rather like a large pear supported by two matchsticks. Most of the 215 pounds I was carrying seemed lodged in my waist and hips, so that when I stripped and looked down at my belly, my belly button peered back at me. I was naturally a bit reluctant to go on the track the first day, since I had a mental image of dozens of fleet, sinewy athletes staring contemptuously at me as they went by. But fleet, sinewy athletes do not, thank the Lord, train on indoor tracks that go 24 laps to the mile. They cannot run fast enough to suit themselves on such a tiny oval. When I stepped gingerly onto the track and began walking a few laps to warm up, I found that I was not the fattest one there, by quite a few pounds.

There are traffic rules on these tracks that are much more rigidly observed than the rules of the road, as I discovered at once. I had just started walking when a potbellied little man with white hair trundled around me and shouted "track!" in my ear at the top of his voice. I smiled and waved at him, a bit surprised that he should say something so obvious, but as I did, someone behind me yelled "track!" again and shot by.

Finally, Andy Crichton, a fellow editor who had been zipping around the outside at a fearsome pace, slowed up and explained that they were not greeting me as a new recruit. "You run on the inside and walk on the outside," he said. "When they holler 'track,' it's just a polite way to say, 'Get the hell out of the way.'" I skipped to the outside and walked six laps before I began to jog again, and moved in on the pole. My jogging pace was not a great deal faster than my walk, but as long as you give the appearance of trotting instead of walking, you are free to stay in the inside lane.

After the first day I decided I would have to figure out a graduated system of walking and jogging, one designed to cut back on walking time and add to running time. And I felt as tired and discouraged after that workout at the Y as I had in Santa Barbara.

By the end of the first week I managed to do two miles in 23 minutes and 55 seconds but discovered to my dismay that, despite the exercise, I had gained two pounds. My ample belly still bounced in counterrhythm to my stride and my belly button still looked up accusingly when I looked down.

Like most people I had thought running, especially in the heat of early September, would melt off pounds, but that is a fallacy. Actually, going two miles at my snail's pace, I was probably burning up only a little more than 100 calories per session. The exercise and the knowledge that I was taking it encouraged me to add more than that to my regular diet.

During each of the next three weeks I added a lap of jogging and deducted a walking lap until, at the beginning of October, a month after starting the workouts, I was running eight laps and walking only four. On Oct. 1 I finished the two miles in about 23½ minutes and felt reasonably well doing it. Breathing was still difficult, but not nearly as labored as it had been. My heart thumped noisily for a while after I finished running, but I had no chest pain.

Where I had pain was in my knees. This began after I had been working out for about 10 days. At first my knees ached, but I supposed this was just part of the toughening-up process. But as the days went by and the muscular soreness subsided, my knees hurt more and more.

I was determined not to miss a workout, so I continued to run. I often had trouble getting out of bed in the morning, and before going to the track I would take a couple of aspirin to deaden the pain a little. The throbbing would be intense as I began to jog, then die down after about half a mile. As long as I jogged, it was bearable, but the acute soreness would return when I walked.

The bad knees helped in one way. Since it hurt more to walk than to run, I decided to run a full mile before walking and found, to my surprise, that I could. Now I would run a mile slowly, then do the second mile by walking four laps and jogging eight in each half. I was still wearing the thick-soled shoes I had bought in Los Angeles.

The pain was most severe just at the top of the kneecap, but it hurt on both sides of the joint as well. Early in October my knees became so stiff that one day I could not force a foot into its running shoe. I knew that if I could get onto the track and jog a while, the pain would ease and my stiffness would disappear, but there is a rule against running barefoot at the West Side Y. I finally solved the problem by buying a pair of judo slippers for a couple of dollars. These are very light, canvas slippers that have almost no padding in the soles. They are useless for road running, but they worked very well for a while on the smooth surface of the indoor track.

The first time I ran in the slippers I did the two miles almost a minute faster than I had run it before. My knees continued to trouble me, but the pain seemed to subside much more quickly than it had before. So I ran in the judo shoes. The soles of my feet were tender from the lack of padding, but that was not nearly as uncomfortable as aching knees.

The improvement was only temporary. The judo slippers allowed me to go faster, but the discomfort in my knees persisted. I finally checked with one of the team doctors in the National Football League to find out if there was anything seriously wrong.

"How long has it been since you did any real running?" he asked.

"Maybe 30 years," I said.

"Your ligaments are like dried leather," he said. "They're stretching now, and the stretching hurts. When they loosen up enough the aching probably will go away."

"How long will that take?"

He shrugged. "You can't tell," he said. "It depends on your age, your tissues and how much you run."

"I don't know about my tissues," I said. "I'll probably keep on running two miles a day. And I'm not young. So what do you think? Another week or month?"

"It could be another year," he said cheerfully.

The knees continued to bother me off and on for three months. By Oct. 24, a little less than two months after I had begun jogging, I was able for the first time to run two miles without stopping. On that day my knees were very bad, and I went two miles because I did not want them to stiffen up when I walked. I went slowly and covered the distance in a little less than 21 minutes; three days earlier I had broken 20 minutes and just gone under 190 pounds.

So now I was at least 20 pounds lighter and five minutes faster than I had been. My heart had not given me any trouble at all. When I started running, my pulse rate was around 90 beats a minute; now it had been reduced to the low 80s — still not good, but better than I had expected so soon.

By the end of the first year I had run a total of 714 miles. I had spent 105 hours, 17 minutes, 4.2 seconds on the track and probably three times that much time boring people talking about it. I had bought a stopwatch and a lap counter. Both are useful in trying to avoid the tedium that accompanies indoor running. And I had gotten rid of the judo slippers.

Toward the end of that first year of jogging I was sent to England on a story. I went to a track meet in which Ron Hill, the magnificent English distance runner, and Derek Clayton, the Australian marathoner, were competing. I wondered how they viewed the amazing amount of miles they cover in preparation for their world-record tries.

"It's no lark," Hill said. "Running is certainly never that. It's a bloody bore at best and damned painful at worst, but then I don't even approach Clayton's training schedule."

Clayton had run the fastest marathon in history, covering the 26 miles 385 yards in an almost unbelievable two hours, eight minutes, which works out to slightly less than five minutes per mile. Since I knew very well that I would be lucky to ever approach seven minutes for one mile, I looked at Clayton as if he were superman, which indeed he is.

"He doesn't talk much about it," Hill said, "but I've trained with him in Australia. On my long day I go up into the hills in the morning and run a 27-mile course, going a good pace, and Derek runs with me. For me that's the lot for the day. Derek goes back in the afternoon and runs another 20."

"You must love to run," I said to Clayton. I could not conceive of anyone running 47 miles in a day without getting some pleasure from it. "I hate it," he said. "Absolutely. But I want very much to be the best in the world at something, and I'll make the sacrifice for that."

I spent a month in London staying at a flat in Chelsea. The London Y does not have an indoor track. There is, for that matter, only one indoor track in all England, since the British are a hardy race, regarding any temperature over 75° as a heat wave. They have many more joggers per capita than we do in America, and they train in appalling weather. They consider it bracing.

I wound up jogging at the Duke of York's Headquarters on — or rather, in — the King's Road. Our flat was only a few blocks from the track, and at first I used to take my running gear with me in an airline flight bag and change in the dressing room. But I found out rather quickly that the English do not believe in coddling their athletes.

The dressing quarters at the Duke of York were small and bare, a room with wooden benches along the side and hooks on the wall for clothing. There were two showers and a toilet. After three or four days of shivering showers under a thin, lukewarm stream of water and a freezing 10 minutes while I toweled frantically and dressed like a fireman, I decided I would rather put up with the scorn of the local runners than catch pneumonia. From then on I walked to the track in a heavy nylon sweat suit, ran in it until I warmed up, then stripped to my running suit to finish, putting the sweat suit back on under a raincoat for the walk home.

Once an elderly lady who was standing with me waiting for a chance to cross the King's Road looked curiously at my blue sweat suit and red running shoes.

"What kind of costume is that, sir?" she asked.

"It's a sweat suit, m'am," I told her.

"A sweat suit?" she said doubtfully.

"Yes, m'am," I replied, wondering if I should try to explain.

"Coo," she said. "You Americans! Imagine wearing a proper costume just to perspire in!"

It was much easier to progress from jogging three miles a day to six to 10 miles a day than it had been to go from scratch to three. The only problem as the months went by was to find enough time to get in all the running I wanted to do. For a slow, middle-aged runner with a scarred heart, about an hour and a half is needed to go 10 miles. Add to that another hour or so getting to the Y, dressing, showering and dressing again, and a heavy running schedule can account for nearly three hours of the day.

By the time I had reached these distances, however, I had fallen into the syndrome that can easily overtake a jogger, no matter what his age or state of health. In the first few months I was trying only to defeat myself, in the sense that I had to fight a desire to quit jogging and start walking. I did not pay much attention to the other runners on the various tracks where I tortured myself. If a younger or better runner lapped me a few times during the course of my three miles, it never occurred to me to resent it. But as time passed, I found myself changing. Runners who had lapped me when I started were now going only a trifle faster and, as my heart and lungs quit laboring and engaging all the attention of my mind, I became more and more aware of them. And, of course, the stopwatch that I wore on a lanyard around my neck began to assume more and more importance.

The first runner I managed to pass at the West Side Y was Bob Cooper, an attorney who runs despite the pain of a circulation blockage in his legs. I am sure Cooper was never aware I was competing with him. As I consciously began to compete, I would pick out a runner a bit faster than I and set a time goal — so many weeks or months — to match his pace. At first, I would decide to stay with him for the last half-mile of my run, building in a strong finish, and would do my best to pass him in the last two or three laps. Sometimes he would accelerate when I did and make it impossible for me to edge by him. Now and then I would pass a runner and have him pass me back, he looking ahead, seeming to pay me no attention.

As my speed increased, I was able to catch and lap others — a small, dark man whom I referred to mentally as the bank clerk, and another, faster runner who was very tall with a tremendous stride. Then I went after a muscular, compact man who lost about 15 pounds in the six months it took me to reach his speed and go beyond it. He had a square, tough face so that I always thought of him as a policeman, although I never found out either his name or occupation. And so it went, step by step.

I now recognize most of the regulars at the Y by their shoes and the shape of their backs and the rhythm of their strides. On a small track, whether you are passing or being passed, what you see is the rears of the other runners. It is only when I have finished running and am walking around the track to warm down that I look at their faces.

It is perhaps because of this sense of competition that I have kept pace and continued to jog. In any case, it is now six years after my heart attack and I am thriving on the competition and the routine. My doctor is astonished at the good condition of my heart and body.

I guess it took a long time for the medical profession to get over the notion that a postcardiac patient should spend the rest of his life as a semi-

invalid. It is my theory that the damaged heart mends with long, slow exercise.
To have that idea accepted may take a long time, too.

    I hope to live to see it.

THE ORIGINAL LITTLE OLD LADY IN TENNIS SHOES

Melvin Maddocks

ROY DECARAVA

One of the nation's best and busiest book critics, Bostonian Melvin Maddocks
has found time to write about motorcycling, hockey and, here,
about one of the most Bostonian achievers ever to come out of California.

Late in the afternoon, when the sun starts to dip and the energies of normal people slump, a relentless rhythmic thudding begins in a brown-shingled garage only a couple of desperate lobs, three or four wild smashes, and maybe a tricky drop shot from the Longwood Cricket Club in Brookline, Mass. Plop-a-BOOM, plop-a-BOOM, plop-a-BOOM. The beat is so regular you could set a metronome to it.

What is this native drum so stubbornly saying to suburban Boston? Open the door at the left side of the garage and walk in. Half a dozen teen-age and pre-teen-age girls form an awed semicircle — apprentice priestesses, some in tennis whites and others in faded blue jeans. They come in the usual sizes and shapes. Fireplugs with determined red faces you wouldn't want to meet on a hockey field. Pale, languid, don't-muss-my-hair types — sex goddesses of Beaver Country Day School. But all have one thing in common: a tennis racket in hand, clutched like the Holy Grail.

In the middle, towered over by the taller girls, stands a Little Old Lady in Tennis Shoes. Plop-a-BOOM, plop-a-BOOM, plop-a-BOOM. A scuffed tennis ball is being propelled with controlled fury against a square of unpainted plywood at the back of the garage. Like a computer-directed missile the ball keeps hitting precisely the same spot — a little to the right of center — then arches back, bouncing obediently onto the face of the waiting racket as if magnetized.

Little Old Lady has the voice of a genteel marine drill sergeant. As she strokes her flawless forehand she lays it on the recruits. Plop-a-BOOM. "Be ready!" Plop-a-BOOM. "Move! Move!" Plop-a-BOOM. "Do I give the impression I have lots of time?" Plop-a-BOOM. "I have, I *have.*"

Now it is the pupils' turn. God have mercy on them, Little Old Lady won't. Her fierce cries rattle the garage windows:

"Where did you aim that ball?"

"Don't cross your feet! Don't ever let me see you cross your feet."

"Be determined! Be determined! You're the master of the ball."

What did these poor teeny-tennis-boppers do to bring into their nice permissive little lives this sadistic perfectionist? As they lunge under those gray-blue eyes that miss nothing, absolutely nothing, they become total believers. They are (plop-a-BOOM) in the presence of a superhuman, who certainly, beyond a doubt (plop-a-BOOM), was *there* when the first tennis ball bounced on American soil.

Well, this is not far wrong.

Hazel Hotchkiss Wightman, also known as the Queen Mother of U.S. tennis, was born in Healdsburg, Calif. 85 years ago, just 12 years after a Long

Island socialite named Mary Ewing Outerbridge, back from winter-watering in Bermuda, brought through New York Customs a suspicious bundle — the first tennis rackets and balls to enter the U.S. The epoch-spanning Wightman chronology goes like this:

In 1902, when her present pupils' great-grandmothers were teen-agers themselves she won her first tournament.

About the time pupils' grandmothers were being born, she was copping her four U.S. Women's Singles championships (1909, '10, '11, '19).

In 1923, when grandmother was just learning to run around her backhand, Hazel Wightman introduced team competition between women of the U.S. and Great Britain. (The silver vase she donated as a trophy has come to be known, of course, as the Wightman Cup. Mrs. Wightman was playing captain of the American team five times between 1923 and 1931 and nonplaying captain eight times between 1933 and 1948.

In 1952, when the pupils' mothers were the pupils' age, she shared her ninth Women's Veterans' Doubles championship — her 43rd national title.

American tennis is almost 100 years old. The tiny, squarish frame of Hazel Hotchkiss Wightman has stood figuratively and often literally on center court for 70 of those years — a player, a myth, a monument. She even has a club named after her: The Hazel Hotchkiss Wightman Tennis Center, Inc. of Weston, Mass.

What, O Lord, is an American woman tennis player? Treacherous and irresistible question. Can any general profile include all the particular profiles from Mary Ewing Outerbridge to Billie Jean King? There may not be even a half-satisfactory answer. But if there is, it must have an awful lot to do with the answer to that other irresistible — and treacherous — question: What is a Hazel Hotchkiss Wightman?

If she was not there — not quite — when Mary Ewing Outerbridge turned in her croquet mallet for a tennis racket, Hazel was there when tennis was a hoity-toity game, claimed as the exclusive property of those effete Eastern aristocrats of Boston, New York and Newport. The old printmakers caught the tone of a pastime a Henry James heroine might have indulged in before tea, discreetly swaddled in ankle-length skirt with one hand on her racket and one on her haute couture hat. Strictly no sweat.

Hazel was also there when — like well-coordinated doubles partners — tennis as a social institution and tennis as a game began to change styles: when Mary Ewing Outerbridge was succeeded by Althea Gibson, out of Harlem's Blue Book, and when the ladies who once went pitty-pat began to go slam-bang.

The degenteelization of Hazel and American tennis began in a backyard in Healdsburg in the 1890s. The childhood of most women tennis players contains one of two tormentors: nagging parents who make the mothers of child movie stars seem unambitious; or mean, mean big brothers. The parents of Suzanne Lenglen, French champion of the 1920s, were monsters, mesdames and messieurs. Monsters! Nancy Richey's father is a notable later case of tennis Tartar. Hazel's father was a benign man who tended to his grapes and spinach, founded a small canning company (later amalgamated into Del Monte) and allowed his daughter to use the space between dormer windows as a bangboard. What Hazel had were brothers — four of them, three older. She played football and baseball with them, filling the roles of the junior-lackey athlete: blocking back and fungo hitter.

Hazel was a beneficiary of the "Watch Sis" syndrome. For example: "Watch Sis climb this ladder with her *hands*."

"Sis may not have had it in the beginning," Hazel Wightman likes to recall. "But she sure got it in the end."

For a while Hazel ran more on motivation than muscle. Woman athlete, thy name is frailty. One day psychologists will run the health records of women tennis players through the old computer and confound themselves. Suzanne Lenglen, naturally, was a comparative physical wreck, dying at 39. Alice Marble had TB. Helen Jacobs suffered from pleurisy. Hazel was so sickly as a child that she spent more time out of school than in.

By the time she started tennis, her delicate days were behind her. But her health cure — composed of pole vaulting as well as ladder climbing, baseball and football — was so strenuous that she has continued for 70 years to regard sports as a kind of obstacle course for the character. It seems perfectly consistent that her first court was a rough rectangle of gravel, divided by a rope stretched from her house to a rosebush. "You didn't dare risk a bounce — you had to volley," Hazel remembers gratefully. "Best training I could have had."

Another blessing well disguised was that once she got into tennis seriously, Hazel had to rise at 5:30 and sprint for a court at the University of California a mile away. In those pre-Lib days, girls were allowed to play only until 8 a.m.

Once a woman tennis player has overcome illness, satisfied her brothers and/or father (Hazel's brothers spurred her on by calling her "Rotten!") and battled for her space on the court, she is likely to flash a winning temperament that makes most male competitors look like milksops. And nothing hones her to a razor's edge like an Arch Rival. Helen Wills Moody had her Helen Jacobs. Hazel had her May Sutton.

Hazel's ground strokes (plop-a-BOOM) were automaton-steady, but her serve was what you might expect from a girl just over five feet. So she won by doing what no lady was supposed to do in those days: hitching up her petticoats and storming the net. With her vincible serve, Hazel was never quite fast enough to reach the net in one sprint. Here the old gravel-court training paid off. "Be ready! Be ready!" Hazel was. She could half-volley an opponent's return in that no man's land between the baseline and the net — a feat few players even today can manage consistently. Then she would make it to the net for her opponent's second return — and WHAM!

A 1910 photograph shows what May Sutton and the other tigers of Early American tennis were up against. Hazel wears a kerchief tied no-nonsense around her hair. Her mouth is set in what might be described as a pleasantly menacing smile. Even standing still in a prim ankle-length skirt, she exudes force — a kind of hunger for combat. The daughter of a man who crossed the country from Kentucky in a wagon train, she looks through the camera with the cool, farsighted gaze of a pioneer woman herself.

What did England make of Hazel when she first sailed over in 1905, regaling her fellow passengers from the ship's keyboard with her version of *The Maple Leaf Rag*? What did Boston make of her when she married George Wightman and moved East in 1912? The records are lost in time or blurred by polite nostalgia. But even New England must have been daunted by Hazel, the exuberant Californian who outdid the natives in Puritan will.

During her championship years she managed to bear — and breast-feed — five children. (She now has 13 grandchildren and seven great-grandchildren.) And between family and tennis a veritable lifetime of Good Works has been squeezed in. A compulsive cross-stitcher and cookie-baker, she earned a 50-year service pin with the Red Cross, working in hospital canteens during two World Wars, dishing up a couple of dozen hot dogs at once ("Be ready! Be ready!"), manning 20 or 30 tubs of ice cream. Perhaps her fondest Spartan dreams relive her hostess duties at the docks or at the airport, comforting the troops with coffee and doughnuts at 5 a.m. in the dead of winter.

She has a "hopelessly grooved zeal for helping her neighbor," one Hazel watcher has summed up. As the years have gone by, this zeal has manifested itself as a positive passion for teaching. Her record might well make her the most successful instructor in the history of American tennis, and certainly the cheapest — she has never taken a cent.

Tennis coaching, particularly among women, can be a Byzantine business, full of blood-oath allegiances and murderous fallings-out. More than once Hazel has found herself coaching Arch Rivals. Helen Moody was her star pupil, but she also drilled Helen Jacobs. She even entertained the two Helens and their mothers as her house guests — a situation roughly comparable to sleeping-in four Lady Macbeths. During tournament week at Longwood, Hazel has put up — on window-seat mattresses, on sofa cushions — as many as 14 protégées and Arch Rivals.

Being a great teacher demands not only superlative tact but extra supplies of stoicism. What does teacher do when two pupils are battling it out with each other? "I usually want the one who is playing better tennis to win," Hazel wrote bravely in her peak teaching days, "but sometimes I have been so divided in my mind as to suffer at mistakes on both sides. This is so exhausting that I have been forced of late to cultivate an indifferent attitude while the play is on."

Tennis teachers, like theologians, can be divided into three general categories: fundamental, neoorthodox and liberal. The liberals say God gave every man his own unique style for hitting a ball with a racket. *Be natural. Be yourself.* There is no "right" way or "wrong" way. If you get the ball over the net and in the court, that's right. The neoorthodox say sure, that's all well and good. But there are, ahem, certain principles, certain laws of physics. No one way is absolutely right — but would you believe two right ways, or even three? Then, with a light but firm hand on the sleeve of your warmup jacket, they give you the allowable options. For instance: the Eastern grip (like shaking hands with the racket) or the Western grip (hand a quarter of a turn back on the handle). And so on. The fundamentalist has found the Truth, and he sees no reason not to share it. He has tested his Truth under fire, and until you can show him a better way — and you never will — he is going to stick with his.

Hazel, at times, can sound like a liberal. She will say of very young children learning the game: "If they're not told something else, they'll do it right themselves — like walking." But her notion of early learning is extreme, even by present educational standards. (Just last fall she sawed off the handle of a racket and presented the shortened instrument to a former pupil's baby on her first birthday.)

At other times, Hazel can sound neoorthodox. She will speak with a nice latitude of "economy of motion" and "rhythm" — that cover word for all athletic directors. She can play it as broad as anybody with tactics: "Use whatever shot will keep your opponent at her worst."

But by modern tastes at least, Hazel is more nearly a fundamentalist than anything else. In fact, she began teaching half a century ago rather in the spirit of a revival meeting. She would grab rackets, balls, whatever Wightman tot was on the scene, and hop a streetcar to her next improvised clinic — Beaver Country Day, Windsor, Brookline High. Five afternoons a week she taught girls in gyms, on hard-surface playgrounds, anywhere a ball would bounce. Then for four decades of Saturday mornings she conducted mass classes at Longwood, climaxing in an astonishing organizational feat: one-day tournaments involving up to 100 children, supervised with a jolly iron hand by Hazel, who describes herself thus: "I like to be businesslike and have fun."

Her own upbringing plus all those years of plop-a-BOOM have made Hazel, if not quite a fundamentalist, a fellow traveler to one. Her intuitions about what makes a champion are crystallized in a book she wrote called *Better Tennis.* The pages bristle with imperatives:

"Shoulders high, arms out."

"The left hand must hold the racket at the throat."

"Skip before and after hitting."

But what really strikes a reader is the way technical advice keeps slipping into a kind of metaphysics:

"Cultivate a buoyant spirit."

"Your footwork is life."

In the end Hazel gives license to the copybook moralist struggling to come out and includes an appendix of "Slogans and Maxims":

"Make excuses for others, never for yourself."

"Don't worry over your mistakes. Overcome them."

The burden of Hazel's moral injunctions have been borne not only by her pupils but by her doubles partners. Her greatest gift as a doubles player, cynics have sneered, was to choose brilliant partners — including Helen Wills Moody and Bill Tilden. But her partners, for their sins, have had to suffer the divine dissatisfaction Hazel feels for anything short of perfection. "It is hard to express in words the comfort there is in playing with a partner who helps at every stage," she has written. "But how few such partners there are!"

Not that Hazel is a bad loser. "Be a considerate winner and a cheerful loser," saith the Slogans and Maxims, and Hazel always practices what she preaches. But how she wants to be a considerate winner.

The terrors and pleasures of playing with Hazel have not excluded what one partner called "jocular battle cries." When badly down in a game, she likes to shout cheerfully: "Forty-love is no lead." When badly down in a set — say, 5–0 — her half-serious idea of a bon mot was to ask her opponents: "Give up?"

"I have even known a player to ask her partner to keep still," she once wrote in slightly shocked disbelief.

To this day Hazel can't honestly understand why the whole world doesn't feel about tennis as she does. She remembers — practically her first memory — how fascinated she always was by a ball, "anything round." The toss, the recoil, the bounce, the brief, marvelous defiance of gravity. She would love to turn every child who can stand into a ball freak like herself. She points to the refrigerator — she calls it "ice box" — and tells a great-grandson, "If you can keep 20 going without missing, "I'll give you a penny." To the child's mother she explains the advantages of indoor volleying: "The risk of a broken vase or lamp makes skill and accuracy even more of a challenge."

As a teacher, Hazel has been less a Svengali-maker of champions than a converter of the heathen, an evangelist preaching to the gawky and the shy, the sickly and the listless, salvation through tennis. She is in love, not with those who win but with those who want the most to win, the fighters, the scramblers — the Casalses, the Goolagongs ("I sense what's inside her").

A skill fanatic herself, she cannot resist those who are fanatic about different skills. For instance, Ted Williams: "He had such an exact knowledge of himself, of what he was doing." Or Bob Cousy — above all, Bob Cousy: "He was so far ahead of everybody, and he kept giving back what he had." These are her saints — and the figure of speech is barely that. For tennis is practically a religion to Hazel, at the very least a holy "channel of intensified life."

In 1906 she was asked to play a match for $300. "Of course I can't" she replied. "I play for the love of it." This is 1972, and amateurs — people who play for the love of it — are mostly waiting for the right moment to cash their virginity in. Frank Merriwell is dead. *Psychology Today* researchers prove that sports have nothing to do with character, and vice versa. And the New Jock pronounces that the game — any game — isn't worth the candle, any candle.

Hazel is aware of all this, without understanding it. She knows that there are other things in life than sports, and that sports have become Big Business. But she can't help herself. At 85, as at 15, her notion of heaven is a world where courage, gallantry, intelligence, even love — every facet of character — is defined by a girl's relationship to some kind of ball and to her opponent on the far side of that ball.

Who is this fugitive from an old sports reel and why is she saying those awful things about us? What does she know that we don't know that makes a game — a game — so worth it?

As she performs her small miracle — ball-to-target-to-racket-to-target — she puts the question oh, so guilelessly in her own way, partly to the silent young statues around her but maybe mostly to the ball: "What (plop-a-BOOM) do you think (plop-a-BOOM) Billie Jean King will be doing (plop-a-BOOM) when she's my age?"

WHAM!

POP, POP, HIT THOSE PEOPLE

Don DeLillo

Don DeLillo has been acclaimed as one of the finest
young fiction writers in America, and this excerpt
from his novel End Zone is testimony not only to his
intimate feeling for the nuances of football but also a
desire "to explore the limits of language."

DAVID NOYES

Taft Robinson was the first black student to be enrolled at Logos College in West Texas. They got him for his speed.

By the end of that first season he was easily one of the best running backs in the history of the Southwest. In time he might have turned up on television screens across the land, endorsing $8,000 automobiles or avocado-flavored instant shave. His name on a chain of fast-food outlets. His life story on the back of cereal boxes. A drowsy monograph might be written on just that subject, the modern athlete as commercial myth, with footnotes. But this doesn't happen to be it. There were other intonations to that year, for me at least, the phenomenon of anti-applause — words broken into brute sound, a consequent silence of metallic texture. And so Taft Robinson, rightly or wrongly, no more than haunts this story. I think it's fitting in a way. The mansion has long been haunted (double metaphor coming up) by the invisible man.

But let's keep things simple. Football players are simple folk. Whatever complexities, whatever dark politics of the human mind, the heart — these are noted only within the chalked borders of the playing field. At times strange visions ripple across that turf; madness leaks out. But wherever else he goes, the football player travels the straightest of lines. His thoughts are wholesomely commonplace, his actions uncomplicated by history, enigma, holocaust or dream.

A passion for simplicity, for the true old things, as of boys on bicycles delivering newspapers, filled our days and nights that fierce summer. We practiced in the undulating heat with nothing to sustain us but the conviction that things here were simple. Hit and get hit; key the pulling guard; run over people; suck some ice and reassume the three-point stance. We were a lean and dedicated squad run by a hungry coach and his seven oppressive assistants. Some of us were more simple than others; a few might be called outcasts or exiles; three or four, as on every football team, were crazy. But we were all — even myself — we were all dedicated.

We did grass drills at 106° in the sun. We attacked the blocking sleds and strutted through the intersecting ropes. We stood in what was called the chute (a narrow strip of ground bordered on two sides by blocking dummies), and we went one-on-one, blocker and pass-rusher, and hand-fought each other to the earth. We butted, clawed and kicked. There were any number of fistfights. There was one sprawling free-for-all that the coaches allowed to continue for about five minutes, standing on the sidelines looking pleasantly bored as we kicked each other in the shins and threw dumb rights and lefts at caged faces, the more impulsive taking off their helmets and swinging them at anything that moved. In the evenings we prayed.

I was one of the exiles. There were many times, believe it, when I wondered what I was doing in that remote and unfed place, that summer tundra, being hit high and low by a foaming pair of 240-pound Texans. Being so tired and sore at night that I could not raise an arm to brush my teeth. Being made to obey the savage commands of unreasonable men. Being set apart from all styles of civilization as I had known or studied them. Being led in prayer every evening, with the rest of the squad, by our coach, warlock and avenging patriarch. Being made to lead a simple life.

Then they told us that Taft Robinson was coming to school. I looked forward to his arrival — an event, finally, in a time of incidents and small despairs. But my teammates seemed sullen at the news. It was a break with simplicity, the haunted corner of a dream, some piece of forest magic to scare them in the night.

Taft was a transfer student from Columbia. The word on him was good all the way. 1) He ran the 100 in 9.3 seconds. 2) He had good moves and good hands. 3) He was strong and rarely fumbled. 4) He broke tackles like a man pushing through a turnstile. 5) He could pass-block — when in the mood.

But mostly he could fly — 9.3 speed. He had real sprinter's speed. Speed is the last excitement left, the one thing we haven't used up, still naked in its potential, the mysterious black gift that thrills the millions.

(Exile or outcast: distinctions tend to vanish when the temperature exceeds 100°.)

Taft Robinson showed up at the beginning of September, about two weeks before regular classes were to start. The squad, originally 100 bodies, soon down to 60, soon less, had reported in the middle of August. Taft had missed spring practice and 20 days of the current session. I didn't think he'd be able to catch up. I was in the president's office the day he arrived. The president was Mrs. Tom Wade, the founder's widow. Everybody called her Mrs. Tom. She was the only woman I had ever seen who might accurately be described as Lincolnesque. Beyond appearance, I had no firm idea of her reality: she was tall, black-browed, stark as a railroad spike.

I was there because I was a Northerner. Apparently they thought my presence would help make Taft feel at home, an idea I tended to regard as laughable. (He was from Brooklyn, having gone on to Columbia from Boys' High, a school known for the athletes it turns out.) Mrs. Tom and I sat waiting.

"My husband loved this place," she said. "He built it out of nothing. He had an idea, and he followed it through to the end. He believed in reason. He was a man of reason. He cherished the very word. Unfortunately he was mute."

"I didn't know that."

"All he could do was grunt. He made disgusting sounds. Spit used to collect at both corners of his mouth. It wasn't a real pretty sight."

Taft walked in flanked by our head coach, Emmett Creed, and backfield coach, Oscar Veech. Right away I estimated height and weight, about 6′ 2″ and 210. Good shoulders, narrow waist, acceptable neck. Prize beef at the county fair. He wore a dark gray suit that may have been as old as he was.

Mrs. Tom made her speech.

"Young man, I have always admired the endurance of your people. You've a tough row to hoe. Frankly I was against this from the start. When they told me their plan, I said it was bushwa. Complete bushwa. But Emmett Creed is a mighty persuasive man. This won't be easy for any of us. But what's reason for if not to get us through the hard times? There now. I've had my say. Now you go on ahead with Coach Creed, and when you're all through talking football you be sure to come on back here and see Mrs. Berry Trout next door. She'll get you all settled on courses and accommodations and things. History will be our ultimate judge."

Then it was my turn.

"Gary Harkness," I said. "We're more or less neighbors. I'm from upstate New York."

"How far up?" he said.

"Pretty far. Very far in fact. Small town in the Adirondacks."

We went over to the players' dorm, an isolated unit just about completed but with no landscaping out front and WET PAINT signs everywhere. I left the three of them in Taft's room and went downstairs to get suited up for afternoon practice. Moody Kimbrough, our right tackle and offensive captain, stopped me as I was going through the isometrics area.

"Is he here?"

"He is here," I said.

"That's nice. That's real nice."

In the training room Jerry Fallon had his leg in the whirlpool. He was doing a crossword puzzle in the local newspaper.

"Is he here?"

"He is everywhere," I said.

"Who?"

"Supreme being of heaven and earth. Three letters."

"You know who I mean."

"He's here all right. He's all here. Two hundred and fifty-five pounds of solid mahogany."

"How much?" Fallon said.

"They're thinking of playing him at guard. He came in a little heavier than they expected. About 255. Left guard, I think Coach said."

"You kidding me, Gary?"

"Left guard's your spot, isn't it? I just realized."

"How much does he weigh again?"

"He came in at 255, 260. Solid bronze right from the foundry. Coach calls him the fastest two-five-five in the country."

"He's supposed to be a running back," Fallon said.

"That was before he added weight."

"I think you're kidding me, Gary."

"That's right," I said.

We ran through some new plays for about an hour. Creed's assistants moved among us yelling at our mistakes. Creed himself was up in the tower studying overall patterns. I saw Taft on the sidelines with Oscar Veech. The players kept glancing that way. When the second unit took over on offense, I went to the far end of the field and grubbed around for a spot of shade in which to sit. Finally I just sank into the canvas fence and remained more or less upright, contemplating the distant fury. These canvas blinds surrounded the entire practice field in order to discourage spying by future opponents. The blinds were one of the many innovations Creed had come up with — innovations as far as this particular college was concerned. He had also had the tower built, as well as the separate living quarters for the football team. (To instill a sense of unity.) This was Creed's first year here. He had been born in Texas, in either a log cabin or a manger, depending on who was telling the story, on the banks of the Rio Grande in what is now Big Bend National Park. The sporting press liked to call him Big Bend. He made a few All-America teams as a tailback in the old single-wing days at SMU and then flew a B-29 during the war and later played halfback for three years with the Chicago Bears. He went into coaching then, first as an assistant to George Halas in Chicago and then as head coach in the Missouri Valley Conference, the Southeastern Conference and the Big Eight. He became famous for creating order out of chaos, building good teams at schools known for their perennial losers. He had four unbeaten seasons, five conference champions and two national champions. Then a second-string quarterback said or did something he didn't like, and Creed broke his jaw. It became something of a national scandal, and he went into obscurity for three years until Mrs. Tom beckoned him to West Texas.

It was a long drop down from the Big Eight, but Creed managed to convince the widow that a good football team could put her lonely little school on the map. So priorities were changed, new assistants were hired, alumni were courted, a certain amount of oil money began to flow, a certain number of private planes were made available for recruiting purposes, the team name was changed from the Cactus Wrens to the Screaming Eagles — and Emmett Creed was on the comeback trail. The only thing that didn't make sense was the ton of canvas that hid our practice sessions. There was nothing out there but insects.

The first unit was called back in, and I headed slowly toward the dust and noise. Creed up in the tower spoke through his bullhorn.

"Defense, I'd appreciate some pursuit. They don't give points for apathy in this sport. Pursue those people. Come out of the ground at them. Hit somebody. Hit somebody. Hit somebody."

On the first play Garland Hobbs, our quarterback, faked to me going straight into the line and then pitched to the other setback, Jim Deering. He got hit first by a linebacker, Dennis Smee, who drove him into the ground, getting some belated and very nasty help from a tackle and another linebacker. Deering didn't move. Two assistant coaches started shouting at him, telling him he was defacing the landscape. He tried to get up but couldn't make it. The rest of us walked over to the far hash mark and ran the next play.

It all ended with two laps around the goalposts. Lloyd Philpot Jr., a defensive end, fell down in the middle of the second lap. We left him there in the end zone, on his stomach, one leg twitching slightly. His father had been All-Conference at Baylor for three straight years.

That evening Emmett Creed addressed the squad.

"Write home on a regular basis. Dress neatly. Be courteous. Articulate your problems. Move swiftly from place to place, both on the field and in the corridors of buildings. Don't ever get too proud to pray."

Rolf Hauptfuhrer coached the defensive line and attended to problems of morale and grooming. He approached me one morning after practice.

"We want you to room with Bloomberg," he said.

"Why me?"

"John Billy Small was in there with him. Couldn't take the tension. We figure you won't mind. You're more the complicated type."

"Of course I'll mind."

"John Billy said he wets the bed. Aside from that there's no problem. He gets nervous. No doubt about that. A lot of tension in that frame. But we figure you can cope with it."

"I object. I really do. I've got my own tensions."

"Harkness, everybody knows what kind of reputation you brought down here. Coach is willing to take a chance on you only as long as you follow orders. So keep in line. Just keep in line — hear?"

"Who's rooming with Taft Robinson?" I said.

"Robinson rooms alone."

"Why's that?"

"You'll have to ask the powers that be. In the meantime, move your stuff in with Bloomberg."

"I don't like tension," I said. "And I don't see why I have to be the one who gets put in with controversial people."

"It's for the good of the team," Hauptfuhrer said.

I went up to my room. Bloomberg was asleep, on his belly, snoring softly into the pillow. He was absolutely enormous. It was easy to imagine him attached to the bed by guy wires, to be floated aloft once a year like a Macy's balloon. His full name was Anatole Bloomberg, and he played left tackle on offense. That was all I knew about him, that plus the fact that he wasn't a Texan. One of the outcasts, I thought. Or a voluntary exile of the philosophic type. I decided to wake him up.

"Anatole," I said. "It's Gary Harkness, your new roommate. Let's shake hands and be friends."

"We're roommates," he said. "Why do we have to be friends?"

"It's just an expression. I didn't mean undying comrades. Just friends as opposed to enemies. I'm sorry I woke you up."

"I wasn't asleep."

"You were snoring," I said.

"That's the way I breathe when I'm on my stomach. What happened to my original roommate?"

"John Billy? John Billy's been moved."

"Was that his name?"

"He's been moved. I hope you're not tense about my showing up. All I want to do is get off to a good start and avoid all possible tension."

"Who in your opinion was the greater man?" Bloomberg said. "Edward Gibbon or Archimedes?"

"Archimedes."

"Correct," he said.

In the morning Creed sent us into an all-out scrimmage with a brief inspirational message that summed up everything we knew or had to know.

"It's only a game," he said, "but it's the only game."

Taft Robinson and I were the setbacks. Taft caught a flare pass, evaded two men and went racing down the sideline. Bobby Iselin, a cornerback, gave up the chase at the 25. Bobby used to be the team's fastest man.

Through all our days together my father returned time and again to a favorite saying.

"Suck in that gut and go harder."

He never suggested that this saying of his ranked with the maxims of Teddy Roosevelt. Still, he was dedicated to it. He believed in the idea that a simple but lasting reward, something just short of a presidential handshake, awaited the extra effort, the persevering act of a tired man. Backbone, will, mental toughness, desire — these were his themes, the qualities that insured success. He was a pharmaceutical salesman with a lazy son.

It seems that wherever I went I was hounded by people urging me to suck in my gut and go harder. They would never give up on me — my father, my teachers, my coaches, even a girl friend or two. I was a challenge, I guess, a piece of string that does not wish to be knotted. My father was by far the most tireless of those who tried to give me direction, to sharpen my initiative, to piece together some collective memory of hard-won land or dusty struggles in the sun. He put a sign in my room:

WHEN THE GOING GETS TOUGH
THE TOUGH GET GOING

I looked at this sign for three years (roughly from ages 14 to 17) before I began to perceive a certain beauty in it. The sentiment of course had small appeal, but it seemed that beauty flew from the words themselves, the letters, consonants swallowing vowels, aggression and tenderness, a semi-self-re-creation from line to line, word to word, letter to letter. All meaning faded. The words became pictures. It was a sinister thing to discover at such an age that words can escape their meanings.

My father had a territory and a company car. He sold vitamins, nutritional supplements, mineral preparations and antibiotics. His customers included about 50 doctors and dentists, about a dozen pharmacies, a few hospitals, some drug wholesalers. He had specific goals, both geographic and economic, each linked with the other, and perhaps because of this he hated waste of any kind, of shoe leather, talent, irretrievable time. (Get cracking. Straighten out. Hang in.) It paid, in his view, to follow the simplest, most pioneer of rhythms — the eternal work cycle, the blood hunt for bear and deer, the mellow rocking of chairs as screen doors swing open and bang shut in the gathering fragments of summer's sulky dusk. Beyond these honest latitudes lay nothing but chaos.

He had played football at Michigan State. He had ambitions on my behalf, and more or less at my expense. This is the custom among men who have failed to be heroes; their sons must prove that the seed was not impoverished. He had spent his autumn Saturdays on the sidelines, watching others fall in battle and rise then to the thunder of the drums and the crowd's demanding chants. He put me in a football uniform very early. Then, as a high school junior, I won All-State honors at halfback. (This was the first of his ambitions, and as it turned out the only one to be fulfilled.) Eventually I received 28 offers of athletic scholarships — tuition, books, room and board, $15 a month. There were several broad hints of further almsgiving. Visions were painted of lovely young ladies with charitable instincts of their own. It seemed that every section of the country had much to offer in the way of scenery, outdoor activities, entertainment, companionship, and even, if necessary, education. On the application blanks I had to fill in my height, my weight, my academic average and my time for the 40-yard dash.

I handed over a letter of acceptance to Syracuse University. I was eager to enrich their tradition of great running backs. They threw me out when I barricaded myself in my room with two packages of Oreo cookies and a girl named Lippy Margolis. She wanted to hide from the world, and I volunteered to help her. For a day and a night we read to each other from a textbook on economics. She seemed calmed by the incoherent doctrines set forth on those pages. When I was sure I had changed the course of her life for the better, I opened the door.

At Penn State, the next stop, I studied hard and played well. But each day that autumn was exactly like the day before and the one to follow. I had not yet learned to appreciate the slowly gliding drift of identical things; chunks of time spun past me like meteorites in a universe predicated on repetition. For weeks the cool clear weather was unvarying; the girls wore white knee-high stockings; a small red plane passed over the practice field every afternoon at the same time. There was something hugely Asian about those days in Pennsylvania. I tripped on the same step on the same staircase on three successive days. After this I stopped going to practice.

The freshman coach wanted to know what was up. I told him I knew all the plays; there was no reason to practice them over and over; the endless repetition might be spiritually disastrous; we were becoming a nation devoted to human xerography. He and I had a long earnest discussion. Much was made of my talent and my potential value to the varsity squad. Oneness was stressed — the oneness necessary for a winning team. It was a good concept, oneness, but I suggested that, to me at least, it could not be truly attractive unless it meant oneness with God or the universe or some equally redoubtable superphenomenon. What he meant by oneness was in fact elevenness or twenty-twoness. He told me that my attitude was all wrong. People don't go to football games to see pass patterns run by theologians. He told me, in effect, that I would have to suck in my gut and go harder. He mentioned, 1) A team sport. 2) The need to sacrifice. 3) Preparation for the future. 4) Microcosm of life.

"You're saying that what I learn on the gridiron about sacrifice and oneness will be of inestimable value later on in life. In other words, If I give up now I'll almost surely give up in the more important contests of the future."

"That's it exactly, Gary."

"I'm giving up," I said.

It was a perverse thing to do — go home and sit through a blinding white winter in the Adirondacks. I was passing through one of those odd periods of youth in which significance is seen only on the blankest of walls, found only in dull places, and so I thought I'd turn my back to the world and to my father's sign and try to achieve, indeed establish, some lowly form of American sainthood. The repetition of Penn State was small stuff compared to that deep winter. For five months I did nothing and then repeated it. I had breakfast in the kitchen, lunch in my room, dinners at the dinner table with the others, meaning my parents. They concluded that I was dying of something slow and incurable and that I did not wish to tell them in order to spare their feelings. This was an excellent thing to infer for all concerned. My father took down the sign and hung in its place a framed photo of his favorite pro team, the Detroit Lions — their official team picture. In late spring, a word appeared all over town. MILITARIZE. The word was printed on cardboard placards that stood in shop windows. It was scrawled on fences. It was handwritten on loose-leaf paper taped to the windshields of cars. It appeared on bumper stickers and signboards.

I had accomplished nothing all those months, and so I decided to enroll at the University of Miami. It wasn't a bad place. Repetition gave way to the beginnings of simplicity. (A preparation thus for Texas.) I wanted badly to stay. I liked playing football, and I knew that by this time I'd have trouble finding another school that would take me. But I had to leave. It started with a book, an immense volume about the possibilities of nuclear war — assigned reading for a course I was taking in modes of disaster technology. The problem was simple and terrible: I enjoyed the book. I liked reading about the deaths of tens of millions of people. I liked dwelling on the destruction of great cities. Five to 20 million dead. Fifty to 100 million dead. Ninety percent population loss. Seattle wiped out by mistake. Moscow demolished. Airbursts over every SAC base in Europe. I liked to think of huge buildings toppling, of fire storms, of bridges collapsing, survivors roaming the charred countryside. Carbon 14 and strontium 90. Escalation ladder and subcrisis situation. Titan, Spartan, Poseidon. People burned and unable to breathe. I became more fascinated, more depressed, and finally I left Coral Gables and went back home to my room and to the official team photo of the Detroit Lions. It seemed the only thing to do. My mother brought lunch upstairs. I took the dog for walks.

In time the draft board began to get interested. I allowed my father to get in touch with a former classmate of his, an influential alumnus of Michigan State. Negotiations were held, and I was granted an interview with two subalterns of the athletic department, types familiar to football and other paramilitary complexes, the square-jawed bedrock of the corporation. They knew what I could do on the football field, having followed my high school career, but they wouldn't accept me unless I could convince them that I was ready to take orders, to pursue a mature course, to submit my will to the common good. I managed to convince them. I went to East Lansing the following autumn, an aging recruit, and was leading the freshman squad in touchdowns, yards gained rushing, and platitudes. Then, in a game against the Indiana freshmen, I was one of three players converging on a safetyman who had just intercepted a pass. We seemed to hit him simultaneously. He died the next day and I went home that evening.

I stayed in my room for seven weeks this time, shuffling a deck of cards. I got to the point where I could cut to the six of spades about three out of five times, as long as I didn't try it too often, abuse the gift, as long as I tried only when I truly felt an emanation from the six, when I knew in my fingers that I could cut to that particular card.

Then I got a call from Emmett Creed. Two days later he flew up to see me. I liked the idea of losing myself in an obscure part of the world. And I had discovered a very simple truth. My life meant nothing without football.

We stood in a circle in the enormous gray morning, all the receivers and offensive backs, helmets in hands. Thunder moved down from the northeast. Creed, in a transparent raincoat, was already up in the tower. At the center of the circle was Tom Cook Clark, an assistant coach, an expert on quarter-backing, known as a scholarly man because he smoked a pipe and did not use profanity.

"What we want to do is establish a planning procedures approach whereby we neutralize the defense. We'll be employing a lot of play action and some pass-run options off the sweep. We'll be using a minimum number of sprintouts because the passing philosophy here is based on the pocket concept and we don't want to inflate the injury potential, which is what you do if your quarterback strays from the pocket and if he can't run real well, which most don't. We use the aerial game here to implement the ground game whereby we force their defense to respect the run, which is what they won't do if they can anticipate pass and read pass and if our frequency, say on second and long, indicates pass. So that's what we'll try to come up with, depending on the situation and the contingency plan and how they react to the running game. I should insert at this point that if they send their linebackers, you've been trained and briefed and you know how to counter this. You've got your screen, your flare, your quick slant-in. You've been drilled and drilled on this in the blitz drills. It all depends on what eventuates. It's just 11 men doing their job. That's all it is."

Oscar Veech burst into the circle.

"Guards and tackles, I want you to come off that ball real quick and pop, pop, hit those people, move those people out, pop them, put some hurt on them, drive them back till they look like sick little puppy dogs squatting in the mud."

"The guards and tackles are over in that other group," I said.

"Right, right, right. Now go out there and execute. Move that ball. Hit somebody. Hit somebody. Hit somebody."

Garland Hobbs handed off to me on a quick trap, and two people hit me. There was a big pileup, and I felt a fair number of knees and elbows and then somebody's hand was inside my face mask trying to come away with flesh. On the next play I was pass-blocking for Hobbs, and they sent everybody including the free safety. I went after the middle linebacker, Dennis Smee, helmet to groin, and then fell on top of him with a forearm leading the way.

Whistles were blowing, and the coaches edged in a bit closer. Vern Feck took off his baseball cap and put his pink face right into the pileup, little sparks of saliva jumping out of his whistle as he blew it right under my nose. Creed came down from the tower.

One day in early September we started playing a game called Bang You're Dead. It's an extremely simpleminded game. Almost every child has played it in one form or another. Your hand assumes the shape of a gun, and you fire at anyone who passes. You try to reproduce, in your own way, the sound of a gun being fired. Or you simply shout these words: Bang, you're dead. The other person clutches a vital area of his body and then falls, simulating death. (Never mere injury: always death.) Nobody knew who had started the game or exactly when it had started. You had to fall if you were shot. The game depended on this.

It went on for six or seven days. At first, naturally enough, I thought it was all very silly, even for a bunch of bored and lonely athletes. Then I began to change my mind. Suddenly, beneath its bluntness, the game seemed compellingly intricate. It possessed gradations, dark joys, a resonance echoing from the most perplexing of dreams. I began to kill selectively. When killed, I fell to the floor or earth with great deliberation, with sincerity. I varied my falls, searching for the rhythm of something imperishable, a classic death.

We did not abuse the powers inherent in the game. The only massacre took place during the game's first or second day when things were still shapeless, the potential unrealized. It started on the second floor of the dormitory just before lights-out and worked along the floor and down one flight, everyone shooting each other, men in their underwear rolling down the stairs, huge nude brutes draped over the banisters. The pleasure throughout was empty. I guess we realized together that the game was better than this. So we cooled things off and devised unwritten limits.

I shot Terry Madden at sunset from a distance of 40 yards as he appeared over the crest of a small hill and came toward me. He held his stomach and fell, in slow motion, and then rolled down the grassy slope, tumbling, rolling slowly as possible, closer, slower, ever nearer, tumbling down to die at my feet with the pale setting of the sun.

To kill with impunity. To die in the celebration of ancient ways.

All those days the almost empty campus was marked by the sound of human gunfire. There were several ways in which this sound was uttered — the comical, the truly gruesome, the futuristic, the stylized, the circumspect. Each served to break the silence of the long evenings. From the window of my room I'd hear the faint gunfire and see a lone figure in the distance fall to the ground. Sometimes, hearing nothing, I'd merely see the victim get hit, twisting around a tree as he fell or slowly dropping to his knees, and this isolated motion also served to break the silence, the lingering stillness of that time of day. So there was that reason above all to appreciate the game; it forced cracks in the enveloping silence.

I died well and for this reason was killed quite often. One afternoon, shot from behind, I staggered to the steps of the library and remained there, on my back, between the second and seventh steps at the approximate middle of the stairway, for more than a few minutes. It was very relaxing despite the hardness of the steps. I felt the sun on my face. I tried to think of nothing. The longer I remained there, the more absurd it seemed to get up. My body became accustomed to the steps, and the sun felt warmer. I was completely relaxed. I felt sure I was alone, that no one was standing there watching or even walking by. This thought relaxed me even more. In time I opened my eyes. Taft Robinson was sitting on a bench not far away, reading a periodical. For a moment, in a state of near rapture. I thought it was he who had fired the shot.

At length the rest of the student body reported for the beginning of classes. We were no longer alone, and the game ended. But I would think of it with affection because of its scenes of fragmentary beauty, because it brought men closer together through their perversity and fear, because it enabled us to pretend that death could be a tender experience, and because it breached the long silence.

It's not easy to fake a limp. The tendency is to exaggerate, a natural mistake and one that no coach would fail to recognize. Over the years I had learned to eliminate this tendency. I had mastered the dip and grimace, perfected the semi-moan, and when I came off the field this time, after receiving a mild blow on the right calf, nobody considered pressing me back into service. The trainer handed me an ice pack, and I sat on the bench next to Bing Jackmin, who kicked field goals and extra points. The practice field was miserably hot. I was relieved to be off and slightly surprised that I felt guilty about it. Bing Jackmin was wearing headgear; his eyes, deep inside the face mask, seemed crazed by sun or dust or inner visions.

"Work," he shouted past me. "Work, you substandard industrial robots. Work, work, work, work."

"Look at them hit," I said. "What a pretty sight. When Coach says hit, we hit. It's so simple."

"It's not simple, Gary. Reality is constantly being interrupted. We're hardly even aware of it when we're out there. We perform like things with metal claws. But there's the other element. For lack of a better term I call it the psychomythical. That's a phrase I coined myself."

"I don't like it. What does it refer to?"

"Ancient warriorship," he said. "Cults devoted to pagan forms of technology. What we do out on that field harks back. It harks back. Why don't you like the term?"

"It's vague and pretentious. It means nothing. There's only one good thing about it. Nobody could remember a stupid phrase like that for more than five seconds. See, I've already forgotten it."

"Wuuuurrrrk. Wuuuurrrrk."

"Hobbs'll throw to Jessup now," I said. "He always goes to his tight end on third and short inside the 20. He's like a retarded computer."

"For a quarterback, Hobbs isn't too bright. But you should have seen him last year, Gary. At least Creed's got him changing plays at the line. Last year it was all Hobbsie could do to keep from upchucking when he saw a blitz coming. Linebackers pawing at the ground, snarling at him. He didn't have what you might call a whole lot of poise."

"Here comes Cecil off. Is that him?"

"They got old Cecil. Looks like his shoulder."

Cecil Rector, a guard, came toward the sideline, and Roy Yellin went running in to replace him. The trainer popped Cecil's shoulder back into place. Then Cecil fainted. Bing strolled down that way to have a look at Cecil unconscious.

Later we watched Bobby Hopper get about 18 on a sweep. When the play ended, a defensive tackle named Dickie Kidd remained on his knees. He managed to take his helmet off and then fell forward, his face hitting the midfield stripe. Two players dragged him off, and Raymond Toon went running in to replace him. The next play fell apart when Hobbs fumbled the snap. Creed spoke to him through the bullhorn. Bing walked along the bench to look at Dickie Kidd.

I watched the scrimmage. It was getting mean out there. The players were reaching the point where they wanted to inflict harm. It was hardly a time for displays of finesse and ungoverned grace. This was the ugly hour. I felt like getting back in. Bing took his seat again.

"How's Dickie?"

"Dehydration," Bing said. "Hauptfuhrer's giving him hell."

"What for?"

"For dehydrating."

I went over to Oscar Veech and told him I was ready. He said they wanted to take a longer look at Jim Deering. I watched Deering drop a short pass and get hit a full two seconds later by Buddy Shock, a linebacker. This cheered me up, and I returned to the bench.

"They want to look at Deering some more."

"Coach is getting edgy. We open in six days. This is the last scrimmage, and he wants to look at everybody."

"'I wish I knew how good we are."

"Coach must be thinking the same thing."

Time was called, and the coaches moved in to lecture their players. Creed climbed down from the tower and walked slowly toward Garland Hobbs. He took off his baseball cap and brushed it against his thigh as he walked. Hobbs saw him coming and instinctively put on his helmet. Creed engaged him in conversation.

"It's a tongue-lashing," Bing said. "Coach is hacking at poor old Hobbsie."

"He seems pretty calm."

"It's a tongue-lashing," Bing hissed to Cecil Rector, who was edging along the bench to sit next to us.

"How's the shoulder?" I said.

"Dislocated."

"Too bad."

"They can put a harness on it," he said. "We go in six days. If Coach needs me, I'll be ready."

Just then Creed looked toward Bing Jackmin, drawing him off the bench without even a nod. Bing jogged over there. The rest of the players were standing or kneeling between the 40-yard lines. Next to me, Cecil Rector leaned over and plucked at blades of grass. I thought of the Adirondacks, chill lakes of inverted timber, sash of blue snow across the mountains, the whispering presence of the things that filled my room. Far beyond the canvas blinds, on the top floor of the women's dormitory, a figure stood by an open window. I thought of women. I thought of women in snow and rain, on mountains and in forests, at the end of long galleries immersed in the brave light of Rembrandts.

"Coach is real anxious," Rector said. "He knows a lot of people are watching to see how he does. I bet the wire services send somebody out to cover the opener. If they can ever find this place."

"I'd really like to get back in."

"So would I," he said. "Yellin's been haunting me since way back last spring. He's like a hyena. Every time I get hurt, Roy Yellin is right there grinning. He likes to see me get hurt. He's after my job. Every time I'm face down on the grass in pain, I know I'll look up to see Roy Yellin grinning at the injured part of my body. His daddy sells mutual funds in the prairie states."

Bing came back, apparently upset about something.

"He wants me to practice my squib kick tomorrow. I told him I don't have any squib kick. He guaranteed me I'd have one by tomorrow night."

They played for another 15 minutes. On the final play, after a long steady drive that took the offense down to the eight-yard line, Taft fumbled the handoff. Defense recovered, whistles blew and that was it for the day. The three of us headed back together.

"Hobbsie laid it right in his gut, and he goes and loses it," Rector said. "I attribute that kind of error to lack of concentration. That's a mental error, and it's caused by lack of concentration. Coloreds can run and leap, but they can't concentrate. A colored is a runner and leaper. You're making a big mistake if you ask him to concentrate."

A very heavy girl wearing an orange dress came walking toward us across a wide lawn. There was a mushroom cloud appliquéd on the front of her dress. The dress was brightest orange. I thought she must be a little crazy to wear something like that with her figure. I recognized the girl; we had some classes together. I let the others walk on ahead, and I stood for a moment watching her walk past me and move into the distance. I was wearing a smudge of lampblack under each eye to reduce the sun's glare. I didn't know whether the lampblack was very effective, but I liked the way it looked and I liked the idea of painting myself in a barbaric manner before going forth to battle in mud. I wondered if the fat girl knew I was still watching her. I had a vivid picture of myself standing there holding my helmet at my side, left knee bent slightly, hair all mussed and the lampblack under my eyes.

GOSPEL OF FALSE PROPHETS

Bil Gilbert

JOHN HUEHNERGARTH

Miffed by what he considers arrant misuse of the word ecology, the author, an outdoorsman, natural scientist and certainly no foe of bird, beast or tree, challenges the word-warpers and their goals.

Ernst Haeckel, a 19th century zoology professor, created the word. While promoting Darwin's theories of evolution he hammered together two Greek fragments, and "oecology" had its beginning. In recent years few words have been so ill-used as the professor's brainchild.

After Haeckel coined it in 1869, "ecology" (the initial "o" was soon dropped) lay around quietly for a time. Then botanists rummaging in the academic attic discovered it and put it back in service. Ecology then, and theoretically still, is the study of the relationships between living things and their environment and of the effect of various life forms on one another. Take any animal or plant as an example, and other animals and plants constitute an important part of its environment, *e.g.*, fox and rabbit, woodpecker and oak. Ecology is a science of the present, the immediate. In the time it takes for one to say DDT, patterns and relationships change and new ones are created. Since the subject in its entirety is beyond our present powers of comprehension, scientists in the field have sensibly avoided calling themselves ecologists.

It is too late to finger the responsible individuals, but in the mid-1950s media men trying to sound scientific or scientists trying to sound like media men seized the tender word and fragile concept and began to peddle it publicly. The age of pop ecology had begun. It was a fad, like keeping gerbils. All sorts of people — politicians, preachers, boy scouts, revolutionaries, ad men, fashion designers, corporate executives, housewives, teachers — went out and got themselves a little ecology. Sometimes the faddists collected two ecological concepts, bred them, so to speak, and began to sell or give away the mongrel offspring.

In 1950, for example, the *Readers' Guide to Periodical Literature* included only four references under the subject heading Ecology. Twenty years later there were four dozen such listings. By 1965 few publications did not feel obliged to make a passing reference to the magic word. Like an all-purpose seasoning, ecology was sprinkled on essays about poverty, racism, dope smuggling, military strategy, professional football, etc. Suddenly there were ecology T shirts, soaps, executives, fund raisers, lawyers, lobbyists. Civil disturbances in the name of ecology popped up all over the landscape like mushrooms after a warm spring rain.

A society for the prevention of cruelty to words and ideas should be established, though it is, no doubt, too late to save ecology. We have trifled with it to the point that it has become an irrevocably loose and fallen word. However, while the intellectual atrocity is still fresh, there is perhaps some value in recalling how we have heartlessly overworked and mutilated this interesting and useful concept. The misuses and abuses of ecology are all but innumerable. But among the cruelest should be noted:

Ecology is a thing.

Within the past year advertisements have appeared for an "ecology testing kit." The inference is that ecology is a substance like chemical compounds in air, soil or water (which is what the ecology kit really is designed for testing). In fact, ecology can no more be seen, tasted, touched, weighed or substantively identified than can a square root. Both are abstractions used to describe an abstract relationship. This may seem a niggling point, but there are a great many people who think ecology is alive and substantial somewhere out in the big woods.

Ecology is a beautiful thing.

A ranger assigned to the Grand Canyon recalls spending an idle hour asking visitors to one of the park overlooks what they particularly liked about the place. Three people explained they had come to enjoy the ecology and certainly were.

Ecology is a nutritious thing.

In Tucson, and very likely elsewhere, there is a health-food store that sells ecology bread. This is catering to the currently widespread belief that ecology is some kind of heavy vitamin. All over this fruitful land there are people munching away on barely digestible items — kelp, sun-dried bananas, sunflower seeds, freaky grains and grasses. They seem to believe that by so insulting their taste and stomachs they are behaving ecologically.

Ecology is a clean thing.

A recent issue of *Scope,* a mod periodical for high school students, devoted an article to *Word Power.* The piece was illustrated by a photograph of what at one time was known as Hermie's Dump (in the village of Monticello, state unspecified). Towering over the original hand-lettered Hermie's Dump sign was a much larger, cleaner one giving the place its new name, MONTICELLO ECOLOGICAL SITE. Without taking sides in the matter, *Scope* noted that this was a good example of the use of plain and fancy words, which it is.

Ecology is conservation.

Ecology as a thing, ecology bread and ecological sites perhaps can be explained, if not excused, by our weakness for pretentious language or plain commercial high spirits. However, the ecology-is-conservation notion is something altogether different. It has been pushed assiduously by pop ecologists and the Bless the Birds Beasts and This Very Green Land crowd. The chief result of the campaign, if not its intent, has been to debase the concept of ecology and spread confusion about biological realities.

The system of relationships between living things that seems to operate in this world is dynamic. So far as anyone has been able to determine, the only stable element within it is change. New forms are forever being created and existing ones modified; extinction and death are a part of the system. There are, for example, no life forms presently inhabiting the earth that have been here from the beginning. This must be considered a blessing by those of us living now, since we would have had great difficulty getting a toehold on a planet loaded to the gunwales with the accumulated biological cargo of the ages past. If things seem crowded these days, consider what they might be if assorted tree ferns, dinosaurs, saber-toothed tigers and worse had not cleared out. The world has always been a kind of transient hotel in which client species come and go in brief cycles of half a million years or so.

Conservation has of course nothing to do with this, with evolution or ecology. Conservation, in fact, does not reflect or describe any known biological process. It represents a rather pathetic attempt on the part of man to hold back the forces of change. Averting the extinction of the whooping crane has been a *cause célèbre* for the past 40 years. We have been led to believe that we must save these birds, which apparently are no longer vigorous enough to save themselves. It is said that we must conserve something called the gene pool (which is the sum total of genes in all things presently alive) and that this pool will be critically reduced if the genes of the 80 remaining whooping cranes are lost. This seems a bit of an exaggeration, since if there is such a pool it has managed nicely for a long time without, say, brontosaurus genes. Some conservationists believe quite intensely that the passing of the crane will leave an irreparable rent in the ecological web of life, causing any number of other strands to snap and shrivel. They declare that the extinction of the birds would be an unnatural happening, since man had caused it. If the cranes are allowed to go by the board this will be a crime against nature and, so the theory goes, man can expect to be and should be punished by nature.

This nonsense has been promoted by a number of people who should know better. To repeat: extinction is as natural as creation and, so far as we can determine, as necessary. The ecological system is self-adjusting; existing relationships are always being modified or replaced with new ones. The remaining cranes are so few in number and so feeble as to be of minimal ecological significance. They could disappear tomorrow as the pterodactyl did a few yesterdays ago, causing scarcely a ripple. Any gap they left in the web would be filled almost instantly.

In objective terms, conservation or attempted conservation might be considered anti-ecological since it represents an effort to meddle with or thwart natural processes. However, it seems biologically harmless since it is such a hopeless endeavor. Then, too, in human terms there is something constructive to be said for the human conceit of conservation. The crane and that sort of thing give some men pleasure. They enjoy having them around, and trying to keep them around makes many people feel righteous and moral. As such, these are useful pursuits and motives. If conservationists would simply acknowledge that whooping cranes, redwoods and wilderness vistas are their thing and that they would like to enjoy them for as long as possible, then they would be entitled to the same tolerance as nudists, vegetarians or horseplayers. However, when conservationists begin to bully and frighten people into believing their hobby is ordained by natural law and that ecological vengeance will be had on those who do not share their interest, then they become intellectual extortionists.

Ecology is a pie in the sky.

The actions of pop ecologists — the things they want to save, the changes they oppose, the laws for which they lobby — suggest that many believe there was a time when all relationships were pure, sweet and perfect. In America this ecological utopia is thought to have existed sometime between 1492 and the demise of the passenger pigeon in 1914. The exact dates can be filled in according to individual taste.

Utopias, of course, are static phenomena. They cannot be improved since they are perfect. If they are changed, they become imperfect and by definition something other than utopian. This changeless character accounts for the fact that utopias are found only within men's imaginations.

In appearance, ecological Camelots are most often described as having been wild, woodsy, scenic places, chock full of vigorous mammals, birds and noble savages and void of noxious insects and scrubby thickets. The better models are said to look very much like Unspoiled Nature, as first identified by 18th century Romantic painters, poets and essayists. When they speak of "our once healthy ecology," pop ecologists are usually talking about the world as Jean Jacques Rousseau perceived it. This is seldom mentioned since it reduces the discussion to the level where it belongs — personal esthetic prejudice.

All of us tend to do a little mooning about how green and glorious things must have been on the other side of time. There is nothing wrong with such fantasizing; actually there may be a good bit to be said for it. If a man likes to think he is Napoleon, more power to him. However, if the delusion becomes so strong that he insists that the rest of us form columns and start marching toward Moscow, he becomes a nuisance. Figuratively, this is what has happened with the pop ecologists. The commands are somewhat jumbled but we are given to understand that utopia has been despoiled, and we must at the pain of ecological disaster drop what we are now doing and head back toward the lost paradise. The pop ecologists will lead us, providing us with a list of what to bring along and what to leave behind. If anyone thinks about it, this is likely to be a long, silly and profoundly frustrating trip.

There is as much ecology now as there ever was. A National Park Service rustic picnic table may not be esthetic but it is not an ecological catastrophe and may, in fact, provide a home for deserving wood borers and sow bugs. A freeway may impair the romantic prospects of a wilderness for some, but it creates nice deer, butterfly, blackberry and poison-ivy habitat; a whole new series of relationships flourishes there. These days are no worse, or better, than the good old ones — only different. Tomorrow will also be different; if it is not, we are in real trouble. Ecology is not concerned with esthetics or antiquarianism.

Man is vile, ecologically speaking.

The theme that man is a "bad 'un" has occurred regularly throughout history. It always has been a slippery thought, composed of a series of contradictory premises, unprovable value judgments and guilty emotions. Recently the notion has been adopted by pop ecologists.

The argument runs that whatever is natural is good, and the unnatural is bad. The world is composed of nature and of man, by first inference unnatural and by second inference bad. Landslides and guano deposits are natural; bulldozers and septic tanks are unnatural. This peculiar dualism has permeated much of our thought. Thus we have natural history and human, or unnatural, history. There is natural science and in apposition perhaps medicine or psychiatry. There is an organization called The Nature Conservatory whose counterpart might be the Department of Health, Education and Welfare, which under this semantic scheme could logically be called The Unnatural Conservancy. We have natural law, natural beauty, natural curiosity, nature foods, nature walks, nature sanctuaries, the balance of nature, and by implication each of these has its unnatural antonym. In practice, man is not always or entirely unnatural. Thus a man can have a natural golf swing or naturally curly hair. The unnatural elements are generally regarded to be the unique attributes of our species, notably our faculties for abstraction, rationalization, contemplation and our technological talents.

In most respects, the man-is-by-nature-unnatural concept is a continuation of the man-is-vile brief. However, man can choose to restrain his unnatural nature, and when he does he lives in harmony with nature. If we do not restrain ourselves, letting all our unnaturalness hang out, we can destroy nature because we are inexplicably and unfairly stronger than it is. Of late we have been showing very little restraint and have become increasingly bad, unnatural and destructive. Unless we quickly shape up, nature will destroy us; ecological vengeance will be taken.

Set forth so baldly, the foregoing does not seem to make sense. Yet, more cunningly dressed and camouflaged, these notions are at the philosophical heart of the ecological-environmental-conservation crusade that a great many of us have taken very seriously indeed.

Nature is a great deal more than deer, still forests, rippling seas of grass, whooping cranes and pure air. Nature is what is. Man is; the combustion engine is; nuclear fission is; and all are as natural as the next phenomena. Theology may give clues about how things should be but ecology does not. Questions of ecological good and bad are irrelevant.

Ecology is altruism

According to information presently available, it seems likely that we play in the same fields and according to the same rules as every other living thing. A master motivation for individuals and all species seems to be to live as long as possible and to multiply as often as possible. In consequence, each life form is forever adapting, in an effort to cope with the environment, expand its range and defend against the expansionist tendencies of other creatures. If the objective is biological imperialism — total, exclusive occupancy of the planet by one kind — then nobody as yet has come close to achieving it. The prospect of such a victory seems remote. There is a kind of ultimate check, a biological Catch-22, built into the system. Every species is potentially its own worst enemy. A creature who by dint of some dazzling adaptive move opens a big lead over the pack never has held it for long. He is brought back, cut down and often eliminated entirely, usually because he has used up the resources, food and habitat upon which his specialty rests, or because of the debilitating effects (plague, starvation, genetic feebleness, psychological malfunction) of overpopulation. Nevertheless, everyone keeps plugging away at the game that is designed not to have a winner. In a sense it is this old-college-try spirit that seems to have created and sustained the dynamic system of interrelations that we call or should call ecological.

Generally, creatures are singlemindedly preoccupied with their own thing. They may need or be forced to respond to others, but self-interest, not self-sacrifice, appears to be at the root of most of these responses. Two of the pseudoecological problems that greatly exercise us currently are pollution and overpopulation. Our dirtiness and fertility are often cited as irrefutable evidence of our vileness and as we become increasingly dirty and fertile we are creating ecological havoc.

The usual rebuttal applies. Fifty billion men, for example, and whatever waste they would naturally create will not destroy the ecological system, only change it. Woodland ecology might go the way of the whooping crane, but the prospects are that sanitary land fills would provide as much ecology as anybody could possibly want. Just as no one knows what men should be, nobody knows how many or how clean they should be. If we can get away with 50 billion men and their garbage there is no ecological law that says we should not, and there are in fact many ecological pressures urging us on to test the human carrying capacity of the planet. If the earth were to be occupied by 50 billion men and their inevitable works, it seems probable that those multitudes would think, eat, work, play, and be organized much differently than we do or are. A good many of us probably would not like such conditions; we are entitled to our preferences and, of course, can do what is possible to avoid this sort of future. It is a matter of self-interest, but of ecological inconsequence. Whatever the outcome, 50 or 0 billions, we can rest assured that there will still be ecology.

In all of this there is a curious anomaly. Pop ecologists talk a lot about ecology, but there is the strong feeling that they underestimate and certainly do not trust the efficiency of the ecological system. It does not seem immodest to claim that because of our technological skills, man is at present in the position of a creature who has moved quite a bit in front of the rest in the competition for dominance. Perhaps the best evidence supporting this assumption is that we are being troubled, among other things, by overpopulation and pollution (befouling our own nest). These are two processes within the ecological system that historically have worked to chop down temporary leaders. In an objective way, many of the current human problems are not evidence of the weakness and degradation of the ecological system. Rather, they are grim (from our standpoint) and constant reminders of its strength and efficiency.

CONCENTRATE ON THE CHRYSANTHEMUMS

Kenny Moore

ALAN E. COBER

Kenny Moore, a former University of Oregon student, is a world-class marathoner; indeed, he was fourth in the Olympics. Frank Shorter, a leading character in this Japanese idyll, was the Olympic gold medalist.

We came to the island of Kyushu at twilight, gliding above black offshore rocks, lumpy hills, refineries. It was a jarring landing. The road from the airport was lined with palms in dubious health. Leafless persimmon trees still bore their orange fruit. In hundreds of tiny drained rice fields, stacks of straw shook in the cold wind.

As our taxi approached the city we saw bundled peasant women tending smoky fires on street corners.

"I'm excited," said Frank Shorter. "Partly at being in a strange country, but it's more than that." Frank is given to analyses of his mental states.

"This is the first time I've started a trip knowing I couldn't be any better prepared," he said. "I've done more long runs than ever, I'm effective over shorter distances [he had won the national AAU cross-country championship in San Diego the day before] and my weight is right. I'm not torn down by too much racing like I was last summer."

He paused a moment, flinching as the cab cut off a cement truck. "Of course, it's frightening to feel like this. I've followed the program perfectly. If I run lousy, there's something wrong with the program."

This was last November and Frank and I were in Fukuoka, Japan, to test our programs in what amounts to the world marathon championship. Since 1966 the Japanese have invited the cream of the year's marathoners to have at it over a flat course in traditionally cool, fast weather. Derek Clayton of Australia became the first man to run the 26 miles, 385 yards under two hours and 10 minutes (2:09:36.4) in 1967 in Fukuoka. The slowest winning time since was 2:11:12.8 by Jerome Drayton of Canada in the rain in 1969. Six of the eight fastest marathoners of all time have run their best races through the streets of Fukuoka, although Clayton improved his world best — there is no world record in the marathon because of varying terrain — to 2:08:33.6 in Belgium in 1969.

I had been invited on the strength of finishing second in 1970 with 2:11:35.8 and for winning the 1971 national AAU marathon championship. Frank had been second in our nationals with 2:17:44.6 in his first marathon and had won both the 10,000 meters and the marathon in the Pan-American Games.

At the hotel we met Eiichi Shibuya, the official in charge of our arrangements, and handed over two bottles of Johnnie Walker. He bowed. His smile was reminiscent of Teddy Roosevelt's while standing over the lion.

"Mr. Kenneth Moore [my name was pronounced, as it was all week, 'Moo-ah'] remembers the Japanese custom of high import taxes on our favorite whiskey."

While our steaks slowly incinerated upon their heated iron platters, we met the runners from Australia and New Zealand. John Farrington, 29, an administrative officer at Sydney's Macquarie University and fifth here last year, shook hands and looked dourly out the window.

"Look at those flags," he said. "Standing straight out from the poles. Bloody awful conditions."

Jack Foster, 39, a clerk in Rotorua, New Zealand, sought to calm Farrington. "We've got five more days, John. It must stop."

Foster was fourth last year. His large eyes and wrinkled forehead give him an appearance of shyness and uncertainty. In September he had run 80 laps on a track in 1:39:14.4, the world record for 20 miles.

Jack introduced two of his New Zealand teammates, John Robinson and Terry Manners, both 32.

"Not as fancy a field as it might be," said Jack. "Clayton says he's not racing again until Munich. Too much chance of injury. Ron Hill [of England, the only other man ever to crack 2:10] is only doing cross-country this winter. Bill Addcocks [also of England, winner at Fukuoka in 1968 with 2:10:47.8] is injured. Karel Lismont of Belgium [the European champion] didn't answer his invitation, and the Japanese are sworn never to invite Drayton again."

"Why not?"

"Last year, after agreeing to run, he wired that he was injured. And in '69, when he won, he left his trophy. Apparently, the Japanese feel they lost face."

"Things are beginning to fall into place for me," said Frank. "Politics and face and duty-free Scotch."

"Well, it never hurts to make oneself welcome," I said.

"Certainly not," said Jack.

"In any case," said Robinson, "there will be a few men out there Sunday who can run a bit."

Akio Usami, Japan's defending champion and national record holder (2:10:37.8), was at another hotel. A graduate student at Tokyo's Nihon University, he had won marathons in Athens in April and at Munich in September.

Two Finns, two Russians, a West German and another New Zealander were expected.

"They invited four Kiwis?" I said.

"Oh, no," said Robinson. "They only paid for Jack. Terry and I had to put down $1,400 apiece, air fare and expenses, to race here."

"My God," said Frank. "Why?"

When Robinson spoke, all the blue showed in his eyes. "New Zealand can afford to send only 80 competitors to the Munich Olympics. How many will the U.S. send?"

"About 450."

"There. Our athletes are selected on the basis of their world rankings, which is the only way to choose between a swimmer and a rower, for example. We marathoners have to go under 2:16 simply to be considered. That time will put a man in the top 20 in the world unless a dozen do it here [in 1970 10th place at Fukuoka was 2:16]. We can't hope to produce those times in New Zealand because all our courses run over mountains. But if we're any kind of runners we ought to do it here."

"So you paid that kind of money to try," said Frank. "What do you do for a living?"

"I'm a phys ed teacher. Terry is a house painter."

Later, as Frank and I walked to our rooms, he said, "I couldn't do that. Not unless I was positive I'd make it." He thought a moment. "Maybe he's ready."

We tried to run twice a day. I went out before breakfast. Nearby was a park and shrine. Crossing the gentle curve of a bridge I could look east and see canals reflecting red sunrise, silhouetting other bridges. A blue-roofed pagoda rose out of twisted, rope-wound pines. A bronze statue of an ancient Buddhist priest 60 feet high sheltered pigeons. Returning, the growing light revealed the foulness of the canals, shallow slime over broken glass and ordure.

Afternoons we were driven to more distant Obori Park. A lake was spanned by a series of islands connected by more bridges. Willows grew over a cinder path. We ran with schoolboys, soccer teams and karate groups. We were photographed incessantly and on following days our pictures were brought back to be autographed.

Frank, at 5' 10" and 130 pounds, looks fragile (Marty Liquori has called him "a vertical hyphen"), yet he always braved the traffic and ran back to the hotel. Shibuya-san, an occasional jogger himself, was impressed.

"Mr. Shorter has much energy."

"Yes."

"Why do you think it is so?"

"He credits it to his drinking."

"He drinks?"

"Oh, yes. Lots of beer and gin-and-tonic."

"I drink wine. And beer and gin. But no tonic."

"So close, and yet so far."

We had no commitments, yet we were always occupied. Perhaps we are slow, or have lengthy attention spans. We certainly lingered over our meals, in conversation or, in Frank's case, in attempting to eat.

"I'm really up for this race," he said early in the week. "I have no appetite at all." For lunch he usually could get down a chocolate sundae and a gin-and-Coke.

I asked if he had any objection to my publicizing his fondness for gin.

"Well, it's me," he said. "I sip it to relax and I've always done it. But if I bombed out in the race, a lot of red-necks would say, 'See how the lush drank himself out of contention.' It wouldn't be true, but I'd hate to give them the ammunition."

Later in the day the Russians arrived and passed out little bottles of vodka.

The previous year the Russians had been archetype proletariat. One, Yuri Volkov, who finished eighth with a Soviet record 2:14:28, is a metalworker and has a scar, of unstated origin, from jaw to hairline. He made noise when he ran, stamping on the pavement as if killing bugs. We all nodded knowingly the morning after the race when he could not walk, so damaged was one Achilles' tendon.

This year's Russians were smooth. Both were 28, phys ed graduate students and, on five words of English, urbane. Their names: Vassily Shalomilov and Yuri Maurin.

They had brought a manager, a robust, gray-haired man who burst, when least expected, into songs about Volga boatmen. He spoke no English and continually pressed us for autographs. If you happened to have a ballpoint pen in hand, it wound up in his. He did know one English word: "souvenir."

In his room, Frank discussed his feelings toward Russians.

"It is a culturally indoctrinated suspicion. I find myself wondering, 'What are they *really* thinking?' It's hard to articulate, harder to explain. I have to fight it."

I said, "I lost that in Leningrad." Frank and I had run there in the U.S. vs. U.S.S.R. meet the year before.

"Yeah," Frank said. "When Mikitenko gave us those little wood carvings from his children."

Between meals and workouts we were entertained by the press. The marathon was sponsored by the *Asahi Shimbun* newspaper chain, whose Fukuoka offices took up the first seven floors of the hotel building. Our pictures appeared daily and some of the interviews attained a depth seldom reached in this country. Having run second the year before, I drew a lot of fire. When my undergraduate major was exposed, I was pegged "the philosopher-marathoner" and asked such questions as "What is there about you which longs for the suffering of the race?" or "In what way is your soul satisfied by the marathon?"

It was a heady atmosphere and I succumbed. "After every experience," I said, "it's natural to reflect that you might have done better. Only after a marathon can I say I have given everything. Because of the enormity of the attempt, the cleansing of the pain, I can sit, even stiff and blistered, and know a kind of peace."

Farrington added, "Marathoning is like cutting yourself unexpectedly.

You dip into the pain so gradually that the damage is done before you're aware of it. Unfortunately, when awareness comes, it is excruciating.''

"That's why you have to forget your last marathon before you can run another," said Frank. "Your mind can't know what's coming."

We were distracted from these musings by the arrival of the Finns. Seppo Nikkari, 23, and Pentti Rummakko, 28, spoke nothing but Finnish. The Japanese were unable to unearth an interpreter. Nikkari, tall and gawky, with a feathery, blond mustache, did not seem perturbed. Disdaining the dinner menu, he barged into the kitchen and pointed at what he wanted. When people in front of him did not make way fast enough when the elevator reached his floor, he cheerfully propelled them into the wall.

"He does not seem to have perfectly adapted to civilization," said Farrington.

Rummakko was slender and silent, with eyes in great dark hollows and gaps between his teeth. Fourth in the 1970 Boston Marathon with 2:14:59, he has raced internationally for years.

"It's unnerving," said Robinson. "You get the idea these fellows don't live for anything but running."

Nikkari seemed to develop an affection for Farrington, jumping in his taxi to the park, pounding on his back at unpredictable intervals when they ran.

"I don't really *detest* the bloody ox, you know," said John. "I mean I haven't struck him between his blinking eyes. I will, however, take pleasure in thrashing him by a few minutes."

Shorter discerned a plan. "The kid's got Farrington's number," he said. "You have to put so much effort into this race that you can't afford to dislike your opponents. It's a waste of energy."

One afternoon the phone woke me from a nap.

"This is cork."

"Who? From Ireland?"

"No. Cork, on ninth froor robby."

Tentatively: "Clerk?"

"Hai. You are Mr. Moo-ah?"

"Yes."

"You have visitor. Prease come down."

It was the man from Tiger. Mr. Yoshihiko Hikita provided us all with leather bags stuffed with his company's racing and training shoes. Not more than 25 and rigid within his black blazer, Hikita-san seemed awed by us.

"Just say, 'This shoe rubs a bit.' '' Farrington whispered to us, "and in two minutes he's back with another pair. Meanwhile, you've tucked away the first. That goes on and on. I brought practically no luggage."

"A bloke could get really spoiled over here," said Robinson, clutching half a dozen shoe bags to his chest. By the end of the week he had filled a packing case with shoes, track suits and camera equipment.

Hikita-san was proud of his new "Ohbori" model, named, roughly, for the park where we trained. He had sent a pair to Foster and me earlier and we had promised to race in them. Foster pointed out the shoe's ventilation.

"People at home asked me what all the little holes were for. I told them that's for the blood to run out."

Frank tried on a pair.

"Mr. Frank Shorter," said Hikita, "in your real opinion these are best shoes?"

"Yeah, they're great. But a little too wide."

"Ah so. But it is not possible to make narrower so soon before the race."

"I think they'll do."

That afternoon Frank ran a hard hour through the park in his regular, non-Tiger training shoes. After dinner Hikita-san was waiting for us in the lobby. He gave Frank a searching look.

"Why," he asked in a low voice, "did you wear Adidas shoes today?"

Frank gently reassured him that he would race in Tigers. He had simply preferred not to run 10 miles in brand-new shoes. He mentioned again that his feet were very narrow.

Hikita withdrew and returned shortly with pieces of string and rice paper. He carefully traced the outline of Frank's foot and measured its circumference at the ball and around the arch, marking the string with red ink. Then he retreated, saying, "We will try."

Frank, his bare foot propped on a coffee table, said softly, "I wish I hadn't worn Adidas today."

"Why? I've seen you play Adidas against Puma without mercy."

"They didn't take it like that man."

Runners are usually perpetual convalescents, leading a life of rich, vigorous afternoons, nodding evenings and stiff, groggy mornings. Easing training before a race sometimes humanizes us, but we are incomplete tourists. Our sense of mission makes us unwilling to tire ourselves in search of culture or Christmas presents.

One morning Shibuya-san told us we were scheduled to go to a Shinto shrine to be purified for the race.

"It makes no difference whether or not we are believers?" inquired Frank.

"No difference. It is automatic."

"That sort of thinking might have saved us a few million in crusaders, heretics and Northern Irish," Frank said.

We were greeted by a tiny, energetic man in beige and dark brown robes.

Nobusada Nishitakatsuji explained in rapid, precise English that his family had served as priests at Dazaifu Shrine for 38 generations.

Detecting an accent, Frank asked if he had ever been in the U.S.

"Harvard Divinity School," he said.

He led us through high stone gates and gilded arches to an inner courtyard. Under a sacred plum tree we were given a sip of ceremonial *sake* from a three-tiered golden bowl. Small printed fortunes were selected for us according to the animal of the year of our birth.

Shibuya-san translated my fortune.

"If you desire something a long time, you will get it. Beware of serious illness. Don't sell your house."

The priest excused himself and hurried off.

"Where is he going?" asked Frank.

"I believe he has a Rotary meeting" said Shibuya.

I had not been feeling well. The combination of the San Diego race, in which I finished sixth, the long flight and the seven-hour time change had subdued me. Three days before the race I awoke feeling honestly sick. At breakfast Farrington said, "I tell everyone they're coming apart at the seams, but you really do look pale."

I reported to Shibuya, who took me to a clinic. My temperature was 101°, the diagnosis virus. I received a shot of antibiotic, some orange pills and signed half a dozen autographs for a row of giggling nurses.

I was ordered to my room. Shibuya looked in every couple of hours. I got him to sit on the bed and talk about the Japanese attachment to the marathon.

"We made marathon important because it is one event in which a man needs not to be tall to be great," he said. "In marathon and gymnastics we can do well against the world."

"There is great pressure upon runners to do well?"

"Yes," he said. "Sometimes there is too much."

"Will you tell me about Kokichi Tsuburaya?"

He sighed. "Yes, there were many pressures on Tsuburaya. He came from a small town in the north, Sukagawa City in Fukushima Prefecture. There is only a cigarette factory there. The city had nothing to be proud of except Tsuburaya. There were signs on the buildings that said TSUBURAYA IS OUR PRIDE. When he won the bronze medal in the Tokyo Olympics, there was a great celebration. Everyone said, 'In Mexico, the gold.'

"Tsuburaya was in the Japan Self-Defense Forces. He was in the department of training, a leader with responsibilities. In our tradition, the leader is always the best. The JSDF is very strict and insists on training hard, hard, hard. There is no limit. My own sister trained with other women to challenge U.S. guns with bamboo poles.

"This tradition has been carried on by the JSDF and influenced Tsuburaya. He trained so hard that he injured his Achilles' tendon. His commanders wanted the honor he would win, so he was not permitted to rest. For a year he ran poorly.

"In 1967 he committed suicide by slashing his wrists. He left a simple note to his mother. It said, 'I can't run any farther.' "

I asked how his death affected the Japanese.

"We were sorry."

"Were people sympathetic, or did they think he was crazy?"

"He was not insane. We could understand. We were just sorry he had no friend or leader who could guide him. He had a heavy burden. We criticized his JSDF captain. We said, 'Why didn't you help Tsuburaya?' He said only, 'We never let up.' "

When Shibuya had gone, I slept. In a dream I found myself at the start of the Olympic 5,000-meter final. I had trained in secret for years, preparing for this single race. I tore through the first mile in four minutes even, pulling to a huge lead. In the second mile, despite the pain, I surged harder, responding to the astounded, howling crowd, and ran it in 3:58. Over the last few laps, when I should have dropped, I began to sprint, lapping the earth's best runners, lowering the three-mile world record by a minute. In the stretch, amid the torture of the effort and the screams of the multitude, I delivered the limit of my energy and all my body's chemical bonds burst. Only a wisp of vapor crossed the finish line, leaving my nylon shirt folded across the tape.

When I awoke, my fever was gone.

We had developed a cocoa ritual. Before bed the English-speaking runners gathered in a coffee shop off the lobby to choke down a few more carbohydrates. (The traditional prerace steak has been discredited. Recent marathon records have been set on cream puffs and pecan pie.)

Feeling recovered, I put in an appearance. Farrington was at the window.

"I hope there are a lot of little Japanese down on their knees somewhere praying for the weather," he said.

"Surely you don't have to worry about a fast time?" John was the year's second-fastest runner with 2:12:14.

"It would help my chances for Olympic selection. Our committee has decided to send only 12 men to Munich in track and field. There are 21 events. Once they are selected, no one else can go."

"What if a runner was the best you had in an event, but wasn't selected and offered to pay his own way?"

"The committee would say no. It wouldn't be fair to other unselected athletes who couldn't afford it."

"What if *everybody* could afford it?"

"They would still say no. It's tough to make the Australian team. It's always been that way."

"Do you think it should stay that way?"

"I will if I make it."

This created a silence. Finally Robinson spoke:

"I say, had a peek in at the massage parlor next door? Fabulous!"

In the morning I jogged a few miles. Outside the hotel I found Robinson changing shoes. He ran 100 yards down an alley, returned, sat down and began changing shoes again.

"Foot problems?"

"Oh, no. It's just that to get these back into New Zealand without paying twice their value in duty, they have to be used."

Upstairs, I met Hikita-san coming from Frank's room. I looked in. Frank looked ludicrous in a flowing *yukata* and Ohbori shoes. He seemed dazed.

"They're perfect," he said.

"New shoes?"

"Yes. Somehow they made a narrower pair. But he tried to take my Adidas. He said, 'Since you have no further use for these. . . .' and tried to slip them into his bag. Don't they trust me?"

"When they know you better, Frank."

Usami came to the hotel to be photographed with his foreign challengers. We were made to sit in a row and hold up our bare feet for the camera.

Farrington felt Usami's rock-hard thigh.

"Your legs feel very, very tired," Farrington said.

Usami seemed about to explode with suppressed glee.

"Yes," he giggled. "Very tired."

"Well they ought to be," said Farrington. "You ran 50 kilometers before breakfast."

Usami laughed, throwing his head back. "Yes, yes. Exhausted."

I had regained my will to live, but the will to run is a more delicate flower. In hopes of nourishing it, I bought a bottle of Japanese champagne with dinner. It was sweet, but without the fruity quality of good sweet wines.

"Alcoholic cream soda," said Frank.

"It's better than their red wine," put in Farrington. "That tastes like kerosene."

Soon we were telling stories. I talked about red-necks and bleeding feet in the Olympic marathon ("Gawd damn you, git awn up there where a American ought to be!").

Jeff Julian, the fourth New Zealander and a banker, told a Ron Hill story.

"Ron went to the Munich pre-Olympic marathon in September," said Julian, "but he didn't enter. He simply ran over the course the morning of the race. Then, after Usami won, Hill came up and told him — I imagine a finger wagging — 'You second next year in Olympics. *Second*. Me first.' "

Robinson and I frowned. "Ronnie should know better," I said. "Winning is never so sweet that losing can't be sourer if you get your hopes up like that."

"Right," said Robinson. "I was just thinking it's nice they give 10 trophies here. I'll be perfectly happy to take home any of those at all."

The day before the race we tried out our endurance in the opening ceremonies. In a ballroom before banks of flowers and the flags of the represented nations, we heard from the mayor of Fukuoka, the Japanese minister of education, the president of the Japanese Amateur Athletic Federation and the president of *Asahi Shimbun*. Frank was edgy.

"I have the feeling I got here a day early," he whispered. "I'm ready right now. My stomach is starting to churn."

"Relax. We'll have a drink afterward."

"You know, the winner of this race really will be the favorite in Munich."

"Concentrate on the chrysanthemums and lilies, Frank. Think of the care some tiny, *patient* gardener. . . ."

"We can do it, you know. I really feel it."

"Think how he watered and pruned and fertilized, creating blossoms that invite quiet contemplation. . . ."

"Those Russians look fit enough. I wonder if they're as nervous. . . ."

"Pretend you're that patient gardener, taking pleasure and fulfillment from simply watching. . . ."

"When I think of the start, all those frantic Japanese, ready to die. . . . The way they're going to drive us. . . ."

"Frank. That way lies madness."

"You're right. What were you saying about flowers?"

Race day dawned crystalline and calm. Then at breakfast, in full view of Farrington, clouds scudded up from the southwest and it rained. Frank and I sat by ourselves.

"I don't feel like I have to win this, you know?" said Frank. "I want to, but I'm calm."

We were bused to the stadium, where we would start and finish, and were put in a bare, unheated room under the stands. We slathered Vaseline in our shoes and wherever skin rubs against skin. Remembering the Pan-American marathon in Cali, where he had to seek relief in a cane field, Frank went out to find a toilet.

"It's banjo, isn't it?"

"*Benjô*."

"Yes. Would be embarrassing to get that mixed up."

Farrington was peering at an infinitesimal blister on Robinson's heel and saying, "Now *that's* going to be trouble. . . ." when we came under attack. Fireworks exploded somewhere and a crowd of crazed, clucking officials swept us out onto the field.

We jogged a mile to warm up. The Japanese runners were grim except Usami, who smiled at friends in the crowd. The rain had stopped but not the wind. We were assembled on the line.

The starter's gun refused to discharge. We were reassembled and, finally, set off. More skyrockets detonated overhead. Usami jumped for the early lead. He did not get it. Farrington darted out of the inside lane and stayed in front until we were out of the stadium. Foster and Shalomilov kept close. Frank and I were fifth and sixth until Nikkari elbowed through.

Once on the road, the wind was behind us. The route followed the westward curve of the coastline out onto a flat, sandy peninsula. We were to return over the same road. Usami took the lead and his pace immediately split the field. Farrington and Foster stayed with him. Frank, Nikkari and I surrendered 30 yards.

"What do you think?" I asked.

"It's under 4:50 mile pace."

"World-record pace."

"We can't let them get more than 80 yards."

By two miles we caught them. At 10,000 meters, reached in 29:47, the six of us were together, 100 yards in front.

The crowd was immense, six and eight deep, mile after mile, and it roared at us with sustained fury. It possessed thousands of paper Japanese flags and slashed and beat the air with them in a frenzy of exorcism. The evil spirits surrounding Usami were given, at the very least, headaches.

Moving with us was an entourage of official buses and police motorcycles. The camera truck vented oily, black exhaust. When it came too near we would shout and wave it away. Frank, saving his breath, merely spit on it.

A little butterfly of a Japanese kept fluttering up to us and falling back. At eight miles I dropped back with him, in crisis. The symptoms of midweek had returned, weakness and swimming nausea. I deluded myself. World-record pace would kill them all. It was infinitely more wise to run economically, give them their too costly lead and take it back when it counted.

Robinson and Rummakko passed me.

Manners passed me. In spite of slowing, I felt no better. I was cooked.

The course turned gradually into the wind. Frank took refuge behind Foster and Nikkari. Farrington ran at his side. They had left all settlement and ran now between white sand dunes and low pines. The crowd vanished and they could hear each other's breathing. The pace slowed.

Farrington watched Nikkari's ungainly shuffle and said, as if insulted, "The bloke's got no bloody calves."

Frank said, "Boy when we go around that turn, all hell is going to break loose."

Farrington shot him a look of panic.

Usami had taken them through the last 5,000 meters in 16:21. Frank ran the next in 15:11. Several hundred yards after turning for home, he met me laboring among the stragglers.

"Put it to them," I said, needlessly. There was blood in his eye and he was running with a light, driving precision.

With nine miles to go Frank had gained 200 yards on Usami and Foster, who were running together. The crowd changed in tone. Applause for Frank was warm, but the resounding encouragement behind him was of a different order. He used it to gauge his lead.

"The race is always between 20 and 26 miles," he said later. "My only doubt was that my mind was ready to put my body through that. When I got into it, I still didn't know. There was the pain, and there was a peculiar frustration. I can run a four-minute mile. It was agonizing for a runner like me to not be able to do anything but crawl."

They ran the last three miles into the teeth of the wind. The gritty, powerful Usami shook off Foster and drove on after Frank.

"It was the hardest I've ever run," said Frank. "Even in the heat of Cali, I felt better. Here, I was so helpless."

He won by 32 seconds in 2:12:50.4.

"I finished and a great feeling of thankfulness swept through me. There was no sense of conquest, none of this baloney about *vanquishing* anybody."

Across the line, he waved away blankets and fought off officials and reporters to stand at the finish and embrace Usami.

"My only thought was, 'Here we are, goddamnit! We made it!' This man had suffered as much as I had. We all had."

He stood there and shook hands with every finisher until I came in. I was the 38th person he shook hands with.

In the last hour, I crept. The kilometer times were gibberish, so different were they from what I had expected. I thought about quitting. Ambulances waited every three miles. I remembered being taken from the Pan-American marathon with heat exhaustion.

"I never quit!" I shouted aloud. "Never! Never! Never!" I repeated this every 500 yards to the end.

More Japanese passed. My hip stiffened. The West German, Manfred Steffny, a pale, effeminate runner who had arrived only two days before, passed. He asked me what was wrong.

"Fever, sick, blisters, don't give a damn. . . ."

He left me spouting afflictions. I was the last of the foreigners. People called "Moo-ah, Moo-ah," held their children by the shoulders and pointed them at me. I imagined them saying, "See, even the silver-medal winner of last year can be reduced to a stumbling, tortured wreck." I was a wheezing mortal.

In some places the crowd had departed. Paper flags drifted across the street like candy-stripe leaves. A few children waved sticks from which the paper had been torn.

I watched the hills, the pines rising out of courtyards, trying to mask with images the meaningless pain.

Entering the stadium, I caught a wobbling Japanese. He spurted. I kept close and jumped him in the stretch. Frank was there.

"Are you all right?" he asked.

"Yeah, I never give up."

Foster was third, Nikkari fourth, Manners fifth, Farrington sixth ("The bloody gales. I couldn't move after 20 miles"), Rummakko seventh. The times, because of the wind, were slow. Of the New Zealanders, only Foster cracked 2:16.

The award ceremony was tedious. Frank put up with it somewhat better than I, accepting four trophies and two medals. The top 10 finishers mounted pedestals. Squarely on No. 10 beamed John Robinson.

In the late afternoon, after hot baths, we were escorted to a buffet for congratulations from dignitaries. Oysters cascaded from a Fujiyama carved in ice. The Olympic torch, fashioned out of butter, rose above a track of pâté, upon which raced stuffed lobsters.

Frank was brought a beer by a pretty girl in a kimono.

"She is the most expensive bar hostess in all Fukuoka," said Shibuya-san.

"Why?" asked Frank. The girl fled.

We met Colonel Leonard Fisher, commander of the U.S. Air Force units in the area.

"Frank, my boy," he said, "youse ran a great race. We almost got out of the car to cheer."

After dark we were taken across the street to the Fukuoka Famous Strip Show, during which Frank was heard to utter the following:

"There really was a student discount.

"That is the kind of girl the servicemen take pity on and bring home to mother.

"They do make it subtly worse, don't they?

"I'm getting warm.

"She's not going to do that again. She's going to do it again.

"Agnew said it. 'You seen one, you seen 'em all.' "

The Soviet manager sat in front of us. When it was over, he turned, pondered, "O.K., yeah?"

"My God," said Frank, "I thought he was going to say 'souvenir.' "

We wound up at a dim French restaurant. The Russians demanded vodka, inspected the label and decided, scornfully, *"nyet."* Shalomilov then stood and triumphantly drew a huge bottle from beneath his coat.

"Real vodka!" he shouted.

The New Zealanders fell to screaming Maori war chants. Shibuya sang a Spanish ballad in a steady tenor. The Russians crooned Caspian work songs and one of the Finns (Nikkari, since Rummakko refused to open his mouth) produced something characteristically unintelligible.

Robinson soon announced, "That vodka's great stuff. My blisters have gone away already."

Frank and I, under overpowering duress, sang *Show Me the Way to Go Home* and went home. We fell asleep in the taxi. I remember the last thing he said:

"I get like this after every marathon, so damn tired."

IN A WORLD OF WINDMILLS

Pat Jordan

WIL BLANCHE

In his playing days Johnny Sain was overshadowed, although not outpitched, by Warren Spahn, but now he is second to none as a tutor of 20-game winners — and worrier of managers. An intimate portrait by a bonus baby whose arm went dead.

He searches the hotel room for a round object. Finding none, he picks up an ashtray from the bedside table. "Imagine this is a baseball," he says. The ashtray is black and square. He grips it in his right hand, his first two fingers and thumb encircling three sides of its perimeter, his other two fingers knuckled under its base. "Now, to break off a real fine curveball," he says, "you have to turn your wrist like this." He holds the ashtray at eye level, his right arm not quite fully extended. He tilts it so that his first two fingers are on top, his thumb below, and looks intently into its scooped-out center. Now he begins to rotate his wrist very slowly. His top fingers move away from him and down and his thumb moves toward him and up until the ashtray has turned 180 degrees from its original position, and he is staring at its base. The original position of his fingers and thumb has been reversed, and now the thumb is on top and his first two fingers on the bottom.

"See," he says, "it's a very simple, natural motion." He repeats the procedure, only this time he rotates the ashtray in a more fluid, sweeping manner, and as his wrist turns he draws the ashtray in to his chest. He demonstrates the motion, slowly and very gracefully, almost with tenderness, as a man might draw a beautiful woman to himself.

"It is a natural motion," he says softly. "It's real easy and natural." He repeats it again and again, each time drawing that woman to his chest until it is apparent that the repetition is only in small part for his student's sake and more for his own. With each repetition he seems to be reaffirming the clarity and logic of that motion, and with each reaffirmation he takes great pleasure. As he repeats the lesson, he speaks in that soothing drawl of his, that opiate that softens resistance, that makes men open and receptive to his teaching. It is as if you slept while a foreign language recording played over and over and, on waking, you discovered you had learned a new language. Only it is not really learned, not consciously acquired, but rather absorbed — and absorbed so effortlessly that it seems not new after all. It becomes something natural that one has possessed all along, though it was buried, and this teacher deserves credit only for nudging it to the surface. Then this new possession, rather this old possession newly discovered, becomes in one's mind one's very own in a way nothing learned ever can be.

He stops, puts the ball in his left hand and says, "If you throw it correctly the ball should break something like this." He cups his now empty right hand and draws a backward S in the air. "See, it goes away from a batter and down at the same time." He draws another backward S, then another, and another, each one drawn gracefully, with care, the shape of that beautiful but elusive woman he has committed to memory. He takes the ball in his right hand and, standing beside his bed, he begins his motion. He is wearing a pale blue shirt, a dark blue tie and navy flared slacks. He pumps, reaches back, kicks, moves forward, and at the last possible second pulls that woman to his chest.

Johnny Sain, the 54-year-old pitching coach of the Chicago White Sox, is a big man, almost 6'3" tall and over 200 pounds. He has one of those slight men's builds that with age takes on weight through the chest and arms while the legs remain thin. His face is small-featured, leathery, creased, and his cheeks are lumpy from years of chewing tobacco. He would look to be a very gruff man, without tenderness, if it were not for his smile, which is faint, and his eyes, which are a clear, youthful blue. That smile (not a smile, really, just a show of teeth) and those eyes (wincing, vaguely distant) lend him the air of a man perpetually scanning the horizon for uncertain shapes and shadows, for, quite possibly, windmills, whose presence he is sure of but whose form escapes him.

When Johnny Sain became the Chicago White Sox pitching coach in the fall of 1970 he inherited a staff that during the previous season had recorded the highest earned-run average (4.54) in the major leagues, and in the American League had allowed the most hits (1,554), had given up the most home runs (164) and the most runs (822). The team's most successful pitcher was eight-year veteran Tommy John, who had won 12 games and lost 17.

After a season under Sain the White Sox finished fourth in their league in team pitching and fifth overall. They had reduced the staff ERA to 3.12; had placed three pitchers in the league's top 15; had produced a 22-game winner in journeyman Wilbur Wood, who in his nine previous years in the majors had won only 37 games; and had developed two young pitchers of promise — Tom Bradley, winner of 15, and Bart Johnson, winner of 12. As a team Chicago finished third in its division, and there was speculation that the club's rookie manager, Chuck Tanner, might be voted the American League's Manager of the Year.

Before Sain was hired by Chicago he was working in the minor leagues, having been dropped as pitching coach by a succession of major league clubs — the Athletics, Yankees, Twins and Tigers. It wasn't that Johnny Sain wasn't doing his job. It seemed, in fact, that he was doing it too well. In New York he had coached Jim Bouton, Ralph Terry and Whitey Ford to 20-game seasons, the only times in their careers they achieved such records. In Minnesota, Mudcat Grant and Jim Kaat became 20-game winners under Sain, also for the first and only times in their careers, and Dave Boswell and Jim Perry improved notice-ably and became 20-game winners shortly after Sain departed. Finally, in Sain's years in Detroit, Denny McLain won 31 games and 24 games. Earl Wilson won 22, a mark he never approached before or after in his 11-year major league career. And Mickey Lolich, although only a 19-game winner under Sain, became a 25-game winner after the pitching coach left the Tigers. "Without Sain's help I never would have done it," Lolich says today.

Johnny Sain came from Havana, Ark., a village close by the foothills of the Ozark Mountains, and signed his first professional baseball contract — $50 per month — with Osceola of the Class D Northeast Arkansas League. In the next five years Sain was to play for three other minor league teams, all of which felt he did not have sufficient speed to become a major league pitcher. One major league scout watched Sain hurl a shutout and then wrote his front office saying he hadn't seen a ballplayer on the field. Sain himself did not believe he ever would become a major-leaguer. He regarded his summer ballplaying as just another job. He got better pay as an athlete than as a soda jerk. For a while he was an automobile mechanic like his father, and occasionally he worked as a waiter but usually just to earn enough money to pay his way to still another tryout camp.

Sain managed to put together two winning seasons in Class D ball and then moved on to the AA club in Nashville. But after posting a 6-12 record his manager told him to bring a first baseman's glove to spring training the following year. He had batted .315 as a part-time first baseman. However, that year (1942) so many young pitchers were drafted into the military that Sain was allowed to remain a pitcher. In fact, he was invited to try out with the Boston Braves and he so impressed the club's manager, Casey Stengel, that he was brought North to start the season. At the time Sain was 24; he had a good curveball and decent control but little speed. Used almost exclusively as a relief pitcher, he posted a 4-7 record before he, too, went into the military. He joined the Navy Air Corps along with Ted Williams and Johnny Pesky. However, Sain spent 22 months trying to earn his flight wings while some ballplayers earned theirs in less than a year. "I've always been a slow learner," says Sain. "That's helped me a lot, both as a player and coach. I have to go over things again and again before they stick in my mind. But when they do, they stick better than if I had picked them up quick."

During the war years Sain pitched in service leagues throughout the South, developing an assortment of sliders and curveballs. He improved so rapidly that at one point he struck out Ted Williams three consecutive times in a service game. When Sain returned to Boston in 1946, he astonished everyone by winning 20 games that season. In the five years from 1946 to 1950, when Sain and Warren Spahn pitched together and Boston fans chanted, "Spahn and Sain and pray for rain," Sain won 95 games and Spahn won 86. Yet it was Spahn, younger, more ebullient, with stylish form and a good fastball, who captured the imagination of writers and fans. Even his profile deserved attention by its very sharpness, while Sain, older, reticent, with only modest ability, seemed the epitome of blurred edges. In those years Sain seldom contributed to team discussions of methods for dispatching opposing batters. He never had been coached in the minor leagues (no one considered him enough of a prospect to waste the time) and had had to educate himself, slowly, painstakingly, so he had grown quite parsimonious of his hard-earned pitching knowledge.

Because of Sain's reputation for dependability and his inherent unobtrusiveness, most people were stunned in July 1948 a few days before the All-Star Game when Johnny Sain threatened to quit baseball. "I meant it," he says. "I was going to walk away from the whole thing." What had angered the previously unflappable Sain was the news that Brave Owner Lou Perini had signed an 18-year-old pitcher named Johnny Antonelli for $65,000. Sain, a proven 20-game winner, was playing for $21,500 after an unsuccessful holdout for more. Eventually Sain got the $30,000 he demanded and a two-year contract. It was not the money that mattered to the modest-living pitcher but what it signified to him. He had come to view the respect and loyalty a team had for him in terms of its salary offer. How much did a team respect him and his talent, he wondered, if it gave an untried youth three times what it offered him.

Sain finished out his productive years as a relief pitcher with the Yankees and there became friends with Ralph Houk, who used to warm him up in the bullpen before relief appearances. Houk was a light hitter who was to spend most of his time in bullpens, but he put this to good use. He studied each game carefully, discussed various situations with pitchers, especially Sain, and prepared himself for that day when he hoped to manage the Yankees. Houk's diligence was eventually rewarded. And when he got the job years later he remembered Sain, who was not only a friend but also someone whose pitching knowledge he greatly respected.

Sain played out his career in Kansas City, retiring in 1955, and the Athletics hired him as their pitching coach in 1959. "To become a pitching coach," he says, "you have to start all over again. You have to get outside of yourself. You might have done things a certain way when you pitched, but that doesn't mean it will be natural to someone else. For example, I threw a lot of sliders and off-speed pitches because I wasn't very fast. But that's me. I could also pitch with only two days' rest [he once pitched nine complete games in 29 days] whereas many pitchers need four, although I think they shouldn't. I have never believed much in running pitchers to keep them in shape. A lot of pitching coaches make a living out of running pitchers so they won't have to spend that same time teaching them how to pitch, something they are unsure of. It would be better to have those pitchers throw on the sidelines every day than run. Things like this I learned on my own. I picked up everything by observation, which is the best teacher. Nothing came easy to me. I had to think things over and over more than guys with natural ability did. Maybe this has made it easier for me to get my ideas across to pitchers.

"I don't know any answers. I don't give pitchers answers. I try to stimulate their thinking, to present alternatives and let them choose. I remind them every day of things they already know but tend to forget. I repeat things a lot, partly for them, but also for my own thinking, to make sure what I'm saying makes sense. . . . I don't force anyone to be like Johnny Sain. I want them to be what's natural to themselves. I adjust to their style, both as pitchers and people. I find some common ground outside of baseball that'll make it easier for us to communicate. I used to talk flying with Denny McLain. Once you can communicate with a pitcher it's easier to make him listen to you about pitching. You know him better, too. You know when to lay off him, when to minimize his tensions and also when to inspire him. That's why you've got to know him. Pitching coaches don't change pitchers, we just stimulate their thinking. We teach their subconscious mind so that when they get on the mound and a situation arises, it triggers an automatic physical reaction that they might not even be aware of."

Sain lasted less than a year with the Athletics. At the time Kansas City was considered both a farm team and a burial ground for the Yankees. It seemed that every aging body New York disposed of finished out his days with Kansas City, and that every talented youngster the A's produced was sent to New York to aid the Yankees in another pennant drive. Sain resigned his position with the A's a month before the close of the 1959 season because, as he told sportswriters, he felt the organization wasn't trying to build for the future. "I didn't want to be someplace where I was putting more into an organization than that organization was." The realization that he might be dawned on him one day when he asked General Manager Parke Carroll for four tickets to a game. Carroll produced the guest tickets but asked Sain to pay for them. Sain paid and left the room inwardly furious. As a coach he was making only $12,000. "Well, if they don't care that much about me, I'm going," he decided.

Sain spent the next year in Walnut Ridge, Ark., where he owned a car dealership. However, when Houk was appointed the Yankee manager in 1961, Sain knew he'd have a job in baseball again. Houk did not rehire longtime Yankee Pitching Coach Jim Turner and gave the job instead to Sain.

At first things did not go well for Houk. He was confronted with the problems any manager who had been a bullpen catcher on a team of Fords and Mantles and Berras would face when placed in charge of those same men. Houk turned to Sain for help. One day after a particularly dispiriting loss Sain advised, "Ralph, things look pretty dark right now, but don't let any son of a bitch know it. Let's not panic." A few weeks later, when the Yankees moved into first place, Houk, puffing a cigar, told reporters, "Yeah, things looked pretty bad for me last month, but I wasn't about to let any son of a bitch know it."

The Yankees won pennants in 1961, '62 and '63, and the World Series in 1961 and '62, under Houk's managership. And in 1961 Houk was named Manager of the Year. During that same period Ford, Terry and Bouton had their 20-game seasons. Says Ford of his old tutor Sain, "If you don't know a coach personally, you try his stuff once or twice and if it doesn't work, you stop. But you get so personal with Sain, you admire the man so much that you just have to give his ideas an extra chance. It was Sain's teaching me a hard slider and pitching me with two and three days' rest, instead of the four and five days I needed before, that made me a 20-game winner."

Despite their mutual success, which should have enhanced their friendship, Sain and Houk began to drift apart. Houk confided less and less in his pitching coach, and when he did it was seldom on the personal basis it had been. Sain, as usual, said little. It was during those years that Houk, an ex-Ranger, began to build a reputation as a forceful disciplinarian. (He flattened a slightly drunk Ryne Duren with one punch on the train that brought the Yankees back to New York after their 1958 World Series victory.) Soon, Houk was being referred to by fans and in newspapers as The Major.

Jim Bouton, wearing bell-bottoms and a body shirt of robin's-egg blue, leans forward over his desk at New York's WABC-TV and says, "But does he still like me? I mean, after the book and all. Does Johnny still like me?" Assured, Bouton sits back and says, "Sain taught me everything I know, from how to put on sanitary socks [inside out so as not to get a blister from the lint that forms in the toes] to how to negotiate a contract. I admire him more than any man I ever met. All players like him. Black, white, liberal, conservative, loud, quiet — they all do. Sain gets a pitcher's allegiance before any manager could. Managers don't like this. But it isn't Sain's fault. He doesn't try to undermine a manager's position. He can't help it, can he, if what he is appeals more to pitchers than what their managers are?

"Johnny sees very deeply into things. A lot of managers can't stand to have him around after a while. What general likes a lieutenant that's smarter? Who wants to live with a guy like Sain, always standing off in the corner watching you, and every time you do something lousy to a player, there's John, not saying anything, not revealing what he sees, just looking like some knight in shining armor who knows all. Take Chuck Tanner, for instance. He's a nice guy who didn't know where the bodies were buried when he came to the White Sox. Now he's a successful manager, mostly because of Sain's help. How long do you think he'll want to look over his shoulder and see Sain reminding him just by his presence that he owes part of his success to someone else? It takes a big man to be able to live with that. That's why Ralph Houk got rid of Sain in '63.

"At first Houk sought out Sain because he was insecure. But when he became a successful manager, The Major didn't need a talented coach anymore, especially one who reminded him of the past. All he wanted was someone who was loyal, and Sain is loyal to himself first, his pitchers second and his manager third. When Houk quit and Berra took over, Houk was afraid Berra would be a winner with Sain's help, and that would diminish Houk's success, so he got rid of Sain."

When the Yankees lost the 1963 World Series to the Dodgers in four straight, Sain found it strange that Ralph Houk, always a bitter loser, did not seem particularly upset by that humiliation. Then Sain read in the newspapers that Houk had been promoted to general manager and Yogi Berra had replaced him as field manager for the 1964 season, and he understood. "There was a rumor that Yogi would be the manager that year," Sain recalls, "and I thought, 'No way. The players won't respect him.' When I read about it in the papers I began thinking — Ralph is a man I always believed leveled with me, and here he didn't tell me about Yogi until after I read it in the papers. Houk sent me a letter saying he hoped it wasn't too big a shock, and a while after that I got a letter from Yogi asking me to work for him. I wrote Houk a letter saying that due to increased expenses I needed a $2,500 raise from the $22,500 I was already getting, which at the time I believe was the highest salary ever paid a pitching coach. I also wanted a two-year contract. Houk called me on the phone and said Topping wouldn't go for the extra money. I said, O.K., send me my release. He did. If he had been my friend, like I thought, he would have tried to talk me out of leaving. But he didn't. When Bouton found out, he offered to give me the extra money I had asked for out of his own salary. He thought it was just a salary dispute. They put Whitey in as pitching coach, and after him Jim Turner came back, and I know what Ralph Houk thinks of Jim Turner."

"Jim Turner is the best pitching coach ever," Ralph Houk said emphatically not long ago. "Understand? The best ever! A good pitching coach deals only with mechanics. It can be detrimental to a team if a pitching coach gets too personally involved with his pitchers. He should treat them mechanically. That's why Johnny Sain had his troubles. I've heard a lot of bad things about Sain since he left us. He can't seem to hold a job, can he? Jim Turner's been a pitching coach with the Yankees for years. He knows what I expect of him. We get together, and I tell him how I'm gonna use the pitchers and he does it."

Again Sain sat out a year until, in the fall of 1964, Calvin Griffith, the owner of the Minnesota Twins, offered him a job, asking him to name his salary. Sain signed for $20,000.

Before the season began it had been rumored that Twin Manager Sam Mele would lose his job if he did not produce a winner in '65. When he left home for spring training, Sain remarked offhandedly, "Wouldn't it be funny if Mele became the Manager of the Year?" That season the Twins did win the American League pennant, and Sam Mele was voted Manager of the Year.

Despite both Mele's and Sain's success (Sain had produced his usual 20-game winner in Mudcat Grant, who said of him, "He sure puts biscuits in your pan"), the two men did not get along. Mele distrusted Sain and the power he held over his pitchers. Furthermore, he seldom agreed with Sain's unorthodox pitching concepts, and often the two men had a difference of opinion over the amount of running a pitcher should do, or how many days' rest he might need between starts. But beyond that, Sain felt he was never able to communicate deeply with Mele, that he never knew where he stood with him, which to a man like Sain was disconcerting. After signing a 1966 contract for $25,000, Sain's difficulties with Mele grew until by midseason they were irreconcilable. One day in a game in Kansas City, Billy Martin, then a Twin coach, berated one of Sain's pitchers over a squeeze play. Sain, furious, went to his man's defense. Mele, who was listening to the dispute, told the two coaches to "knock it off." Later, thinking about the incident, Sain became increasingly upset. The following day he moved all his equipment and uniforms out of the coaches' locker room and deposited them in the players' locker room, where he dressed until the end of the season, when he was fired. Ever since then, whatever club he has worked for, Sain has dressed with the players.

When news of Sain's dismissal was made public, Jim Kaat, a 25-game winner that year, wrote an open letter to the Twins' front office that was published in area newspapers. The letter accused the Twins of making a terrible mistake in firing Sain, and it implied that the team's drop to second place that year rested with Mele's inability to communicate with his players, as well as with Sain.

Dave Boswell, a pitcher at Minnesota in 1966, was until very recently a seldom-used reliever for the Baltimore Orioles. A 20-game winner with the Twins, he subsequently damaged his arm so severely that he was given his unconditional release. He was picked up by the Orioles only on a gamble. "If Johnny Sain had any weakness as a pitching coach," says Boswell, "it was that he didn't understand hard throwers as much as he should. He never made us run wind sprints at Minnesota because he didn't believe in running. Some of the pitchers, me and Kaat in particular, didn't run 10 sprints all year, and we came up with sore arms. But that was our fault, I guess. Johnny left it up to us to run on our own if we thought we needed it. He never pressured you to do anything. He didn't bother you a lot, but when he did, when he talked about pitching and the possibilities of a baseball, you could actually see them before your eyes. As a kid you put that ball in your hand and you thought of it just as a ball. But after Sain put that ball in your hand you didn't see it the same anymore. It had possibilities you never dreamed of."

From 1967 to 1969 Johnny Sain coached under Mayo Smith at Detroit. In 1968 the Tigers won the American League pennant and the World Series, Mayo Smith was named Manager of the Year, Denny McLain became the first pitcher to win 30 or more games in one season since Dizzy Dean in 1934 and Mickey Lolich won three complete games in the World Series to become only the seventh man in history to accomplish that feat. Ironically, but predictably enough, Sain was close friends with Lolich and McLain, both of whom he had been warned were "real nuts," and daily he grew more estranged from Mayo Smith, who, he had been told, was "a real gentleman."

"McLain and Lolich both wanted to improve themselves," says Sain, "and that's all I need in a man. Both were very individualistic, and I like that. McLain may have been a little loose off the mound but on it he was all business. And he's got guts. Both he and Lolich. You know that Lolich rides those motorcycles of his, and McLain's got a pilot's license. If McLain was flying an airplane and it died on him you could bet money he'd still be fighting it when it hit the ground.

"It was Mayo I had problems with. He's a fine guy like everybody told me, and I only really disagreed with him once. But still we never got along. When I came to Detroit I had a reputation behind me, and he was relatively unknown and trying to make a name for himself. Every day sportswriters would seek me out for an interview. They were always asking me questions like why didn't I become a manager, which I could never be, and all the time Mayo was hitting that press room trying to be real nice with reporters. Pretty soon I could sense there was friction between Mayo and me. I don't like friction. It lingers with me. It disturbs me if I have to be on my toes with someone, always afraid I might offend them. That's not what life is all about. Mayo had this ability to keep me uneasy all the time. He was so smooth, I never knew where I stood. I'd rather he declared himself, cuss me out, so we could get things in the open. But he never did. He was always a real nice guy."

Mickey Lolich, the Tigers' 25-game winner in 1971, sits down for breakfast at New York's Hotel Roosevelt. He orders four scrambled eggs, four pieces of toast, bacon, a large orange juice and a pot of coffee. At 6 feet, 230 pounds, Lolich refers to himself as a fat man's athlete. "Fat guys need idols, too," he once said. Now, speaking quietly and occasionally glancing across to a nearby table where Manager Billy Martin is eating his breakfast, Lolich talks about Sain. "He made me a 20-game winner. Yet, he never taught me a single thing about pitching a baseball. Maybe that's because John's not a pitching coach, he's a headshrinker. Even when you learn from Sain, you never feel you've learned a thing from him. He lets you think you did it yourself. McLain wouldn't learn from anyone when he was with Detroit, so Johnny just taught him things without letting Denny know it. McLain used to sneak down to the bullpen like a little kid so he could practice what Sain had taught him without letting anyone know it. I'll bet to this day he'll swear he never learned a thing from Johnny. But every pitcher learns from John. Pitching takes on new shades and nuances. Sain loves pitchers. He doesn't maybe love baseball so much, but he loves pitchers. That's why he doesn't get along with the management. He believes pitchers are unique, and only he understands them."

In the spring of 1970, after the Tigers fired him, Sain was offered a job as minor league pitching coach with the California Angels. To the surprise of many, Sain accepted the position. He spent much of the 1970 season driving across the country, stopping at cities like El Paso, Salt Lake City and Idaho

Falls, where he worked with youngsters who were light-years away from the Lolichs and McLains he had been accustomed to. Yet Sain cherishes that experience in which, in his own words, "I rediscovered the country. I had been having marriage problems, and I took that job to get away from things. I'd always thought that in baseball or in life you get to a point where you can relax, level off, but I found you can never rest. You always have the possibility of sinking. This divorce action with my wife has made me stay young as I grow older. She's got six lawyers and she's determined to take my money, my kids and my reputation, and I'm just as determined not to let her. In her thirties she wanted to go back to college, so I encouraged her. But then she seemed to think she was better than me. We always seemed in competition. She said I was too easy, that I like to be kicked around by people.

"I was always an outsider. I was never anyone's glamour boy. I was always looking over my shoulder at some new Dizzy Dean who would make everyone forget me. People were waiting to drive a nail in my coffin. It's a human weakness to hope somebody fails. People are never the way you're taught they should be. We grow up with standards that we find aren't true. I used to believe if you were straight with people they would be straight with you. But they aren't. I hate for people to toy with me, to be superior, but I've got to give them the chance. I don't know why I'm always testing people, but I am. Maybe I'm just playing games with them. Maybe I'm fooling everyone."

Sain, wearing the light blue traveling uniform of the White Sox, stands with his arms folded behind Steve Kealey, who is working steadily off the pitchers' warmup mound at Fenway Park in Boston. Kealey sweats and grunts as he throws. He is 24 with red hair, freckles and the muscled, tapering build of a swimmer. While he sweats, Sain talks softly to him. Kealey does not acknowledge Sain's words, which are few, really only an occasional phrase, an exhortation, rarely a sentence.

"Heh, that had the beginnings," says Sain, "the beginnings." Kealey, impassive, continues to throw a curveball that is flat and does not break down as much as Sain would wish. "He'll get it soon enough," says Sain, speaking just loud enough for Kealey to hear. "It's only a matter of time."

It is mid-July and Kealey is 1-1 with an ERA of 4.35. He is a hard thrower with adequate control, but even he will be the first to admit he is far from being a finished pitcher. But he has confidence that wherever his potential might lie, Sain will unearth it. "He tells me things I never considered before," says Kealey. "They make sense when you think about them, but who thinks of the things Johnny Sain does? John's whole life is teaching pitchers. It's like, by teaching us to get hitters out it proves he could have done it today, too. You know, his success lives on. This is the second year I've worked with him. When I was in spring training with the Angels I talked to him once. But the front office wouldn't let any big-leaguers talk to him. They told us to stay away from Sain."

After Kealey finishes throwing, Sain walks to the outfield where the rest of the Chicago pitchers are standing around, stirring themselves infrequently to retrieve a fly ball in a halfhearted lope, but more often planted, spread-legged, like gray-flanneled pelicans. Sain moves from pitcher to pitcher. He stands beside each one for a few moments, his arms folded across his chest, spitting tobacco juice into the still, sunny afternoon, passing the time in small talk that only occasionally drifts into, then out of, the subject of pitching.

Sain says very little about pitching to Wilbur Wood, the club's 29-year-old knuckleballer, because as Sain admits, "I don't know much about knuckleballs." Wood, a chunky, smiling man, is a nine-year veteran, a castoff of the Red Sox and the Pirates, both of which used him primarily as a relief pitcher. In 1970 as a reliever with the White Sox he was 9-13. The club's '71 brochure said that "some thought was being given to restoring him to a starting role on occasion." That thought belonged to Sain. Sain made one other suggestion to Wood, and it was that he pitch often with only two days' rest between starts. Sain felt that as a knuckleballer, Wood put less strain on his arm than did other pitchers with more orthodox stuff, and therefore he could absorb the extra work with ease. Wood started 42 games in 1971 and won 22 of them. He pitched 334 innings, the most of any White Sox pitcher since 1917 and second in the American League in 1971 to Mickey Lolich's 376 innings. Wood's ERA was 1.91, second in the league to Vida Blue's 1.82.

Sain also says very little to Vicente Romo, the club's 28-year-old, Mexican-born relief pitcher, but for a different reason. Romo, a smooth-skinned man who resembles an overweight bullfighter, is another Red Sox castoff. He possesses a windmill motion, similar to Luis Tiant's, that seems to deliver a thousand different pitches from a thousand different angles. He speaks little English, and for this reason Sain finds it difficult to communicate with him as deeply as he wishes. With Romo he deals primarily with pitching mechanics. To speak to him in more personal terms would be to risk a misunderstanding, says Sain.

Sain talks a good deal with Joel Horlen, the club's 33-year-old veteran. Horlen, a small man with a preoccupied gaze, is at a crucial juncture in his career. He was once the ace of the Chicago staff, winning 19 games in 1967, but he lost speed from both his fastball and his curve and has been losing. Sain is trying to help Horlen make that adjustment all pitchers must make in their mid-30s when the quality of their pitches deteriorates and they must increase their quantity. Sain is working with Horlen on a screwball that he hopes will prolong his career. "He doesn't say much to guys who are going good," says Horlen. "He's a funny guy. He seems to spend more time with guys who are having their problems. Like he always says, he waits for guys to hit bottom before he talks to them." After a 6-16 season in 1970, Horlen posted an 8-9 record in '71, his first year under Sain. (Horlen is now with the Athletics.)

Rich Hinton, a 24-year-old graduate of the University of Arizona, had pitched only five innings at this point of his career (he would be traded to the Yankees). Yet Johnny Sain calls him a terrific prospect if for no other reason than, "He looks at you real straight." Of Sain, Hinton says, "Working under John is the best break I could get. Every club he's been with has had a 20-game winner. The only problem is he's been with so many clubs that all the pitchers he's taught cut each other's throat. It's like telling everyone in a card game the same trick. Pretty soon they'll all use it and nobody benefits. What I like best about John, though, is that he never second-guesses you. He'll come out to the mound and say, 'Don't you worry, that was a helluva pitch. He never should have hit it.' Then he'll say, 'Now, this batter is a poor breaking-ball hitter, but you can throw him whatever you think best. You're the judge.' And when you get the guy out with a breaking ball, you believe it was your pitch, not his. You made that final decision. Johnny Sain lets you make the act of will."

"A LA RECHERCHE DU TANKS PERDU"

Robert F. Jones

HEINZ KLUETMEIER

Twenty years out of the competitive swim, Robert F. Jones, the Splash of this story, goes home again to Wauwatosa, Wis. to rejoin some old high school classmates and hit the water against current Wauwatosa stars.

Because, in a way, we live in an age of arrested development. We tickle our adolescence much in the manner our wives employ when amusing the very young. We cannot let go of it — the game we played or the joy we took in playing it. The 80-yard run or that long, last hook shot that won the game for good old — you name the school. We sprint in our sleep, some of us, like dogs adreaming. But only rarely is the old jock fool enough to reenter the fields of play. Sure, there are the pickup games of touch in the park or of half-court at the Y, these paid for often enough in the coin of pain: a charley horse or a bent nose. The old baseball player wallops the horsehide at the company picnic, sucking down beer between innings, enjoying both the memory and the prospect of hangover.

Ah, but the man who was once a champion swimmer — where does he go to recapture the psychic garlands of his now-drained glory? Usually he ends up swimming laps in a motel pool, a dinky well of nostalgia fraught with kids and chlorine. He hopes his stroke will announce to the world, or at least that portion of it sizzling like pork chops at poolside, that he was once akin to Schollander and Spitz. But at the very moment of his grandest fantasy, he usually clips a little girl on the side of the head with his nifty, bent-armed recovery and hears her porcine papa bellow: "Hey, showboat, look out for my kid. Who do you think you are: Weissmuller?"

The swimmer returns to his laps, chastened, slower, thinking that, after all, the real thrill of swimming was not in the workouts. No, not in those endless, dead-armed hours of ennui punctuated by retching. The *real* thrill was in the race itself, and in the hours leading up to it. He relives the scenario. There was that fine, visceral balance that had to be struck between fear and fury as he shaved down for the meet. Then the dry-throated shimmer of horror when his event was called. Followed by a feeling of calm, yes, of readiness, rising like mercury in the competitive thermometer of his backbone as he mounted the block. A quick glance at the crowd — the grim-faced fathers, the hot-eyed girl friends. And then the climactic moment: the crack of the starter's pistol. . . .

Four ancient swimmers from Wauwatosa, Wis. recently relived those dubious thrills. Hoping against hope, teetering against time, they swam a 200-yard freestyle relay — 50 yards per Methuselah — against four of their inheritors, topflight members of Wauwatosa West High School's 1971 state championship swimming team. The senior citizens lost, as they knew they would, but not so badly as had been predicted. At the same time they won a victory of Proustian magnitude, a successful search for the past — *à la recherche du temps perdu* — without the aid of tea cakes. These four men, whose combined ages totaled a century and a half and averaged 38¼ years, proved that Thomas Wolfe was a liar: you *can* go home again!

The instigator of this juvenile exercise was a man whom I shall call Splash, age 37 and possessed by some strange coincidence of the same fingerprints as this article's author. Splash now lives in the exurbs of the Northeast, but in his day as a high school swimmer he was the fastest 50-yard freestyler in the state of Wisconsin and the fourth fastest high school swimmer in that event in the U.S. Lean, swart and crew cut in those years, Splash affected a sullen mien that he thought would score points with the girls, but at heart he was a happy romantic. He believed in competition for its own sake, and knew that the lad with the best attitude would ultimately win — at anything, anywhere — provided he trained properly. Four years of college, three in the U.S. Navy, followed by many more in the corporate dueling *salles* of New York City had complicated that vision. But Splash was sure his unarticulated major premise was still right, although sportswise, at least, his spreading waistline, balding pate and pallid hide were slowly but surely eroding its credence. "If I could only get back in shape," he would frequently lament over his fifth martini. "If I only had the time. . . ."

Clearly it would take a major psychosocial shock to jolt Splash back into competition. And in the sports world of the 1970s, none of the psychosocial shocks had any impact. He could not feel outraged pro or con over the plight of the black athlete: he had never particularly wanted to hear Duane Thomas talk, or to smoke pot with him either, for that matter. The premature death of Dick Tiger had moved him, but that was more a geopolitical and medical sorrow (Splash had kind of liked Biafra, but he hated cancer). The trades and fades of athletes in any sport, of any color, were interesting but hardly emotional matters. They all could have been stories on the business page for all Splash cared, and probably should have been. He shared the Western world's mild contempt for Avery Brundage and envied Karl Schranz his commercial cunning. Still, the Olympics was "teevee" to Splash. And Splash could take "teevee" or he could leave it alone.

Thus he was surprised when the major psychosocial shock actually hit. It came on the commuter train one morning when, in the tattletale-gray shirt-tails of *The New York Times* sports section, he discovered that a 19-year-old girl swimmer — a girl who had swum the 100-meter freestyle faster than Splash had at the age of 22 — had retired. Retired because she could no longer "get it on" for swimming. The effect was one of instant outrage, followed by a flush of self-doubt.

"How could I have been that stupid to be a swimmer?" he wondered later. "It was like one of those dreams where you suddenly find yourself on Park Avenue in your pajamas. I tore the paragraph from the paper and stuffed it under the seat. I don't even remember the girl's name — Debbie Flyer or one of those cutesy monickers they give the little twerps these days — but I'd known there was a revolution going on in swimming, an earlier start in competition, a tougher training regimen, a total disregard for the sanctity of records, which is as it should be. But this was too much. Over the hill at 19 — my sweet Weissmuller! This one cruel development had undercut all my happy memories of swimming, had curdled the milk of my nostalgia and made me old before my time, as we say. For days I tried to submerge the fact, sublimate it so that my ego might heal, but the ache endured. It was then I realized that we had to swim The Relay."

To Splash, with his love of metaphor, The Relay suddenly seemed to symbolize meaningful transition in an age of instant rejection, a rapid but orderly transfer of confidence and tradition from one man to the next, if not between generations. "I reckoned that if I could get some guys together from our 'Glory Days' and swim them against our counterparts on the same high school's team of today," he said, "then even if we lost, which we surely would, we'd at least know the measure of our decline. And perhaps by swimming out our humiliation, we might drown it like a nagging, unwanted alley cat. And what the heck, it would be a lot of fun just to get together again."

On his next trip to Wauwatosa, where his parents still lived, Splash set about locating his relay team. It was not easy. Just finding three old friends still living in one's hometown after a 20-year absence is pure luck in this age of corporate diaspora. During Splash's youth, Wauwatosa had been a small bedroom suburb on the western outskirts of Milwaukee, a quiet, tidy enclave whose middle-class affluence was as sturdy as its stone houses, as neatly clipped as its putting-green lawns, a town where men often took the streetcar to work, or else walked whistling under the elms. Now Milwaukee's sprawl had locked the town in a crablike embrace and the elms were dying — as much, it seemed, of woe as of blight. Warehouses and ticky tacky covered the fields where Splash had shot prairie chickens; where woods had grown, freeways ran thick with black plastic cars full of pink plastic men in brown plastic suits. Some benevolent authority had placed a concrete bottom in a stretch of the Menomonee River where smallmouth bass had swum.

Yes, much of the past was gone, but not, fortunately, Splash's old high school swimming coach. Not that Robert B. White, 44, of Wauwatosa, is old in any sense of the word. Coach White had been only 23 when he had come north from Indiana University to run the Tosa swim team two decades earlier. He had not changed: energy and wit, an ability to drive kids through the walls of their babyhood, the cruel but kindly scorn of a good coach, even his hairline — none had receded with time's passage. Better yet, the seven-year difference between his age and Splash's, so vast in the old days, had undergone the miraculous shrinkage that is one of the few benefits of aging. Bob White not only remembered Splash, he had often wondered what had become of him. "You might find it hard to believe," he told his young swimmers when Splash arrived, "but this old codger was one of my best freestylers when I first came here during the Boer War." The kids stared at Splash with that steady sneer now known as "cool."

"For a moment there I was put off by the stare," Splash said. "It made me bridle. But then there was a shock of recognition: I had practiced that same look over and over again in the mirror when I was a kid. Instead of going high with dudgeon, I flipped them the bird. It broke them up. Look, this was a damned fine swimming team. They'd won the state championship last year. We old guys had been state champions three years running, and these guys reminded me of us. Their hair was longer, but they had that same cockiness, the same single-mindedness when it came to winning that we had back then. Absurd, that baseless confidence. It's a kind of premature maturity, I guess, but it's one of the best things about sports when you're a kid."

White was keen for The Relay idea — "Oh boy, will we whip you!" he chortled — and, better yet, he knew where three of Splash's peers could be found, all of them former swimming team captains. "I'll bet they'll do it," White said. "They were all dead game."

When Splash telephoned the three men that evening, he found White was right. It was as if the 20 years since the last time the four had raced together had been no more than a break between events. The world had changed radically over those two decades, but it had not affected their bedrock enthusiasm for competition.

Ted Wahlen, for example, at 39 the oldest of the four, had lost a bit of hair but none of his whoop-it-up ebullience. "He had always been a big guy," Splash recalled. "Six feet and change, 200 pounds, wrists like the rest of us have ankles, and a mat of hair on his chest when he was in the eighth grade. He was one of those rare people you meet who never seem to get angry or rattled, never sulk or carry on as if the world is doing a number on them. By the same token, Teddy has not been the quickest of swimmers — his bones and muscles got in the way — but he had grit and wit. No, not wit exactly, more like bonhomie. We were lifeguards together for two summers in the county swimming pools. Best job in the world if you can live on $1.25 an hour. We walked around like God in red shorts, bellowing one-word orders to the 'pygmies' — the little kids — to make them slow down. 'Walk!' we would roar, and they'd put on the brakes. Every now and then some pygmy would start to drown, and you'd dive in, deadpan, slap a cross-chest carry on him, haul him ashore and take down his name and address so you could write a letter to his folks. 'Dear Sir and/or Madam, Your son and/or daughter nearly drowned in Hoyt Pool this morning

and/or afternoon. We suggest swimming lessons, available at the pool . . . etc.'
A rescue was called a 'jump,' and the best jumps were for teen-age girls, thanks
to the cross-chest carry. You kept a record of jumps, and there was a kind of
status that accrued to the guard with the most. More status for the girls. Teddy
seemed to get the best jumps, because he was so good looking. Teddy and I
shared a mutual enthusiasm for early Debra Paget movies, the ones where she
was always getting killed by cowboys or volcanoes because she wasn't supposed to be white and couldn't marry the hero. Real romantics. Korea was on
then, and Teddy went into the Marines.''

Now Ted Wahlen was back in Wauwatosa, big and shaggy as ever (except on top), married and the father of four sons, one of whom was on Coach
White's swimming team. "Yeah," said Ted, "my boy Kurt swims the back, the
free and the IM'' — the IM being what we used to call the injividdle medley.
Wahlen himself worked as a timer for the home meets and often swam laps
during the workouts of the age-group swim club White ran at the pool. "I'm in
fairly decent shape," he said. "But I've got this strange business — I wash air-
planes, buildings, school buses, dump trucks and big things like that. I'm called
'Mr. Porta,' and I've got my own truck. It takes a lot of time and I'm afraid it
tightens up my muscles. But yeah, I'd love to swim another relay.''

Robert Carl Montag, 39, of the U.S. Postal Service, was just as willing,
maybe more so. Montag had been one of Splash's three closest friends during
the swimming years; the others had disappeared, one to become an eye doctor
on the West Coast, the other a lawyer somewhere south of Wauwatosa. In those
days Montag was known as Moonbeam for his round face and ready grin. A
long, jolly kid whose father was an immensely popular butcher on the old
German North Side of Milwaukee, Montag possessed not only charm but three
very valuable commodities: a .300 Savage lever-action deer rifle, a deck of
pornographic playing cards and a 1934 Ford sedan. Up in Rhinelander, Wis.,
where Montag's parents had a lakeside cabin, the boys shot guns on the winter
ice and pool in the local saloons. In Wauwatosa, rendered mobile by Moonbeam's machine, they were the original "lonely teen-age broncin' bucks.''

Montag remembers: "Gee, in a lot of ways high school was the best time
of my life. That old '34 Ford — the way we used to do spins on purpose when
the roads were icy or go down to the South Side and look for fights with those
Polish kids! I could never grow a D.A. because my hair was too curly. I don't
know what it was — we were *daring* then. Now I'm a letter carrier. I walk 15
miles a day. I've got Mace for the dogs, but you'd have to be Billy the Kid to
use it, the way they come up on you. You have to hit 'em in the face. In weather
like this — it was 22° below last week — the Mace turns into a Popsicle. A dog
bit me a couple of years ago. The lady who owns him was walking her other
dog and her big one came around the corner of the house and blindsided me.
'Does it hurt?' she asked me. 'Lady,' I said, 'get the dog offa me.' She came up a

bit closer, smiling kind of nice. 'I hope he isn't hurting you,' she said. I said 'Lady, would you please get him *offa* me?' The leg puffed up like a loaf of bread. I'm afraid of every dog now, and they know it. Even cats chase me sometimes.''

Bob Kelbe was the final member of The Relay, and far and away the best "natural athlete" of the lot. At the age of 38 he weighed less (166 pounds) than he had when he was swimming in high school (170). Although he now wore glasses, Kelbe's hairline had not receded half an inch and the spring in his long, wiry shanks, which had given him the best start Splash had ever seen, was coiled as taut as ever. Kelbe was now the vice-president of a family-owned heavy-equipment business. In the lot outside the raw, concrete-block headquarters of Kelbe Bros. Equipment Co., Butler, Wis. stood a 140-foot crane. "You can have it for just $124,516.25,'' Bob told Splash. "That includes tax.''

Kelbe's twin brother Ray, who had been known as Whitey, was now living in California. The twins had probably been the most dynamic sporting duo Wauwatosa ever produced: hockey, football, track, golf, skiing and swimming, they had excelled at each. What's more, they were musical. Whitey played the trumpet, Bob the sousaphone. Both had married their high school sweethearts and produced handsome children. "You couldn't help but envy them their skills,'' said Splash. "I remember watching them play a pickup game of hockey on the Menomonee River. It was one of those windswept Wisconsin days when even the crows weren't flying. Those guys had all the dekes I had ever seen, and when they checked a guy he ended up in the catbriars on the river bank. I used to chase them downhill on skis at Currie Park. They wore through the trees like those proverbial wraiths you read about on the sports pages. I ended up with one ski on either side of a pine trunk. When I started breaking Bob's freshman swimming records — he was a year ahead of me at Tosa — I couldn't quite believe it. Maybe he'd spread himself too thin, while I was concentrating my energy on swimming. I always knew he was a better jock than I was.''

Kelbe recalls it differently. Watching Bob White's team working out one day before The Relay, he marveled at the endurance of the kids. "When I first tried out for the swimming team I wanted to be a diver,'' he said. "Coach said I was too skinny — I couldn't compress the board hard enough. He gave me a time trial for 25 yards, and I couldn't even sprint the whole distance. These kids go flat out for 200 yards at the age of 10. But you know, swimming taught me something. Remember how it was when you'd see some other guy's arm, just a blur, a brown blur, flashing ahead of you during a race? Sometimes it was an optical illusion, a psychological quirk, but you'd pull all the harder — keep trying, don't let that son of a gun beat you. It taught me to keep at it. Teachers and grownups always told you to 'keep at it,' but you couldn't believe them until you felt it, and I first began to feel it in swimming. I swam at the University of Wisconsin, but it wasn't the same, the pool was a bathtub. I studied 'light construction' in the business school — we didn't have to take history or English or psychology or any of that stuff. I had one course in forest products where as a test we had to sniff and taste 30 pieces of wood and identify them. I'm now an expert on 'Toothpicks of North America.' "

Then it was time for the workout. The kids would cover 5,000 yards that afternoon, nearly three miles, with variously paced combinations of pulling, kicking and full stroke, no single segment amounting to less than 200 yards. "My God," said Montag with awe, "if we swam 5,000 yards a week we were going some." White chuckled with the friendly sadism of a good coach. "That's one of the main reasons why the sport has changed so much since your time," he said. "Doc Counsilman is the man to blame. He showed that swimming was a softy sport up until the mid-1950s, and he really made his kids work. Swim through the pain barrier, swim until you've puked out all of your self-pity and your natural tendency to coddle yourself." White looked at his boys larruping through their laps, checking their splits on the big pace clocks at the starting end of the 25-yard pool. "I can tell them to swim four 200s at four seconds above their best time, and they can do it, some of them without even looking at the clock. As the season wears along and we get closer to the state meet, I'll reduce the workouts to 2,000 yards, shave 'em down and peak 'em up. This is the fast lane, here. Why don't you guys drop in at the tail end of the line and see how fast they go?"

They went plenty fast enough. Splash found himself a slot in the round-robin line behind a backstroker, a lanky, easygoing kid who seemed to be dawdling. "I thought I'd outfox them," he said. "A freestyler swimming behind a backstroker — I could take it easy in the wake of his toes. But those big feet kept pulling away from me after the first 50 yards. I put on a bit more power, but it wasn't there. It was like hitting the gas pedal when the tank is empty. It turned out later that the backstroker was a 16-year-old named Mark Unak who was the fastest 100-yard backstroker in the state, with a time of 56.2. Finally I just let myself fall behind slowly, enjoying the memories. The smell of chlorine and warm water and the hollow sound of kicking and pulling: they had been natural parts of my life from the age of 11 to 22, but I had not been aware of them then, no more than I am now of the stench and clangor of the commuter train. These were the better sensations. After a few laps your mind goes into a kind of free-association trance. Great gobs of unconscious material drift into sight, as if your hands were digging up the sediment of memory with every stroke. I found myself thinking of the summer outdoor meets — the sun on the hard blue water with schlock music over the loudspeaker and the girl swimmers, whom we saw only at those kinds of meets, with their strong tanned necks and their nipples showing under their nylon tank suits. The memory eased the sting of that little girl going so fast, that damned Diana Dryad."

Leaving the workout that evening, the oldsters had another memory stirred. It was cold and black in the high school parking lot, with that sharp frigidity of the northern winter that makes nostrils tick at each breath. Their muscles were loose from swimming and steam rose from their coat sleeves and collars. "Hey," yelled Montag suddenly. "Look at the halos! I'd forgotten the halos." Sure enough, every light in Wauwatosa wore a subtle nimbus, the gift of the chlorine in the warm water reacting on their now-bloodshot eyeballs. It is the single most distinguishing — and indeed formative — psychophysical attribute of the competitive swimmer. After every workout the world seems to have achieved instant sanctity through his dreary, weary eyes, thanks, no doubt, to his own hard work and the commensurate grace with which he was rewarded. Kelbe, at least, could no longer be deceived by the halos. "When I get home," he said wryly, "my wife and kids will take one look at my eyeballs and figure I've been out drinking, that's all."

Three afternoons under Coach White's tutelage did little to return the old swimmers to their former speed. Except, that is, for Kelbe, who had never lost it. The others managed to recover a few lost skills, like flipping their turns and snapping their towels. "These guys aren't that tough," Montag confided after one workout. "Why don't we make it a double event — the relay and a towel-snapping contest? So what if they beat us swimming, we can take our revenge afterward!" He cracked his towel with the long, deft wrist snap that had made him the terror of Wisconsin swimming two decades earlier and neatly removed an inch-deep gouge from a bar of soap in the shower room. "Touché, you athletic little creep!" He had pecked out the "i" in Lifebuoy.

So it was all back together, finally — the smells and the colors, the work and the play, four friends who had remained teammates through 20 years. All that remained to be done was the swimming of The Relay itself, and the psychological game that would have to precede it if the recapture of the past was to be complete.

"I really doubted that I could 'get up' for it after all those years away," Splash confessed later. "I mean, we knew we couldn't beat them, and without at least the illusion of possible victory, how could we pretend to ourselves that defeat would hurt? Still, by God — and this is one of the greatest things I've ever gotten out of anything in my experience — it was there, it didn't fail me. I looked at my watch when I felt *it* start. Just 23 minutes after noon on the day of The Relay. Regular as clockwork, as they say, just like it was in the old days. At first it was only a flicker, a brief preoccupation, a butterfly emerging from its cocoon. I helped it along with some of the old rituals. A few curses, as obscene as I could make them, directed not only against my opponents and my coach but against myself for letting me get into so grave a confrontation. The butterfly grew stronger with every obscenity. I fed it further with a mug of hot, strong tea — Earl Grey, as I recall — so thickly laced with honey that you could feel it in your wrist when you stirred. I hadn't shaved or brushed my teeth that day, another of the old rituals. Makes you meaner and tougher, we used to believe. The butterfly began to flap its wings down at the base of my spinal cord, and pretty soon there were a dozen more kicking and flapping at the top of my gut.

"The afternoon wore along with perfect symmetry. I was alone in my father's house, watching the Wisconsin winter through the big picture windows — goldfinches and cardinals at the bird feeder, flights of mallards rising and circling and landing on the Menomonee across the road, icicles dripping from the eaves and then freezing again as the sun went down — but I wasn't seeing a bit of it. I was seeing instead the hard blue water of the near future, with Montag coming out of the turn at the far end of the pool and lurching back toward me with his fast, awkward stroke, me waiting on the block to take my own start. Sometimes in my reverie Montag would stop cold in the middle of the lap and drown: dead of an exploded memory, the victim of my nostalgic madness. Other times he would put on a surge reminiscent of Don Hill or Dick Cleveland back in my college swimming days, and give me a body length's lead when it was my turn to start. Mostly I just scowled and sat and felt the butterflies trying to get out."

By the time Splash joined his grizzled buddies at the pool that evening, all of them were up and ready. They were outfitted in the same cardinal-red tank suits they had worn on the old team, while the young swimmers wore a newer, hipper green and gold. (During workouts, White allowed the whole team to wear whatever color or patterns they preferred, a concession to the New Generation many less successful coaches have been loath to make.) It was obvious that the old guys were feeling competitive. "We used to drink our tea and honey to get charged up," said Kelbe, watching the youngsters. "They probably do this. . . ." And, laughing, he shot an imaginary hypodermic needle into his forearm.

White had spared his old swimmers nothing. Kelbe, lead-off man for the ancients on the strength of his start, would face Mark Unak, the deceptively quick backstroker who, it turned out, was also a considerable freestyler. Wahlen would go against Mark Irgens, also 16, a sub-24-second freestyler over 50 yards. Montag was pitting his mailman's stride (not to mention his beer drinker's gut) against a mere sophomore, 15-year-old Bob Sells, who had swum the 50 in 22.4 just a week earlier (as against Montag's best-ever 24.8). In the anchor slot, Splash would be up against Coach White's very own son, Tim, age 16, who has done 1:52.9 over 200 yards freestyle. God and the coach only knew what young White could do for 50. "Don't worry," Tim whispered to Splash as they lined up for the race. "I was out sick for the past few weeks and I probably won't even finish." Then he rippled his muscles and laughed uproariously. "It was a nightmare," Splash said later.

But nothing proved more nightmarish than when Splash overheard the team manager — a tall, pale kid — wagering that the youngsters would beat the ancients by two lengths of the pool. The kid was carrying a calendar —

"the better to time you with." In Splash's day the team managers had been fat, sycophantic types. This one was as sly as Teddy Brenner. "Do you mean that your anchor man will finish before our anchor man takes off?" Splash asked. "Yeah," said the kid. "How much you bet?" asked Splash. "Well, let's say two bits." Splash hesitated a moment, the horror of that quarter looming beyond loss in his mind. "O.K., you're on," he sighed. The tall, pale kid smirked and clicked his stopwatch. Or was it his bubble gum?

The crowd that had gathered for The Relay — word of which had filtered through the school's 1,150 students and among the old swimmers' kinfolk — included enough longhairs and graybeards to belie the generation gap. It was difficult to judge who was the prettier, the wives of the old swimmers or the girl friends of the young, particularly since Kelbe's high-school-age daughters were sitting near their mother. "By this time my mind was doing time trips," Splash said later. "I could see Kelbe's wife — I'd known her as Kathleen Berger in high school — up in the stands and these other girls just beneath her. Kathleen would suddenly look to be about 16, and then she'd look severe, matured, and then she'd look 16 again. I'd look at Wahlen's boys laughing in the grandstand, and I'd see Teddy laughing it up on the lifeguard stand at Hoyt Pool, but then Teddy was standing next to me, grave and balding with his happy eyes, saying, 'Let's go get 'em.' I didn't know if I was 15 or 50. Unak was just finishing his warmup, and he snapped me back into focus. He climbed out of the pool and rubbed his eyes, which were red with chlorine, and said in a very loud, smart-aleck voice, like I had when I was his age: 'They used this chlorine on the Germans in World War I and now they're using it on us!' It was right then that I knew what time it was."

The time, real time, started a minute later, when White brought the swimmers to their marks and fired his gun. If there were a writer's equivalent of slo-mo, it would be nice to freeze those few instants between words and the gun. Kelbe took his mark with the control of a yogi, bending at the waist until his fingertips were aligned with his toes, his fingers spread slightly and flexed, his eyes bent uncompetitively, almost obsequiously, downward. But in the instant of the gunshot, his eyes flicked up and out, toward the pool, as his arms came backward and around and his legs uncoiled in the start. "Hawk's eyes make for hawk's flight," Splash said later. "Kelbe whipped that kid off the block by half a body length. The old guys suddenly bought the whole box of hope — maybe we *could* win! Kelbe stayed with Unak into the turn, but when we were swimming you had to touch the wall with your hand, which Kelbe did. Now they can flip their turn a yard from the wall, letting only their feet hit the wall for the pushoff. Unak flipped very nicely. . . . "

And that was it for hope — but not for competition. Wahlen, starting half a body length in arrears, whaled the water to a froth, his heavy muscles pulling against his will to win — heart against buoyancy, as Splash saw it. Montag took off with half the pool to make up and no hope of collecting it.

He moved with the rolling stroke of a modern swimmer, his arms snapping into the water with the bite of his towel snaps; he hit his turn with precision and came streaking out of it like the Montag of old. Splash got up on the block, waiting for his chance to swim. Montag was 15 yards away when Timmy White took off beside Splash.

"I knew there wasn't any way they could double-lap us now," Splash recalled. "I knew I'd collect my quarter from that manager. And when Montag came up to the finish of his 50, I was hell-bent on catching Timmy even though he was almost into his turn before I'd even started. I think I fouled my start, but that didn't really matter — I'm a cheat at heart. When I hit the water, there was this splat of fat and energy. Then it was all just blue and anger. The first 25 yards went in a blaze. I screwed up my turn something awful, trying to flip it a yard outside like the kids were doing. I didn't have the momentum to get me into the wall deep enough for a good pushoff. But I swam the last gasp, I mean the last lap, as hard as I ever had. The psych I'd given myself — that the other guys had given me — was so strong, so absurd, that I actually thought I was swimming fast, that I was catching up to the kid. I put on a conscious surge at the end, over the last 10 yards, and slapped my hand into the wall as hard as I'd ever done during the Cold War. Gee, it was fun."

The young guys had beaten the old guys by enough of a margin to break — unofficially — the existing state record for the 200-yard freestyle relay. Their time: 1:34.2, two-tenths of a second below the mark set only a week earlier in the state-wide Cardinal Relays. And this after a full day's workout of 5,000 yards, followed by dinner, homework and chlorine jokes. The old guys had swum their 200 yards in 1:52.2, only 10 seconds slower than their best collective time two decades earlier, followed by war, marriage and nostalgia.

"After The Relay we went down to Karl Ratzsch's restaurant to celebrate our defeat," said Splash. "It was a fitting conclusion, as they say. After all, most of our training over the past 20 years had been in saloons like this one, many of them less elegant. I had my five martinis and a few Asbach Uralt brandies to boot, and of course I felt an immense affection for these guys, not just Wahlen, Montag and Kelbe, but Coach White, too. I still don't know how much of that affection was booze and how much was simple exhaustion, but it felt mighty nice.

"The nicest thing, though, was right after The Relay, when the kid I'd bet with came up to me to pay off his quarter. I sould see it gleaming in his hand, a sandwich of copper-on-nickel, the coinage of the present, baser perhaps than the coinage of the past. But it had a halo around it, by God! Anyway, I told the kid to keep it. I told him to buy himself a peanut butter-and-jelly sandwich next time he ate lunch in the high school cafeteria. I told him it might arrest his development."

THE GRADUATES
John Underwood

RICH CLARKSON

NEIL LEIFER

They were heroes of uncommon dimensions, these Nebraska football players. As they approached graduation they looked back at what their football and their college years had meant to them — and might mean to their future lives.

The offensive right guard said he would remember the Oregon game, how hot it was, and how the blonde in the end zone had such a short skirt and as the team drove downfield toward the blonde there was more than casual reference in the Nebraska huddle to the quality of her limbs. And the Colorado game, when it was 35° and raining in Lincoln and cold, and the crazy Nebraska fans lined up their empty booze bottles on the concrete steps in the north end zone and you could see them there, glistening. He said for all the gravity of big-time college football it was amazing how observant you could be in a huddle. And he said within his treasure chest would live forever the lines of Raquel Welch, who declared she dug quarterbacks like Joe Namath over "dumb guards." "If I had Raquel Welch here, I'd punch her out," he said, and everybody in the room leaned back to enjoy the specter of the guard pummeling Miss Welch.

The split end, sitting on the bed with his legs crossed, said he would remember all the attention they received before the Oklahoma game — television cameramen running around, magazine covers, The Game of the Century, Howard Cosell — and how the pressure finally got to him and he quit going to class because he could not concentrate on the two things at the same time. But he said that after the season, their last at Nebraska, he actually enjoyed and got a lot out of some of the courses he took — Zoology, Kinesiology, Physiology of Exercise 284. The guard and the tackle laughed at him and told him to come off it.

"Who likes school?" said the tackle. Of the three, he was the only one with enough credits to graduate.

"I hate it," said the guard. He said he figured it out and he was "exactly 24 hours" (about two semesters) short of his degree. "Or 26."

"Or 28," said the tackle.

The tackle said he would remember Bob Devaney. He said he was convinced it was a special thing about Coach Devaney that brought it all home — the national championships and the indulgence of the Nebraska fans, who made themselves obvious not just in the stands but everywhere: on the streets, in drugstores, dentists' offices, gas stations. He said even the Nebraska students were nuts about the football team.

He looked around the room at the memorabilia they had accumulated (red-and-white player dolls, No. 1 clocks, Big Red bath mats), the spoor of Nebraska's football zealotry. They were clearing it all out now. He said the funny thing about playing football at Nebraska was that eventually you went over the line and became a fan yourself. He said the answer had to be Devaney, but after close surveillance he had not been able to figure out what the man did, except to scare him (the tackle) to death.

He corrected himself, exhaling over the lip of his can of beer. "No, not exactly scare," he said.

"Yes," said the guard. "S-c-a-r-e."

The guard asked his girl, a platinum blonde named Jeannie who had been helping with the cleanup, if she would please get some more beer. The guard's name was Keith Wortman. He had come to Nebraska from Whittier, Calif. and Rio Hondo Junior College, an affable, quick-witted young man with densely lashed brown eyes. At 21 he had grown to be 6′ 3″ and 250 pounds and, as the logical extension of his training at Nebraska, had acquired a contract to play for the Green Bay Packers. Over his bed was a crinkled photograph laminated onto a piece of wood, which Jeannie had made him, that showed the guard at the sublime moment of his employment at Nebraska: on the ground after completing a block for Halfback Jeff Kinney, who is shown soaring over the top to score a touchdown against Oklahoma. Wortman's number — 65 — is visible in the picture between the legs of an official.

Also on display was one of Wortman's athletic supporters Jeannie had embroidered with a red N.U., a No. 1 and a cluster of oranges symbolizing the victories over LSU and Alabama in the last two Orange Bowl games. Jeannie was a very talented girl, Wortman said. He planned to drop by Pershing Auditorium the next day to watch her graduate, something he himself would have to put off. He wasn't trying to bull anybody — his ambition when he came to Lincoln was to play football. "I don't consider myself dumb," he said. "I'll get my degree when the time comes." He said much of his academic life had been a series of false starts. "I had five majors. English, sociology — I couldn't pronounce the word — business and then P.E."

"That's four," said the split end.

"Math wasn't one of them," said Wortman.

One positive effect Nebraska had on his development, Wortman said, was a birth of confidence. "I'd never been on a winner in my life until I came here, then all of a sudden I was surrounded by them." He said it transformed him. In high school he had thought himself a clod, and there was always someone around willing to support that view. In those days he had dreamed of being a fullback. One of his coaches told him, "Wortman, you're a lineman, and you will always be a lineman." He said when he missed making All-League by one vote, his head coach told him it was he who didn't vote for him. "My own coach! I was just a big fat insecure kid until I came here to Nebraska."

"So what's changed, Chubby?" said the tackle.

The tackle's name was Carl Johnson. Blond, blue-eyed and massive (6′4″, 255 pounds), he had come from Phoenix Junior College and played next to Wortman on the Nebraska offensive line; played well enough to be drafted in the fifth round by the New Orleans Saints. He had also completed the requirements for a degree in business. His father and mother and grandmother were in from Phoenix to see him get it. The grandmother wore an orchid corsage for the occasion.

The split end's name was Woody Cox. He was, by the standards of his roommates, lilliputian: 5′ 9″, 167 pounds. He had been told many times, even before he got to high school, that he was too small to play football but had never been convinced. Wortman remembered playing against him in junior college, when Cox starred for New Mexico Military. "I saw him twice — running past me to touchdowns." In his last season at Nebraska, Cox caught 26 passes for 378 yards, second high on the team. Since then, free from team restrictions, he had let his curly brown hair spring out from his head like chicory. He had not been asked to play professional football, Cox said, so he was going home for the summer to sail on a friend's new $150,000 yacht. "Woody owns Grosse Pointe, Michigan," said Keith Wortman.

Cox was 10 hours short of his degree. His grades were good, and he would be back in the fall to finish up. He would, at the same time, help coach the Nebraska team as a "graduate assistant." He said it was the least he could do after learning such advanced techniques on the field: "All this knowledge . . . it would be a shame not to pass it on."

The three players had shared the apartment for nine months, along with an occasional freeloader such as Van Brownson, the quarterback, whenever Brownson tired of living out of his automobile, and a fairly consistent ebb and flow of coeds. ("Girls go for football players around here," Jeannie said.) The apartment's inventory of goods during that time had multipled to include a line of empty Strawberry Hill wine bottles on the board-and-cinder-block bookcase, a superabundance of colored bath towels, a worthwhile stack of popular records (Cat Stevens, Chicago) and, on the toilet tank, a tall, yellowing pile of *Playboy* magazines.

Now, preparing to quit the apartment, the three roommates sat around hashing over their experiences, letting memories trigger memories. The success of Nebraska football, said one, was due not so much to dedicated players as it was to dedicated coaches. "Football's a big business here. The whole state is involved. The coaches know it, and they coach that way."

"More meetings, more films, more everything."

"The coaches made themselves accessible. 'I need help in this science course.' They got you a tutor. 'Where do I go to buy tires.' 'What am I going to do about this girl.' They were there always."

"The big thing was the closeness. The players got along. No race problems, no nothing."

"When you made a block for Kinney, he let you know he appreciated it. Tagge was the same."

"We were a partying team. Devaney knew it. I think he encouraged it. He's strict, but he knows what it's all about."

"Nobody really hassled you, but there was kind of an unspoken rule. As long as what you did didn't wind up in the newspapers you were safe."

"Nebraska's not as conservative as you'd think," said Carl Johnson. "It's not Berkeley, but the girls behave the same here as anyplace. And when they have a demonstration, all five or six campus radicals show up."

"Most college kids are a bunch of bull shooters," said Keith Wortman. "You think they're really saying something, or being involved, but they're just giving you a lot of bull. I do it myself."

"I'll say," said Woody Cox.

That night the roommates and their dates celebrated, perhaps for the last time as a group in Nebraska, by taking in a steak at Tony and Luigi's, one of the nicer restaurants in town. They drank a little (Cox abstaining), and one of them recalled the night they went swimming in Broyhill Fountain after loading up with beer. Wortman said he would miss that, and a lot of things. Getting psyched up for a big game. Double-teaming some opponent with Carl. He said it hadn't been so bad being a guard after all. "Fridays were the best days," Johnson said. "They let all the linemen play catch at practice."

"The challenge was to see how long we could keep the ball up in the air without dropping it," said Wortman, "31, 32, 33 . . . duhhhh."

College life, said Cox, was a series of these challenges.

Bob Terrio's mother came from Los Angeles for the graduation. His father, George, flew from Las Vegas, where he is shift boss in the Keno game at the Las Vegas Hilton. "This is what we've lived for," said George as they pulled two lounge tables together at the Misty the night before graduation. The Misty has a reputation for prime ribs that is Lincoln-wide and is known as a good place to sit around after hours. "I wouldn't have missed this for the world," said George Terrio, smiling happily. He is a tall man, deeply tanned, with a Don Ameche mustache, and he wore a flowered shirt with the tail out. The Terrios had been divorced when Bob was a child. Mrs. Terrio kept the name by marrying George's brother Bill, but they had all remained close over the years, sharing a common interest in Bob.

The mother was in a reminiscent mood. She, too, is tall and lean, with flesh-colored hair and horn-rimmed glasses. She recalled with delight the time she fell over the railing at a Pop Warner League football game cheering one of Bob's feats (a crucial run, as she recalled). She recited from "the greatest story ever done on him," in the hometown paper when he was a fullback at Fullerton J.C. "In the story they called him The Mudder," she said, because he was always at his best when playing conditions were worst. "The Mudder," she repeated, looking at Bob.

She told about the time she almost fell out of the Orange Bowl on New Year's night 1971 when Bob intercepted a last-ditch LSU pass to save Nebraska's victory and first national championship. She was jumping up and down, she said, and almost lost control.

Bob Terrio said he remembered the first day he arrived in Lincoln, on a flight from Los Angeles, three years ago.

"It was January," he said, "and the sun was shining like today. Bob Newton and I got off the plane in our shirtsleeves. It was 5°. We looked at each other. 'We ain't staying here,' I said."

Nevertheless he did, partly out of appreciation for Devaney's attractive program (bowl games; trips to Honolulu) and partly because the University of Southern California had not asked him. He remembered falling in among the redwoods Devaney had recruited that year. "I thought *I* was big," he said. (He is 6′ 2″, 215 pounds.) At the first practice session he was matched one-on-one with a 6′ 8″ 280-pounder. His compensation was a swollen eye that did not open for two days.

A scar on Bob's right cheekbone, from an encounter years ago with an opponent's front teeth, stood out in the blue glow of the lounge, contributing to a general swarthiness that made him look older than his 22 years. Terrio, he said, was not an Italian name; it was shortened from Therialt, and the bloodlines were French Canadian and Indian. One of his Nebraska coaches had said there was also a creditable strain of American Stubborn. The coaches had redshirted him his first year at Nebraska, risking the chance that he might run home to sunny California.

"It was a terrible letdown," Bob said. "I'd always been first string wherever I played, whatever I played. I thought, 'Do I have to put up with the weather and this, too? For an extra year? Why am I here?' I did think of going home. But I had never quit anything in my life, and I didn't want to start.

"That Easter, Diane and I got married, and in the fall, even though I was a redshirt, Coach Devaney included us on the Sun Bowl trip. We had a great time. I never really thought about quitting again."

Ultimately, Terrio was told he was not going to be a fullback anymore, but a linebacker. "It meant I had to start all over. I'd never played defense in my life, and there were guys around who were bigger and harder nosed than me. But I thought, what the hell." Terrio was laboring on the third team when an assistant coach, John Melton, ordered him to take off his green practice jersey and put on a black one. Black shirts are worn only by the first team at Nebraska. He said he would not forget that day.

Thereafter, the good times far outnumbered the bad for Bob and Diane Terrio. An A student in high school, he breezed through Nebraska's physical-education courses. "I never had to study. I learned to be satisfied with Bs."

His teammates were also his classmates and the friends he socialized with. It was a pleasantly insulated life — hunting and fishing together, drinking, fooling around. Bob and Diane rented a house at the Lincoln Air Base eight

Important as immediate news is and will continue to be, there has always been a place in SPORTS ILLUSTRATED for a more contemplative kind of graphics. The camera (or palette) is freed from the constraints of the day, the hour, the moment, to seek beauty, insight, atmosphere; to explore activities that will not necessarily make headlines but are woven into the texture of sport and leisure. The following pages offer a tapestry of the best such for 1972.

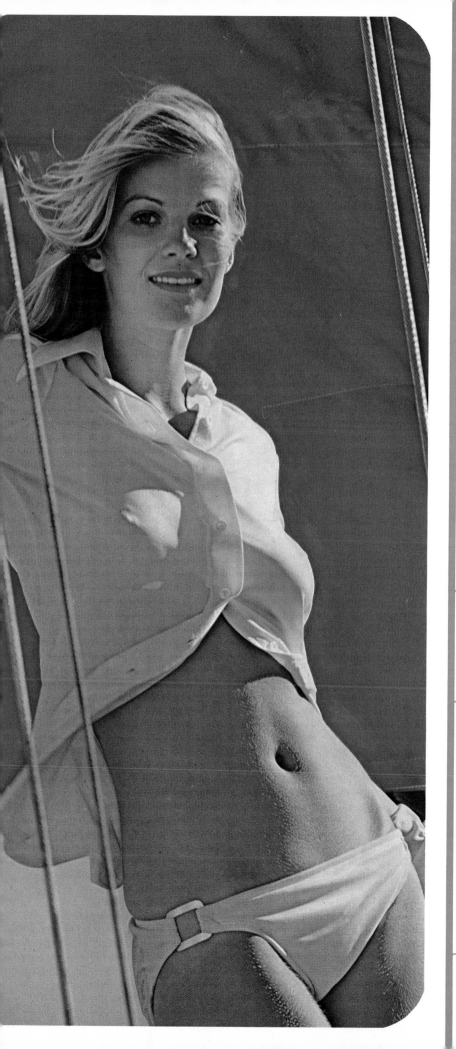

SI's annual inquiry into feminine winter vacation fashions found these new delights on and by the water.

Of the five million recreational skiers in America, who's best? Well, no list could omit Aspen's resident hippie, Jim Biebl (left) or the Sun Valley sensation Barbara Amick (above). Biebl, a college dropout who sweeps a restaurant to pay for lift tickets, is Aspen's No. 1 exponent of the superjet turn, a lean-back, skis-out, full-speed-ahead maneuver. Biebl says some of his friends learned the stunt on mescaline. "You hear music when you jump," he says, "and man, you stay up a long time." Barbara, who works as a waitress to support her ski habit, began running the trails of Sun Valley when she was 3. Result: a style of beauty and complete technical security. She says: "I concentrate on carving my turns. I don't like radical, flashy moves." *Looks* flashy enough.

"Legs, shouts. The scrape and snap of Keds on loose alley pebbles seem to catapult their voices high into moist March air." Novelist John Updike's aging Rabbit Angstrom spoke the words. The photographer stalked city streets and suburbs across the country to give them life. He found "a fantasy, an addiction."

When it comes to sports locomotion some like it hot,
as in off-road racing on the deserts of the U.S.
Others obviously prefer the cooler climate of trotting,
which is nowhere more orderly and elegant than at the
great French training establishment of Grosbois, near
Paris. At right a trotter jogs between glassy pond and
woods where deer and boar abound amid Grosbois' 1,100 acres.
Below, an off-road racer lashed to a dust-kicking dune buggy of
lunar look rips across the desolate moonscape behind Las Vegas
in an event known as the Mint 400. It is axiomatic that the off-road
men seek escape, freedom in the desert. Yet to be free they first
must be bound — cocooned within roll cages in a web of safety
harness. Then they are indeed free to swoop and soar and slide,
and to thumb their noses at the drones back in the hives. Parnelli
Jones, an Indianapolis 500 winner, is the king of the desert, and
though it sounds paradoxical, one can understand what he means
when he says, "It's real peaceful out there."

They call him Tom Terrific: Tom Seaver, the perennial 20-game winner of the New
York Mets; a thrower of lightning,
a man of intense dedication to his craft, and the person most responsible for
the little miracle of 1969, when
the Mets won the World Series. Seaver got his 20 in 1972 despite injuries and
a failing team. And Yaz!

Carl Yastrzemski, the chief architect
of another astonishment — the Boston Red Sox' American League pennant of 1967.
Yaz was back in the news in 1972 as
the Sox made a desperate run at Detroit, Baltimore and New York in the last weeks
of the season, only to lose to the Tigers
on the next-to-last day.

If show biz is an element of sport, some of its most intriguing aspects during the year were the Mona Lisa smile of Jockey Robyn Smith, the continuing reign of Softball King Eddie Feigner (who at a recent count had struck out 85,000 men, women and children — 15,000 while he was blindfolded); the highfalutin Texas Stadium, new home of the world champion Dallas Cowboys, where one could buy a 16' by 16' box for $50,000 and have a legal sip while the common folk went dry; and the frightening menace of the Oakland Raiders' 280-pound offensive tackle, Bob Brown. But perhaps nothing and no one could outglitter — or outgiggle — Jack Nicklaus and Arnold Palmer, who cut a comic rug one night in Palm Springs. That's Mr. Nicklaus in the wig.

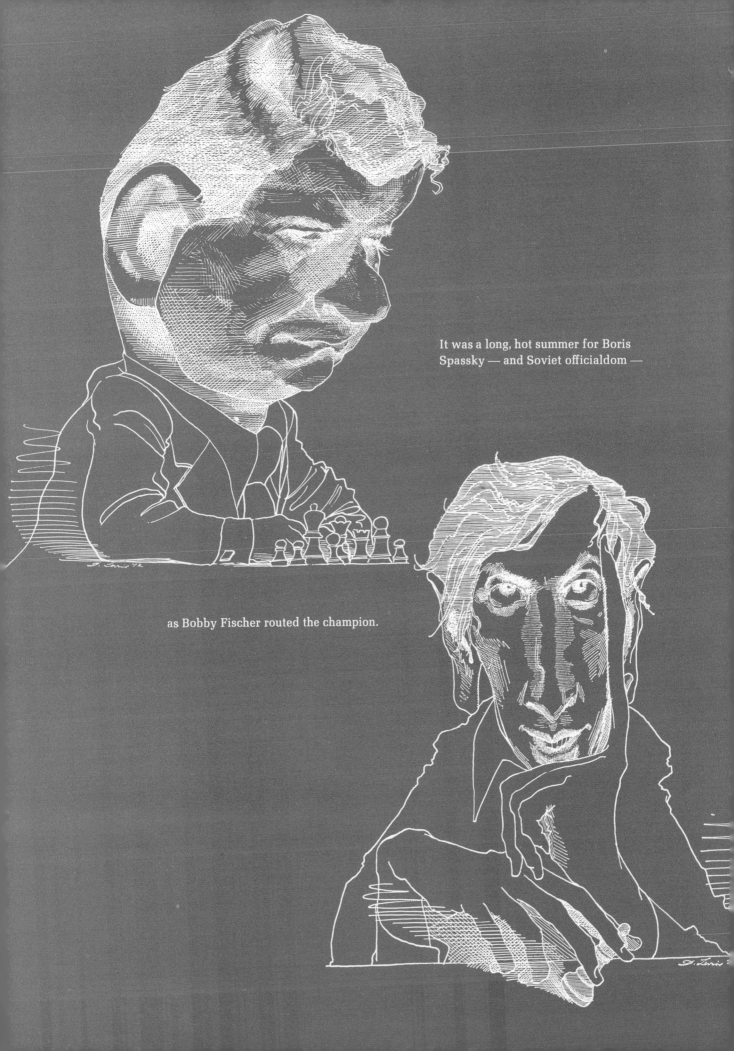

It was a long, hot summer for Boris
Spassky — and Soviet officialdom —

as Bobby Fischer routed the champion.

Panache that passeth understanding
went into drag boats like the 100-
mph ''Grim Reaper'' and its racy peers.

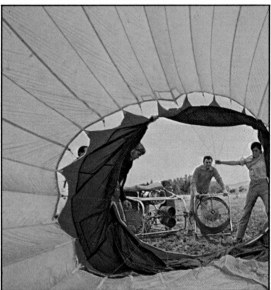

Ballooning is a sweet anachronism in this desperate and hurried age, a remarkably delicate, gentle, civilized amusement practiced by persons of good taste and romantic sensibilities. There are only about 250 active balloonists in the U.S. today and not more than 100 hot-air balloons for them to fly. Little girls do well to watch in wonder as they untie themselves from the busy Earth and drift up and away. Sailing across the quiet skies, borne aloft in a basket, one exercises a minimum of control. Beckoning are leisurely exploration or high adventure — as long as the hot air holds out.

Top cat in New York's prestigious Empire show was this Persian, Fanci-Pantz Petti Girl of Araho, who stuck out her tongue at a record turnout of feline lovers, while top fish to many an angler was, is and will be the elusive bonefish, who moves like a gray-green ghost from the deeps to the flats and back again.

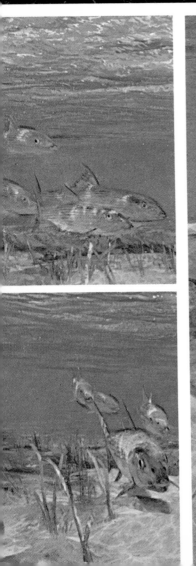

miles out of town for $63.95 a month. The water pipes were in the ceiling. There was no money to burn, but they paid their bills. Diane worked as a telephone operator, and they drove a Volkswagen, and the couples they ran with were expert at cut-rate entertainment. Of an evening, the girls would gossip, the guys would play pitch and drink some beer, and then they would all join in for a hot game of charades. "You'd be surprised how wild charades can get," Terrio said.

He said he learned to appreciate Nebraska. He said, most certainly, he learned to appreciate Nebraska football fans.

"People would see you in a place like this and come right up to you. 'Say, you're Bob Terrio. Let me buy you a drink.' 'Hey, Bob. Siddown over here. Want a beer?' " There were stores, he said, that gave players discounts on clothing, and car dealers who would give you a break. "I bought a car for $1,995 and traded it back a year later, and they allowed me $2,300."

George Terrio said he had kind of hoped to have a pro football player in the family.

"No way," said Bob. "I'm a family man." In June, Diane Terrio had produced Robert Ryan Terrio, and Bob Devaney had invited the baby's father to help coach the Nebraska team in the fall while he works on his master's degree. Bob Terrio said it was enough to make a man proud to be a University of Nebraska graduate.

The proprietor of the restaurant came to the table then and, calling Bob by name, ordered drinks for everybody. On the house.

Van Brownson had let his hair grow almost to his shoulders since the football season and wispily down his forehead in the front; he was working on a goatee but had a way to go. He said girls like long hair; "they all tell you so." One, an eye-catching brunette in pants and a halter, was present in the apartment. The apartment was that of his friends, Wortman, Johnson and Cox, but Brownson at the time had the run of it.

Brownson said there were times when he did not care to live out of his gold Toronado. There were other times, however, when he had felt there were "more worthwhile things than paying rent." He said he had almost totaled out his living quarters late one night (or early one morning) in West Omaha when he hit an icy spot, slammed over a retaining curb, hit a sign and jumped a 10-foot drainage ditch. When he appeared in court, the spectators recognized him and applauded. He told the judge he fell asleep at the wheel. He pleaded not guilty and paid a $10 fine.

The story made the local papers, he said, but he got the car fixed himself rather than go through insurance channels because he didn't want his father to get wind of it. His father was back in Shenandoah, Iowa, "the nursery capital of the world," and did not always appreciate Van's adventures in paradise.

"A lot of guys get into trouble," he said, smiling, his leg slung over a chair, "but I am the one who always gets caught." His lean (6′ 3″, 195 pounds) lizard's body was covered with a Hawaiian shirt, faded red Bermudas and a pair of two-tone blue-suede string-up shoes with square toes. "Ninety percent of the players drink beer. I drink quite a bit. I wonder sometimes how many brain cells all that beer has killed."

For the record, Van Brownson was listed as a senior. He had completed four years of football at Nebraska and had been drafted in the eighth round by the Baltimore Colts. For two years — as a sophomore and junior — he had shared the quarterbacking with Jerry Tagge, and they had made a formidable, even spectacular, duo, unbeaten in 19 games. But injuries nagged Brownson, and in the spring before his senior year he suffered a shoulder separation. After that Tagge pretty much had it to himself, and Nebraska won 13 more. The experience of stepping from spotlight into shadow cost Brownson a dear thing, he said.

"I lost my confidence. I never lost my determination — I'm as determined as ever — but I lost my confidence. I lost confidence in my body. I always liked contact. I liked running the ball. Now I was getting hurt. My elbow, my shoulder. I got bursitis. I lost confidence in my passing. I knew where to put it, but I wasn't getting it there on time. I thought, 'If I could just throw as well as I did in high school.' "

His strikingly clear blue eyes, so blue as to appear luminescent, darted back and forth. In the context of his experience, one might have said he appeared shell-shocked, except that his tongue was facile. He said he had come to the point where he had abandoned all pretenses.

"No," he said, "I don't want to go to class. No, I don't go to class. I don't need a degree to play football." He said he had attended only 10 classes in the fall semester, all in the same subject — the professor threatened to drop him and that would have cost him his eligibility. Since the season, he said, he had gone to New Orleans for Mardi Gras, and to the Colts' rookie camp in Tampa. He spent some time in L.A.

The trouble with being a fun lover, he said, is that you get a reputation. Rumors start. They get all the way back to Shenandoah, Iowa. He said that Devaney had put up with a lot. "He'd hear rumors and he'd call me in. We were in the Suite IV Lounge in Omaha one night to see this hypnotist. He got me up on the stage, doing crazy things. I was out, but not from hypnotism. I yelled some profanity. They had my picture in the paper on the stage. Devaney called me in. 'You can't go around making a spectacle of yourself,' he said. Actually, he was very understanding."

Brownson said that his eventual comedown in football was as much a blow to his father as it was to him. His father, a tractor and implement dealer, was living in Lincoln when Van was born and the father, an alumnus himself, caught the passion. "He was more frustrated than I was. He'd continually say things — 'if you had only been in there. . . .' How could it matter? We never lost. I heard he went to the coaches a couple times. A real pain.

"I wouldn't change anything I've done," he said. "Nothing at all. I want to live my life the way I want to live it, and if others don't agree, well. . . ." He shrugged and lounged back in the chair. "In many ways these have been the most enjoyable four years of my life. I've made so many friends. Fraternity guys, football players. It's not just eat, drink and be merry. I worry about tomorrow. I don't worry about getting married. I came to college to get smarter, not dumber. But I worry about whether I'm going to make it professionally, whether I'll be economically stable. I'd like to make it in pro football. I wonder if I can. If I will. What I will do if I don't. I think about those things.

"I'd like my coaches here to have good memories of me. Hopefully, they'll remember me as a good athlete. As an intelligent person. I'm not sure they'll think of me as a responsible person. But I think I understand more now."

Ten years from now, Brownson said, he would remember those two national championships, and his contributions. He would especially remember the time in 1970 when Nebraska was down 20–10 to Kansas, and he brought the team back to win 41–20. Those heroics, which won him Big Eight Back of the Week honors, began with an 80-yard touchdown pass to Guy Ingles. Brownson remembered he got the pass away just as he was knocked off his feet and didn't see it, but the game movies showed it to be a perfectly thrown ball, the kind quarterbacks deliver in their dreams. Ingles had one step on the defender and never had to break stride.

Then a very funny thing happened, Brownson said. That spring the Nebraska football-highlights film, the one that makes the rounds of luncheons and banquets, came out, and included in it was Brownson's great pass. At the appropriate moment, as the play flickered on the screen, the announcer said, "Now, here it is: Jerry Tagge's perfect 80-yard touchdown pass to Guy Ingles."

Brownson said the irony had not been lost on him.

He was born in the south Nebraska town of Oxford (pop. 1,116), which is on the Republican River, where the bass fishing is good. There is nothing else Jeff Kinney can think to say about Oxford except that it has a big turkey feed every summer. His father, a brakeman for the Burlington Northern Railroad, raised the family upriver in McCook, a town distinct from Oxford in that it has 7,000 more people. There Jeff Kinney grew to be a star quarterback and a fine all-round athlete. Devaney himself came to McCook to see him ("It was like entertaining the President," Kinney recalls), and Devaney gave him a scholarship to Nebraska, where Kinney starred again, this time as a halfback.

He married his high school sweetheart, whose name is Becky, as all high school sweethearts should be, and Becky gave him a son, Jeffrey Scott. And the Nebraska football fans gave him unremitting attention. In his senior year

Kinney made All-America; he ended his career with the finest record for running the football in the history of the school (2,420 yards, 35 touchdowns) and was drafted in the first round by the Kansas City Chiefs. "Things have always fallen into place for me," said Jeff Kinney.

But with the encroachment of adulthood, Kinney found that a hero's work is never done, and that the ascent is never as direct or as painless as that brief résumé would indicate. To be objective about it, one would have to say that between the joyful noise of hands clapping together, one would have to include the sleepless nights and the family budget; the realities of a classroom education and the harder realities outside. One summer he took a job with a section gang for the railroad, changing ties in the steaming rockbeds around McCook. The temperature reached 118°. He learned to appreciate the shade. Another time he worked as a policeman in Lincoln, riding a squad car at $3.50 an hour, and experienced the sensation of being called a pig. He said as a policeman he had a very hard time controlling his temper.

On the afternoon before the Nebraska class of '72 was to be graduated — graduating without him, he said, with a trace of indignation, because he had fallen behind due to the demands on a football hero's time — Kinney sat in the stark two-bedroom brick bungalow on Cleveland Avenue, the one he and Becky had rented (a bargain at $55 a month) two years before, and with the window-unit air conditioner buzzing at his back, he recalled that even the greatest triumphs were not without postscripts.

"A lot of us don't realize yet the full impact of that Oklahoma game," he said. "Maybe we never will." Surrounding him on the walls and furniture tops of the living room were the engraved plaques and trophies and pictures (one showing him with President Nixon) that certified his rank as a football star. Becky sat on the chair next to him. They had been packing for the move to Kansas City. Becky had quit her job as a dental assistant. Jeff said: "I know, personally, it was the biggest moment of my life, the Oklahoma game. Not everybody gets to play in a game like that. People around here idolize football players. They'll remember that game. They'll remember and be apt to help you later on, if you ever need help." Jeff Kinney had rushed for 171 yards and scored four touchdowns.

"The whole thing was wild, like being in a different world. The game itself was unbelievable — 35–31. When the plane bringing us home landed in Lincoln, they couldn't get it anywhere close to the terminal because of all the people. Ten thousand of them, yelling and screaming."

Becky said she and three other players' wives had watched the game that afternoon on television. "I almost had a heart attack on that last touchdown drive when Jeff. . . ."

"Don't say it. It wasn't a fumble."

"When Jeff almost fumbled."

The ball had come loose from Kinney's grip near the Oklahoma goal, but it was blown dead because he was already down. Oklahoma players protested vigorously, but vainly. Moments later Kinney scored the winning touchdown.

"I haven't been the same since," Kinney said. His nerves, he said, were a mess. He had been unable to sleep. He hyperventilated. "I'll be in bed at night," he said, "lying there wide awake, feeling like I'm having a heart attack, my fingers tingling. The doctor said not to take deep breaths. Drink a beer. Take a hot bath."

"The whole thing made him a hypochondriac," said Becky.

Jeff Kinney smiled. It is a good smile, on a good face: protrusively jawed, with full lips and sleepy blue eyes under a Buster Brown hairdo. "I've had them all," he said. "Cancer, heart attacks, brain tumors. I saw *Brian's Song*, and actually got a stomachache."

It hadn't been easy for him, Becky said, with all his responsibilities and commitments, trying to get through school and being married, too.

"If I hadn't been married, I would have been enjoying myself too much," Jeff said, still smiling. "Becky was somebody to complain to. She took a lot of heat.

"I'm glad it's over," he said. "It's time to get away. It's been good for us, but it's too small a world. We need to get out. It's just about impossible to get lost in Lincoln."

"A lot of Sundays after a game I'd get up early and go over to the hospital to watch the autopsies," said Linebacker Pat Morell. "After a while the pathologist let me help — I got to remove a liver, or a kidney, and put it on a dish to be examined. They let me in the operating room to watch open-heart surgery. I got to see kidney stones removed. And a vasectomy. The urologist let me cut some sutures and hold back the incision while he worked.

"A lot of guys are filled up with college after four years, but I'm not. I'm anxious to get started again. Medicine excites me. I'm intrigued with the possibilities of having that kind of ability. For a long time I hoped that at this point in my life I would have been drafted by a pro football team and be all geared up to play pro ball, but I don't worry about that anymore. I came to realize I didn't want to make football my life."

The 1971 Nebraska football brochure describes Morell as 6' 2", 215 pounds, "big, tough, mobile and aggressive," a linebacker with a "potential for stardom." The adjoining picture shows him to be clean-cut and clear-eyed with enough strength in his jaw for an alert publicist to suggest "determination." Morell's career at Nebraska is now over. He played well enough to letter three times. He never became a star. For three years he was "almost" a regular; for the last two he marked time behind his friend, Bob Terrio, who had come from the West Coast to steal his thunder. Morell's name did not become a household word in Nebraska. People did not stop him on the street unless he was walking with his buddy Jerry Tagge, the quarterback. When they were roommates their junior year he got an occasional kick out of pretending he was Tagge when the girls called at 2 a.m.

But if waves of applause did not carry Pat Morell into adulthood, an uncommon sense of priority and direction did. He had applied and been accepted into the university's medical school at Omaha. Following an accelerated program, he said, he would have his M.D. in three years.

Morell had been married for almost a year. His wife Debbi is a breath-takingly lovely girl with eyes the color of seawater ("greeny blue," she says), and together they have found a lot to like in the world. They found they like Lincoln ("really nice people, nice-size town," says Pat); they talk about living there. They like to do things together. They even like their parents. They like going to see his folks in Kansas City ("My father is a postal inspector, and the man I admire most in the world") and can't wait to get down to Broken Bow to see hers. Not only does Debbi have a beautiful face, but she has an exquisitely level head. She encourages his studies. She keeps his shirt with the little OB (for Orange Bowl) 71 on the front whiter than white and their apartment spotless. There are books (*An Introduction to Art, A History of Classical Music, The Autobiography of Malcolm X*) and paintings (a large print by Luongo; an original, by a friend, showing horses being led to a race, that hangs over their bed. "There are just so many walls," says Debbi). Missing is the clutter of Nebraska football paraphernalia. Only a couple of team pictures.

Debbi herself was graduating the next day, with a degree in business. She said she planned to be a CPA. She had, in the past, helped some of Pat's teammates. She was capable of being very serious. But she was also capable of giving Pat a hard time in Miami when he wanted to sit by the pool and read *The Godfather* when she wanted to run on the beach. Her argument was that he had already read it once.

"Three outstanding things happened to me in these four years," Morell said as they sat together on the sofa of the apartment, consciously touching. "One, I got married. Two, I got admitted to med school. Three, I was on two national-championship football teams. Some guys might give you that in reverse order, depending on who's with them at the time" — he looked at Debbi — "but I am very, very happy to be married."

Morell said that his disappointment at not being a regular had been keen. "There was so much talent here that first year. Sixty guys, all of them outstanding — All-America, All-State, all this or that. I remember going to Valentino's for a pizza one night with Tagge. He happened to mention that he had been a high school All-America in football. But not only that, he was All-America in basketball, too, and had been offered a pro baseball contract. So many outstanding guys.

"You see things, being less than first string. Nebraska fans, as good as they are, can be as fickle as anybody. If you're in there with the second team and the opponent scores, they start yelling, 'Get the scrubs out.' I experienced that. But I guess I never really reconciled myself to being second team.

"I was bitter for a while, but looking back I feel I really did contribute. And it was worthwhile contributing, too. Football at Nebraska is like pro football. Devaney treated us like men. We responded like men. It can be the other way. It's the same with college life. It can be a farce. You can get by without studying. You can cheat. Some guys cheat all the way through school. Or you can lose your identity. It's a big school. Some classes are so big you don't even sign your name, you give your Social Security number. But you get what you put into it. I thought my education was as good as I could have gotten anywhere, because I put the time and effort into it."

He looked at Debbi.

"I feel the same way about football," Pat Morell said. "It was the third-best thing that ever happened to me."

Bigness, rather than beauty, is the mark of the University of Nebraska campus. It sprawls without rhyme through the avenues and side streets of Lincoln, spreading fitfully under the duress of an ever-increasing demand on its enrollment, now up to 21,000. Its architecture is a rummage of style and shade, its epidermis a variety of brick and stone and, as a concession to modern tastes, glass and metal. Somehow, one is not surprised to find the Hardy Furniture warehouse in the midst of it all. An aerial view is dominated by two enormous grain silos on the north edge of town, and to the west is the Memorial Football Stadium, which has been enlarged five times since Bob Devaney arrived to be coach in 1962. By next fall it will have enough seats (75,000) to accommodate half the population of Lincoln.

To keep those seats filled, Devaney has made Nebraska a national institution — he does not discriminate against a good football player because he lives in San Diego or South Philadelphia. Once they reach Lincoln, he does not require his players to live in a football dormitory, separate from the natural stream of student life. Once they have varsity experience, they may live off campus. They filter into apartments and fraternity houses. Those who wish to remain often gravitate to George P. Abel Hall, the largest of the campus dormitories. Abel Hall is 13 stories high, with musty-smelling corridors and yellow block walls that need paint. There usually is a sign in the lobby of Abel Hall that says something like "Wanted: two roommates to share a mobile home." For John Adkins of Lynchburg, Va., Abel Hall was home for the last two years at Nebraska. "I don't like to cook," he explained when asked about his choice. What does that mean? "Move into an apartment and you wind up cooking."

The morning of graduation, Adkins was in his room, sifting through piles of clothes and supplies, filling a trunk, cleaning out. Still on the bookshelf was a copy of Faulkner's *Light in August* and a large bottle of Hoffman's Hi-

Proteen food supplement. Adkins had fulfilled all academic requirements for his degree in physical education, but he was not going to the graduation. He said it was partly because he owed the university $130 in parking tickets and couldn't get his diploma until he paid up, and partly because he never planned to attend in the first place.

"All they do is tell all the seniors to stand up, sit down and then go to the basement and pick up their diplomas. It's easier to have it sent to you."

John Adkins, nicknamed Spider, is 21, 6′ 3″ tall, 221 pounds, handsome and black. His father drives a garbage truck in Lynchburg. Neither his father nor his mother ever saw John play football, except on television. He lettered every year and was a regular defensive end for Nebraska. He was not drafted by an NFL team.

"That hurt," he said. "I really wasn't planning to play pro football. I was planning to go to graduate school. But that hurt my pride." So when Montreal of the Canadian League called, Adkins signed up.

He had other plans as well. He and a buddy back home and a white teammate named Jeff Hughes hoped to someday develop an area outside the Cherry Point, N.C. Marine base for low-income housing. He said it was no pie in the sky. He was confident that sometime in the future there would be real money in the project. "If there's one thing college has given me," he said, "it's confidence. Confidence to play football, confidence to get my degree, confidence I can do anything."

He said there would be no bad memories of Nebraska. No real problems. His girl friend Cindy was white, he said, and he felt sometimes they received some unusually long looks when they went places together, but he admitted it might have been his own sensitivity that caused him to think so. Certainly there had been no overt discrimination, he said. Black players tended to go their own way, but that was not unusual, and there were white players he considered good friends. He hunted with Larry Jacobson. One thing he especially liked about Nebraska, he said, was the availability of pheasant; one of the most prized of his acquisitions was a 12-gauge shotgun. He said if there was one thing that would bring him back for a visit it would be a pheasant hunt.

One play in his junior year stands out in his memory. Against Oklahoma State, a pass deflected by a teammate floated into his hands — "I don't know how I got it, but I got it and I went with it" — and in order to make it to the State goal he outran a swift back for 57 yards.

After that, he said, the attention that Nebraska football players get began to come to him, too. "Too much attention?" he was asked. "How can you get too much? I liked it," he said. When his senior season was over, he was named to a local columnist's 10-year All-Nebraska team. He said it was no small thrill. But there had been others. It was inspiring, he said, to enter a stadium with 68,000 people, all in red, screaming their lungs out for you. And to play under inspired coaches, with equally inspired teammates. But he said when it came right down to it, for John Adkins, it wasn't necessary. He would have been inspired anyway. "My inspiration," he said, "was myself."

Graduation for the University of Nebraska class of '72 was held May 19 at Pershing Auditorium in downtown Lincoln. It was divided into two sessions, morning and afternoon, because the number to be graduated (2,338) was a record. The auditorium is a bulky sandstone and slate building with a large tile fresco over the front entrance. Relatives and friends of the graduates — some of whom rode into town with bumper tags that read WIN IT THREE TIMES, and some of whom ate the Go Big Red Breakfast at the Ramada Inn that morning — filled the auditorium at both sessions.

There was no great solemnity, no particular majesty to the occasion. The graduates moved down the aisles in waves, according to their colleges. Mothers and fathers popped flashbulbs and in the upper reaches of the auditorium fanned themselves against the heat. No radicals or revolutionaries were seen to make a temper.

The various colleges — arts, sciences, teachers and so forth — rose in groups, were recognized and sat down. Of the special awards given, one for Distinguished Service went to George Sauer of Waco, Texas, a former Nebraska All-America and now a pro football scout, and another, The Nebraska Builder, went to Lyell Bremser for his 33 years of broadcasting Nebraska football games. Praise for Bremser included reference to his "corduroy voice, soft but substantial," his "tremendous enthusiasm" and his "partiality to Nebraska."

Chancellor James Zumberge's remarks to the graduates were brief. He spoke of the tens of thousands of students who had completed study at Nebraska in its more than 100 years of serving the state, and, "for better or worse," told them they would "bear the mark of this institution for life."

Of the 19 football players of the national championship team who were listed as seniors, eight were eligible to receive their degrees. Half that number showed. Defensive Back Jim Anderson, who had a perfect 4.0 average his last semester of play, was already home in Green Bay, Wis., where his father is a mail carrier. His degree would arrive in the mailbox. Larry Jacobson, the All-America tackle with the 3.3 average, was in town but chose to sit by the pool at his apartment.

Bob Terrio was there in his cap and gown, looking no different from any other graduate. His wife and parents watched the ceremony. Phil Harvey, Bill Kosch and Carl Johnson went through the ceremony and then picked up their diplomas in the basement.

Carl Johnson's parents, his grandmother and a girl friend gathered with him afterward for a farewell picture in Memorial Stadium. The grandmother, whose name was Pearl F. Johnson, said it was a particular thrill for her because the day was also her 70th birthday. The orchid corsage, now a couple of days old, was pinned to her coat. "I don't know how much longer this thing's going to last," she said. A friendly bystander said it would be nice if it lasted forever, like the chancellor said about the mark of the school. She said her late husband, who came West in 1907 to found the building business that Carl's dad inherited, would have been thrilled over Carl's success because he had not gotten past the seventh grade.

The object of her pride, college graduate Carl Johnson, then said it was time to go. With the mark of Nebraska on him, he was heading west and did not want to miss his flight. He had plans to spend the weekend in Las Vegas. To get the kinks out.

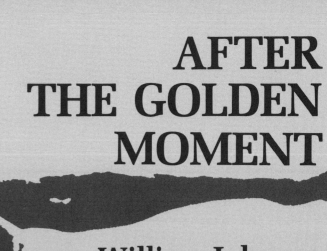

AFTER THE GOLDEN MOMENT

William Johnson

Where are they now,
the Paavo Nurmis, the Eleanor Holms,
the Herb Elliotts whose deeds illuminated
the Olympic Games of yesteryear?
The writer seeks and finds.

ED KASPER

To the world, Olympic heroes tend to endure at their moment of victory. Flushed with youth, exalted by triumph, they are crystallized in time. Perhaps that is the essence of the Olympics — a single, intense, theatrical instant shared by competitor and spectator alike. There are the gold medals — actually gilded silver — the anthems, the flags, the transcendent applause. It is so fleeting and so beautiful. But, of course, there is more. And though our memories of them may not admit it, Olympians carry no marks of identification once the victories are won, the medals given out. Nothing is predictable except that their lives are never again the same. As a group, only one thing can be said of them: their feet are made neither of gold nor of clay, but only of flesh.

Paavo Nurmi, Recluse

He is a legend and newspapers have his obituary on composing-room trays, waiting to be pulled out when he dies. Most have had the type set for years. But perhaps they will not know when he dies, for Paavo Nurmi is a recluse. He is 75 years old and his heart, once perhaps as steady and as strong as any on earth, is feeble. He suffered a massive coronary failure four years ago, others more recently. He cannot get about without a cane.

In Helsinki, where he lives in an apartment overlooking Sibelius Park, Nurmi is considered to be a miser, a shrewd and sour fellow who made a lot of money in real estate and with the Paavo Nurmi shop, a men's clothing store. He won nine gold medals, more than any Olympic runner in history. He also won three silver medals. He entered 12 Olympic races in 1920, 1924 and 1928.

Nurmi was born on the nails of poverty in 1897 in Turku, the old capital of Finland. His father died when he was 12 and he became an errand boy, pushing a wheelbarrow. He began running in the black-pine forests near Turku and soon became so intense about it that people avoided him; where he had been taciturn to the point of glumness, now he did nothing but talk — about nothing but running. After elementary school he became a machine-shop worker, then went into the army where he was a weapons fitter. He never stopped running, but he became more and more withdrawn. He loved classical music and attended concerts frequently, but always alone. He was married for a year, then divorced. Neither he nor his wife remarried. He has one son, Matti, whom until recently he rarely saw.

Perhaps because of his early deprivations, Paavo Nurmi was known as a pothunter. It was once said, "Nurmi has the lowest heartbeat and the highest asking price of any athlete in the world." Nonetheless, he has always been a hero in Finland, a man whose fame put his country on the map of the world. A statue of him was sculpted in 1925. It now stands outside Helsinki Stadium, and recently an old friend, discussing the life of Nurmi, shook his head and said, "Think, for years Nurmi has had to look at his own statue. What would that do to a man?"

In 1952, when the Olympic Games were held in Helsinki, Paavo Nurmi astonished everyone by appearing suddenly at the opening ceremonies to run the final lap with the Olympic torch. He had trained hard for that role and his celebrated stride was unmistakable to the crowd. When he came into view, waves of sound began to build throughout the stadium, rising to a roar, then to a thunder. When the national teams, assembled in formation on the infield, saw the flowing figure of Nurmi, they broke ranks like excited schoolchildren, dashing toward the edge of the track.

A few years ago, after his first severe heart attack, Paavo Nurmi arranged to leave his estate (valued at about $240,000) to a foundation that supports heart research. When he announced the bequest, Nurmi agreed to hold a brief conversation with reporters. One asked, "When you ran Finland onto the map of the world, did you feel you were doing it to bring fame to a nation unknown by others?"

"No," said Nurmi. "I ran for myself, not for Finland."

"Not even in the Olympics?"

"Not even then. Above all, not then. At the Olympics, Paavo Nurmi mattered more than ever."

Eleanor Holm, Ex-decorator

She is 58, saucy as ever, with that stunning, fresh, *huge* smile which captivated the world in 1936 after she was canned from the U.S. Olympic team for drinking and staying up late during the voyage to Europe. "I was drinking *champagne!*" she said. "If it had been whiskey or *gin*, well, all right."

She now lives in a penthouse apartment in a Miami Beach condominium loaded with pink French provincial furniture, carved wooden chests, bureaus and tables, and Oriental lamps. On her walls are two Dalis and a Renoir. Much of this came from her second husband, the late Billy Rose, after they were divorced in 1954.

Eleanor Holm first went to the Olympics at Amsterdam in 1928. She was 14. Her father was a New York City fire captain. She won no medals, but in Los Angeles in 1932 she won a gold in the 100-meter backstroke and she doubtlessly would have won another in Berlin if she had been allowed to compete.

"The afternoon before I was kicked off the team I won a couple of hundred dollars playing craps with the reporters in the first-class cabins," she recalled. "I didn't give it back either, and I'm sure this didn't sit too well with the officials. Of course, *they* were all in first-class cabins and they didn't like my being there. I *tried* to buy my own ticket to go first class, but they wouldn't let me. I was an *athlete!* To them athletes were *cattle* and they had to be fenced off. So they put us down in *steerage,* four to a room, way down in the *bottom* of the boat! God, everything smelled like liniment. *Yukkk!"*

Eleanor Holm speaks almost exclusively in italics and exclamation points, always with gestures and usually wielding a lighted cigarette to lend further emphasis to her remarks. "Well, it was such a *mess!* I was no baby. . . . Hell, I was married to Art Jarrett and he was the star at the Cocoanut Grove and I had been singing for his band before the '36 Games. I'd been working in *night*clubs when I made the team.

"I guess it was the second night out of New York and I was sitting around with the newspaper boys when this chaperone came up and told me it was time to go to *bed.* God, it was about nine o'clock, so I said to her, 'Oh, is it really bedtime? Did *you* make the Olympic team or did I?' I had had a few glasses of champagne. So she went to Brundage and they got together and told me I was fired. I was *heart*broken!"

Well, not *permanently* heartbroken. In Berlin, Eleanor was the belle of the Games. "I had such *fun!* You know, athletes don't think much about politics at all. I *enjoyed* the parties, the Heil Hitlers, the uniforms, the flags and those *thousands* of cleaning ladies with their gray dresses and brooms.

"Goering was fun. He had a good personality. So did the little one with the club foot [Joseph Goebbels]. Goering gave me a sterling-silver swastika. I had a mold made of it and I put a diamond Star of David in the middle."

When she returned to the U.S., she was a celebrity. "Jarrett, my husband, was going to sue Brundage for kicking me off," she said, "but then we started getting all these fabulous *offers* and, well, he dropped it. I did all right after the Los Angeles Games, but 1936 made me a *star* — it made me a *glamour* girl! Just another gold medal would never have done *that!"*

Eleanor Holm has lived in her Miami Beach apartment for 11 years. "I play golf," she said. *"Awful* golf. One hundred and eighteen is my *consistent* score. My *best* is 106. I made a living doing interior decorating for a while. I was pretty good, too. But, my God, going up against those rich, showy broads. They'd have all this *jewelry* dripping off them. To impress them, when I was trying to get their decorating jobs, I'd run down to my bank vault and get out this one big *rock* that Rose gave me. I'd put it on and then go talk with them and I'd sit flashing that big rock back and forth in front of my face. Oh, they'd *notice* that *rock,* all right. Then when I was done selling them, I'd run back to the bank and put my rock back in the vault. I couldn't afford to insure it."

Herb Elliott, Sales Manager

When he was 22, Herb Elliott was the most promising runner since Paavo Nurmi. He won the gold medal in the 1,500 in Rome and he held the world record in that distance and in the mile, an event that he never lost. Then he quit.

Elliott is now 34 and it is as if he had never been anything but what he is today, an ascending and extremely ambitious sales manager for Australian Portland Cement Ltd. He lives with his wife and six children in the Melbourne suburb of Moorabbin. "I believe life falls into categories," he said. "When you are a youngish sort of bloke, as I still class myself, your career has to be developed to a level that makes you happy. I am not happy by any means. There is a family to educate and a home to build and pay off. The first 15 or 20 years of married life must be a selfish sort of existence where job and family come first."

When asked what interest he has in track now, he answered sharply, "Nil." When asked if his celebrity as a medal winner had helped his career, he said, "No."

When asked if he ever appears before athletic associations, he said, "I accept those invitations only if they are for a very close friend or if they will help me in my job or if they will pay me."

Elliott discussed his brilliant running career as if he were discussing a stranger's. "When I first started, my only ambition was to be better than I was. This gradually leads you on until you are satisfied with what you have done. I didn't realize what my goal was until I felt satisfied. I felt satisfied when I won an Olympic gold medal and broke a world record. Once that hunger had been satisfied, I lost interest altogether.

"Every time I ran it was an enormous strain on me, even if it was at a little country meeting. I hate the four or five hours before a race. I was twisted up and knotted up inside. It was a ghastly feeling. The nervousness and the pressure increased as my unbeaten record got longer. The pundits, the damned journalists would say, 'Today's the day Elliott's going to be knocked off,' and in England and all over the world tens of thousands of people would turn up just to see if I would be beaten. It was a drag."

Gazanfer Bilge, Bus Czar

From Olympic champion to a kingdom of buses. . . . On the verge of death, then to prison. . . . In spite of tuberculosis, jaundice, infarctus and bullets perforating liver and lungs, the man is alive and standing on his feet. . . . But this man, a businessman and a millionaire, is guarded day and night by an army of volunteers. . . .

Thus does Ankara journalist Mehmet Ali Kislali put into elegiac summary the life and times of Gazanfer Bilge, 48, the Turkish wrestler and bus mogul. These have been bitter and bloody years for Gazanfer Bilge, a far cry from the radiant hour when he stood upon the podium in London in 1948 and received his gold medal for winning the featherweight division in freestyle wrestling. "I trembled very much," he said.

Ordinarily, Gazanfer Bilge is a man of immense ego and gargantuan

166

self-confidence. When he was asked who had helped him most in his quest for the Olympic medal, he replied, "Nobody did. I have learned every game by myself. The secret of my success is my strength and my intelligence."

It is a bizarre world that Gazanfer Bilge lives in now, and as Kislali writes, "Clouds of anxiety have come to fill his eyes." A bloody feud has erupted among the major bus owners of Turkey. It is the more surrealistic in that all the major parties were, like Gazanfer Bilge, Olympic wrestlers.

Turkish wrestlers have gravitated to the bus business in surprising numbers — among them Kazim Ayvaz, Mustafa Dagistanli, Hamit Kaplan and the Atan brothers, Irfan and Adil, who have come to be the nemeses of Gazanfer Bilge.

After he won his medal the Turkish government rewarded Gazanfer Bilge with a house and 20,000 Turkish liras ($7,142). This resulted in his being disqualified at the 1952 Olympics along with several other Turks who had been similarly honored. He bought a farm, then sold it for a profit and bought two minibuses. He prospered and bought a full-sized bus, then many buses, and today there is scarcely an important route in Turkey that is not serviced by the buses of Gazanfer Bilge.

They are easy to recognize for they are painted with the famed five circles of the Olympics and also with Gazanfer Bilge's name in large letters. He is very rich now, with two villas in Istanbul and other valuable real estate in Ankara. Still, there are those "clouds of anxiety."

The storm center is Adil Atan, 43, who won a bronze medal in wrestling at Helsinki, and his brother Irfan, 45, who finished fourth in the same Games. Adil Atan is not as rich as Gazanfer Bilge, but he owns 50 buses. Adil Atan is a fierce-looking fellow. He is almost bald and he weighs well over 250 pounds. Adil Atan's hobby is keeping canaries. There are dozens of them in his home and it is said that he is as gentle as a little bird himself when he is around them.

There is confusion over exactly what triggered the fighting between Adil Atan and Gazanfer Bilge, but here is the chronicle in the words of Gazanfer Bilge as told to the journalist Kislali. Certainly, this is a prejudiced version, but it is the truth as Gazanfer Bilge sees it:

"The Atan brothers are Abazas, a branch of Circassians; my mother is Circassian, too. We knew each other since we were very young. One day the Atan brothers came to see me. They threatened me, started swearing and asked for half of my company. Of course, I gave them no share whatsoever. They started beating and threatening my drivers. I complained to the authorities, but nothing was done to protect me. . . .

"It was in 1963. It was election day. The law stipulates that on election day nobody is to carry a gun. That very day, wrongly presuming I had no gun, they made me fall into an ambush. . . . I pulled out my gun and started to fire. The bullets entered in the arm and hip of Fethi Atan, the youngest brother, and in the belly of Adil Atan. Whilst I was trying to charge again, they got scared and disappeared. Thereupon I went to the police station and gave myself up.

"In the meantime, I was informed that I had slightly wounded a young girl I did not know and I was informed that Adil's condition was serious. Then I was arrested. I stayed in prison 48 days. I lost 12 kilos (26 pounds). I had tuberculosis of the lungs.

"Two years elapsed from that day. One night I was passing by the Kadiköy post office. All of a sudden I had the impression that a bus was running on me. A bullet fired from the back put my liver into pieces, went through my lung and out my chest. When I turned to face the assassin, a second bullet wounded my arm. I immediately ran behind a minibus and I started firing, too. But the assassin ran away. Later he was captured and sentenced to 12 years. He was the son of the eldest of the Atan brothers. His name was Bahtiyar Atan.

"I was put into the hospital. Siyami Ersek, the world-famous doctor who has undertaken a heart transplant for the first time in Turkey, operated on me. In the meantime, I had jaundice. I was under treatment for three, four years. Also, the hearing of the lawsuit for the events of 1963 was going on. The decision was rendered in 1968. I was sentenced to two years. Finally, after 1½ years, I was released because of my good conduct."

Not long ago, Gazanfer Bilge suffered a heart attack. Now, scarred and weakened, he is taking no chances of being attacked again. Kislali visited Gazanfer Bilge's office recently and he reported, "There are iron bars at the windows. Volunteers are guarding the door. To be able to see Gazanfer one has to overcome four or five obstacles. One has to make an appointment months in advance. The only thing they do not ask for is a password. As for the rest, you have only the impression of entering a top secret military zone."

Micheline Ostermeyer, Pianist

She is 49, a graceful woman with gray hair and horn-rimmed glasses. At London she won two gold medals and a bronze for France — golds in the shotput and the discus, a bronze in the high jump. Then Micheline Ostermeyer went on to become a concert pianist, but her performance at the Olympics remains a magical event. "The Olympics were, no doubt, the biggest moment of my life," she said. "But you must not forget life is not a moment. In a way, I suppose the Olympics was a prolongation of my childhood."

Mme. Ostermeyer was born in Berck in the north of France; her mother was a piano teacher, her grandfather the composer and virtuoso Lucien Laroche. Victor Hugo was a great-uncle. She attended the Paris Conservatory of Music and practiced the piano five or six hours a day. She practiced track five or six hours a week, usually at night. She was married for many years to an Armenian-born kinestherapist, Ghazar Ghazarian, who died seven years ago. She now lives quietly with her two children in an apartment in Versailles. She teaches piano at the Claude Debussy Conservatory. She rarely gives concerts now, although last autumn she did write a note to Count Jean de Beaumont of the IOC asking to play for Olympic competitors in Munich. "I've had no reply, alas," she said.

Her own career as a pianist was not enhanced by her fame as a gold medal winner. "They thought that I was an athlete who happened to play the piano. In reality, I was a pianist who happened to compete in athletics. If I had played tennis or something mundane like that it might have been all right, but other musicians thought — track and field? There was prejudice. I had to show them my diplomas.

"For a long time I could not play Liszt, though, because he was too *sportif*. I knew what other musicians would say — 'Well, *of course*, what else *would* she play?' So I had to play Debussy, Ravel, Chopin. In 1954 or 1955, I finally played Liszt at a recital and I had such a success with it that I thought, 'Oh, why didn't I play it before?' "

Takeichi Nishi, Cavalryman, Deceased

Baron Takeichi Nishi won a gold medal in the equestrian Prix des Nations event in the Los Angeles Olympics of 1932, and he counted Mary Pickford, Douglas Fairbanks Sr. and Will Rogers among his friends. Baron Nishi's widow lives in a small apartment in Tokyo's fashionable Azabu district. She recently recalled that Douglas Fairbanks once said that "one Baron Nishi is worth 10 diplomats."

His widow said that the baron had been downcast after Pearl Harbor, but that he had said, "I have many friends in the United States, but I must go to war for I am first a soldier and second a friend." The baron was killed in 1945 in a cave above a beach at Iwo Jima. As the story goes, one of the attacking U.S. marines knew of Baron Nishi — then a lieutenant colonel — through his Olympic exploits. During a lull in the fighting, he shouted, "Baron Nishi, come on out! You're too good a horseman to die in there!"

His widow said, "Oh, of course, he could not surrender. To surrender is disgrace." She said she was very proud of her husband's courage and that she has been told there is a plaque on a rock along the beach at Iwo Jima that marks the place where he died.

Alain Mimoun, Civil Servant

When the mother of Alain Mimoun was carrying him in her womb, she lived in a dismal mountain village in Algeria. One night she dreamed that she was walking across a desolate, stony landscape lit only by the moon.

The moon was a comfort and she stopped walking to gaze at it. It seemed to drop a little closer to her. It became brighter, more silvery, and it descended gradually toward her, until at last it loomed so close that she reached up and embraced it and held it to her bosom. In the morning she was troubled by the dream. She could not forget it because she could not understand it. She went to see a crone who interpreted dreams. The old woman said, "The child you carry will someday do a magnificent thing."

Alain Mimoun now lives in the Paris suburb of Campigny-sur Marne. His home has a wine cave where he keeps a fine stock of Beaujolais and an excellent champagne, which he purchases from a private supplier. He is 51, a prosperous civil servant in the French national sports program and the most popular sports personality in French history — overshadowing Carpentier, Cerdan and Killy. He has named his daughter Olympe, he calls his home L'Olympe and he has a room filled with his medals, which he calls the Olympic Museum. He says, "If the Olympics is a religion, then the museum is my chapel." He entered four Olympics from 1948 through 1960. He won a silver medal in London, two more in Helsinki. In Melbourne he won the gold medal in the marathon. At Rome he was injured and won no medals.

Mimoun left Algeria when he was 18 and joined the French army. He was named a Chevalier in the Legion of Honor in World War II, but his mother did not tell him of her dream. Over the years he won a record 32 long-distance running championships. She said nothing. She remained silent when he won his silver medals. Nor was he told about the dreams after he became a physical-education teacher in France — a position of magnificence to the peasants of his village. He was 36 in Melbourne, but he was in fine condition. "I knew I was older and I was losing speed," he said. "I am a realist. But I also knew my resistance was as good as ever."

So he ran the marathon. Only his old nemesis, Emil Zatopek, who had beaten him in every Olympic race he had ever run, and a solitary journalist said that Mimoun had a chance to win. When Mimoun entered the stadium and neared the finish line he turned to see if Zatopek was gaining. There was no one in sight. Mimoun shook off the officials who crowded about to congratulate him and stood gazing at the stadium entrance. "I was sure Emil was there at my heels," he said. "I was hoping he would be second. I was waiting for him. Then I thought, well, he will be third — it will be nice to stand on the podium with him again. But Emil came in sixth, oh, very tired. He seemed in a trance, staring straight ahead. He said nothing. I said, 'Emil, why don't you congratulate me? I am an Olympic champion. It was I who won.'

"Emil turned and looked at me, as if he were waking from a dream. Then he snapped to attention. Emil took off his cap — that white painting cap he wore so much — and he saluted me. Then he embraced me."

Alain Mimoun weeps at the memory. "Oh, for me," he said, "that was better than the medal."

The gold medal won in the Melbourne marathon was what the mother of Alain Mimoun had been waiting for. "She said to me, 'That's it! That's what my dream meant!' And then she told me about embracing the moon and of the magnificent thing she had been waiting for me to do. I suffered much, but I knew the real Olympics to be religious games as the Greeks had planned them. You can't fabricate an Olympic champion. You are an Olympic champion in your mother's womb."

Rie Mastenbroek, Housewife

She is an invalid, nearly crippled from an auto accident and unable to work. She is 54 now, heavy and seemingly very tired. Rie Mastenbroek was the most famous woman swimmer in Europe in 1936, a pretty slip of a girl, just 17. She won three gold medals and a silver in the Berlin Games. "I am forgotten," she said. "No one remembers who I was."

She lives with her second husband and a 16-year-old son from her first marriage in an apartment in Rozenburg, a suburb of Rotterdam. Her first marriage was a "disaster" and she was forced to work 14-hour days as a cleaning woman after the war in order to care for her children. The only time she has actually been in a swimming pool in decades was when she waded into a therapy pool at a hospital in an attempt to ease the headache that constantly pounds at the base of her skull.

Yet Rie Mastenbroek remembers the days when she swam. "Sometimes I think, 'oh, dear, oh, dear, how good I must have been, how really *good!*' After me, not one lady swimmer, nobody, not one, ever did it again: three times gold and once silver. Oh, how good I must have been!"

Don Bragg, Boys Camp Owner

Kamp Olympik is in the pine barrens of New Jersey. In the summer it overflows with 270 boys, but in the early spring it is a cold, desolate place. The owner of the camp is Don Bragg, 37, who won a gold medal in the pole vault in Rome in 1960. The medal is now displayed, along with dozens of other trophies and ribbons he won, in the dining hall of his camp. At twilight one evening last spring, Bragg peered at the medal, and when he spoke his voice bellowed and echoed among the rafters of the large empty room. "All I ever really wanted to be was Tarzan. It was my dream. Listen, I broke the world's record because I was Tarzan. I won the gold medal because I wanted to be Tarzan. I knew Hollywood would believe I was Tarzan if I had that medal."

Bragg was very excited. He is an enormous man, with thick, curly black hair, but his sideburns have turned white. While he talked, he strode about the gloomy dining hall and his feet thundered on the floor. "People started calling me Tarzan, which I loved. In the Garden, they'd be yelling up in the galleries, 'Go, Tarzan! Win one for Cheetah!' Once one of those pale little stuffed shirts from the AAU came up to me and said I was going to jeopardize my amateur standing because I had 'Don Tarzan Bragg' printed on my traveling bag. I laughed at him.

"So in Rome I won the medal after eight hours. Eight hours! I went from 198 to 178 pounds, but I won and I let go with this fantastic Tarzan yell. It echoed all over the stadium and the crowd went wild.

"But the gold medal did it for me — Hollywood called. I moved out there to become Tarzan. At this point Tarzan was in my bones. They wanted to straighten my nose and cut my vocal cords. My wife was about to have our first baby and she went home to New Jersey. I was living with Horace Heidt, the bandleader, and one night I took this girl home from some party and some guy took a shot at me. God, the headlines! And I get to thinking what am I doing in Hollywood — Don Bragg from Penns Grove, New Jersey? What am I doing with nose jobs and voice-box tricks? I figured it's all too rich for me, so I came home."

It was very dark now in the dining hall of Kamp Olympik. Bragg paused for a moment, then spoke in hushed tones: "I am home for a week. I go down to the local swimming hole and some kids ask me if I'll make like Tarzan. Could I resist? No, I could not, so I swung out on a rope, dropped and landed on a big jagged hunk of glass and cut my foot so badly I needed 18 stitches and was supposed to stay off my foot for six weeks. So at this point I get this phone call from my old friend Sy Weintraub, the producer, and he said, 'Don, Don, we want you to play Tarzan in *Tarzan Goes to India.*' I was lying in bed with my foot wrapped and I just gulped. 'Don, Don,' said Sy, "we'll forget about fixing your nose because we don't have time and we're leaving for India right now. You ready to go, Don? Don?' I said, 'Well, ah, er, Sy, I can't walk because I got this foot problem. . . .' So he hired Jock Mahoney to play Tarzan.

"Then in 1964 I was talking to some TV types about playing Tarzan in a series. They'd tested Weissmuller's son for the part, but he was too tall, so I got it. Yeah, I was going to be Tarzan. We went to Jamaica to film it and one day there I was, standing on a cliff in my little Tarzan briefs. The cameras were all below me and the director was sitting in his chair and I puffed my chest out and I thought, 'I'm a star! My life's dream — me Tarzan!'

"So not two days after we started shooting they slapped a subpoena or an injunction or something on the whole company — a great legal mess over whether we had the rights to do Tarzan. The company shut down on the spot. I was crushed, of course. I came home to New Jersey and I took a job selling drug supplies for $6,200 a year. What humiliation! People would say to me, 'Say, aren't you Don Tarzan Bragg? What are you doing selling drug supplies?' Oh, it was some ego adjustment. But it still wasn't the worst."

Now it is almost pitch dark in the dining hall and Don Bragg nearly vanishes as he paces. "I was having bad back problems then. My leg had been going numb and the doctor said I had no choice but to go into the hospital for spinal surgery. So I was packing my stuff to check in when I got this phone call from South America. Sy Weintraub. He was calling from Brazil and he wanted to know if I could fly down there and be on location in 48 hours. He said they were shooting *Tarzan the Impostor*. Sy wanted me for the impostor. I gulped again and I told him I couldn't make it just then because I, ah, er, had this back problem. Weintraub couldn't believe it. He hired Ron Ely, and Ely ended up playing the real Tarzan on a TV series."

Bragg shook his head. "I'm no fatalist, but I just wasn't meant to be Tarzan."

Gisela Mauermayer, Librarian

A homemade pullover sweater covers her big frame, and there is in her face a hint of haggardness of age and loneliness and the dry fatigue of a life filled with too much work. Gisela Mauermayer, 58, lives in the row house in Munich where she was born. She is a spinster. Her married sister shares the house; Gisela Mauermayer works as a librarian at the Munich Zoological Society.

Anyone who has seen photos of Berlin's Olympians will never forget Gisela — a 6-foot blonde beauty who won the discus. She was the very flower of Nazi maidenhood and she gave the Nazi salute as the swastika rose on its staff and the stadium roared.

Hitler had made it a state policy to produce gold medal winners for the Games and Gisela was discovered by the Führer's Olympic talent scouts. She spent the year before the Games in intensive training under government coaches. Despite her resolute devotion to the Führer, her gold medal brought her no great material reward. After the Games, Gisela was given the same teaching job she had applied for earlier. She taught in Munich during the war. When American troops occupied the city, her home was robbed of all her medals and trophies. She was removed from her teaching job because of her Nazi party membership. "I started from scratch at the Zoological Institute of Munich University," she said, "and I earned my second doctor's degree by studying the social behavior of ants."

In her home a Bechstein grand dominates the living room; next to it is a cello. Gisela Mauermayer plays chamber music twice a week with friends. "I sorely miss the idealism which ought to be an integral part of sport," she said. "Nowadays, competitive sport has become too commercialized, too specialized and, last but not least, a hazard rather than a boon to health. As a zoologist, I can attest from my scientific experience that no animal exists which could sustain the kind of protracted effort nowadays demanded by a high-performance athlete."

Emil Zatopek, A Czech

Emil Zatopek of Czechoslovakia ran every step of every race as if there were a scorpion in each shoe. After he won a gold medal in the 10,000 and a silver in the 5,000 in London in 1948, Red Smith wrote: "Witnesses who have long since forgotten the other events still wake up screaming in the dark when Emil the Terrible goes writhing through their dreams, gasping, groaning, clawing at his abdomen in horrible extremities of pain."

In Helsinki in 1952, Emil the Terrible let his grand agonies (which were almost entirely a matter of theatrics) transport him beyond the realm of mere human endurance as he won gold medals in the 5,000, the 10,000 and the marathon. No man had ever done such a thing, and it was the more amazing because Zatopek had never run a marathon in competition before. When it was over he said, "The marathon is a very boring race."

In 1967 Emil Zatopek spoke to a reporter from the London *Times* about his appreciation of the Olympics: "For me the 1948 Olympics was a liberation of the spirit. After all those dark days of the war, the bombing, the killing, the starvation, the revival of the Olympics was as if the sun had come out. I went into the Olympic Village in 1948 and suddenly there were no more frontiers, no more barriers. Just the people meeting together. It was wonderfully warm. Men and women who had lost five years of life were back again." For many years Emil Zatopek was a colonel in the Czech army and the toast of the Communist Party. Crowds used to gather around him in the street. Then in 1968 he signed the 2,000 Words Manifesto. After Russian tanks stamped out the rebellion, he was expelled from the party, transferred to the reserves and given a pittance for a pension. He worked for a time as a well-tester, but he lost that job. He became a garbage collector, but people recognized him at his work. They helped him carry the garbage cans. This was viewed as a symbol of solidarity against the regime, so he was fired. Then last year he publicly recanted his liberal views. While this incurred the ire of the Czech public, it prompted Party Boss Gustăv Husăk to say that he held "Zatopek in esteem as a man of character." Zatopek is now working for the Czech Geological Research Institute on oil-deposit research. He says it is an outdoor occupation that allows him to go home to Prague once a fortnight.

Harold Abrahams, Barrister

Harold Abrahams is 72, a dignified retired London lawyer. In the 1924 Olympics in Paris, he won the 100-meter dash, defeating Charles Paddock, then the World's Fastest Human. "The medal had a bearing on my career, of course," he said. "I was a celebrity. People knew me through my victory, but that was not the reason I tried to win. My brothers were both well-known athletes and, eventually, I wanted to show I could do better than they had. When I won, there wasn't any great surge of patriotism in me, though I *was* pleased for Britain.

"But another reason why I hardened myself to win was that there was a certain amount of anti-Semitism in those days. Certainly, now, I didn't run in the Olympics to win for all of the Jews. I ran for myself. But I felt I had become something of an outsider, you know. That may have helped."

Abebe Bikila, Soldier

He will have a seat of honor at the Munich Olympics, but it will be a sad and futile tribute of the type that healthy men pay to the cripples whose still, gleaming wheels line the sidelines at athletic contests.

Abebe Bikila of Ethiopia will be there in his chromium-plated wheel chair, a doubly painful sight because he was so graceful and so strong before he was paralyzed. Now 39, Bikila became a historic figure in Rome in 1960 when he won the marathon: it was the first gold medal for a man from black Africa. He was unforgettable when he ran through the streets of Rome that day. He was barefoot and his stride was easy, though his legs seemed far too thin to carry him over so many miles. His face was set in a gaunt, brown mask that somehow seemed beatific at the same time it was grim. When he won, the mask cracked, bursting into a radiant smile.

He made Olympic history in Tokyo when he won his second consecutive gold in the marathon; there he did a handstand just after he broke the tape. He might have won a third marathon in Mexico City except that he ran with an injured ankle. He did not finish.

Now Bikila is a paraplegic; he cannot move from the waist down. In 1969 an automobile he was driving near Addis Ababa overturned. He was flown to England for special treatment and Haile Selassie himself made a trip to visit him there. But the doctors could do nothing and they say now that his chances of ever moving his legs again are a million to one.

Though he is virtually helpless, Bikila still holds the rank of captain in the Imperial Bodyguard. He was a private in the army when he went to Rome, was promoted to corporal after the gold medal, won promotion to sergeant in the Imperial Bodyguard before Tokyo, was made a lieutenant following that triumph and became a captain after Mexico City. "My life was enriched by the Olympics in that way," said Bikila.

He lives with his wife and four children in a cottage among groves of gum and eucalyptus on the outskirts of Addis. About his house are the shabby huts of his peasant neighbors. There is a seven-foot corrugated iron fence around Bikila's property, and inside, on brilliantly green grass, half a dozen sheep graze, chickens pecking at their feet. Inside the house, the floors are polished to a fine sheen and the walls are hung with war shields. His trophies, stained and discolored by the damp mountain air, are displayed in a cupboard. The scent of incense permeates the rooms.

"Men of success meet with tragedy," said Bikila. "It was the will of God that I won the Olympics and it was the will of God that I had my accident. I was overjoyed when I won the marathon twice. But I accepted those victories as I accept this tragedy. I have no choice. I have to accept both circumstances as facts of life and live happily."

The path leading to Bikila's door is trod by dozens of Olympic aspirants who come to him for inspiration and advice. Little boys and soldiers alike arrive daily to visit him. They wish to run as he did; they wish to win as he did. It is a pilgrimage to Ethiopia's Olympic oracle. And the honor is more profound than any he will receive in Munich.

Jesse Owens, Public Image

The morning was warm and sunny in Binghamton, N.Y. On the infield, runners were warming up, the distance men floating with a long gliding gait, the sprinters chopping furiously through starts. Jesse Owens came down the stadium steps and walked out onto the infield with the short, bouncy, confident stride that appeared so often in the newsreels and movies from Berlin 1936. He was erect, square-shouldered, and all the fluid power that used to explode in his sprints still seemed to be available if he had decided to call upon it. Seemed, but only fleetingly. Jesse Owens was 58, pouched around the eyes and 25 pounds heavier than in 1936. The features of the older man scarcely resembled those of the young. But no one would *ever* be quite like the young Jesse Owens, who electrified the world by winning four gold medals in Berlin, a black man who threw the Aryan racism of Hitler back in his face.

Owens was in Binghamton for a teen-age track meet sponsored by the Junior Chamber of Commerce. Besides the busy legs of competitors warming up, the infield was also alive with the grins of go-get-'em junior executives and the smiles of rising young salesmen. They moved in to shake hands with Jesse Owens and he was enormously friendly, enthusiastic, not unlike a Jaycee himself. There were only 100 or so people in the stands. *The Star-Spangled Banner* was playing through a loudspeaker from a tiny cassette recorder and a Jaycee said rather tremulously into a microphone, "I give you America's greatest Olympic hero, Jesse Owens!"

Jesse Owens spoke in a deep, impressive voice, his words wonderfully well enunciated. He was at work, of course, and he said, "On behalf of the Ford Motor Company and the Lincoln-Mercury Division of Ford, we're glad to be a part of this fine Sport Spectacular here with the Junior Chamber of Commerce of Binghamton . . . a lot of good luck to all of you and God bless."

He left the infield then, grinning, waving, signing every autograph requested, and climbed into the back seat of a Lincoln furnished by the local dealer. The president of the Binghamton Jaycees was at the wheel and he drove Jesse Owens to Schrafft's Motor Inn where he was staying. The red plastic letters on the marquee were arranged on one side to spell DINNER SPECIAL SEAFOOD PLATTER. On the other side they said WELCOME JESSE OWENS. It was time, said Jesse, to eat lunch — a ham and egg sandwich and a bottle of beer.

When Jesse Owens speaks, even with a bite of ham and egg in his mouth, grand oratorical echoes roll out. If you ask him, for example, how he liked the Games in Mexico City, he will reply, "I saw 10,000 people competing there, and it was the aim of every girl and every boy to be victorious. Yet, there they were — eating together, singing together, dancing together, rapping together and I thought, 'If this does not bring the nations of the world together, what ever will?' " Or if you ask what material advantage a gold medal may bring to a man, he will say, "Material reward is not all there is, sir. No. How many meals can a man eat? How many cars can he drive? In how many beds can he sleep? All of life's wonders are not reflected in material wealth. . . ."

This is a natural way of talking for Jesse Owens, unless he is very relaxed. He is a kind of all-round super combination of 19th-century spellbinder and 20th-century plastic P.R. man, fulltime banquet guest, eternal gladhander, evangelistic small-talker. Muted bombast is his stock-in-trade. Jesse Owens is what you might call a professional good example.

For this he is paid upwards of $75,000 per annum. Some of the income derives from the 80 or 90 speeches he gives each year. Some is from the corporate clients he "represents" — meaning, in essence, that he sells them his celebrity and his reputation for use at public events where the client wishes to display its "Jesse Owens image," as one ad man calls it. Among his clients are the Atlantic Richfield Company, Sears, Roebuck and Company, the American League and the Ford Motor Company. In pursuit of his career, he travels 200,000 miles a year. On the average he spends four days of every week sleeping in a hotel bed and taking his meals with Jaycees, salesmen and other strangers.

Jesse Owens spoke of his growth as a public orator: "I was once a stutterer and when I was at Ohio State I took a course in phonetics from a master teacher. I've always admired the great orators of my day even more than the great athletes. Roscoe Conklin Simmons and Perry W. Howard and, of course, Martin Luther King and Adam Clayton Powell." His own style of oratory is grandiose and soaring, perhaps more notable for its delivery than its context. "Mostly, I'd say the substance is sheerly inspirational," he said. "I work for my payday like anyone else and things fall into a routine. I have a speech on motivation and values, one on religion, one on patriotism. I have one on marketing and statistics for sales conventions, pointing out that training for athletics is like training to sell. Parts of the speeches are interchangeable, but I'm talking to kids most of the time and I tell them things like this. . . ."

His voice made a slight adjustment, became deeper, a dignified holler that bounded around the restaurant. "Awards become tarnished and diplomas fade," he said. "Gold turns green and the ink turns gray and you cannot read what is upon that diploma or upon that badge. Championships are mythical things. They have no permanence. What is a gold medal? It is but a trinket, a bauble. What counts, my friends, are the *realities* of life: the fact of competition and, yes, the great and good friends you make. . . ."

He readjusted his voice to show that he was no longer orating but the timbre remained. "Grown men," he said softly, "stop me on the street now and say, 'Mr. Owens, I heard you talk 15 years ago in Minneapolis. I'll never forget that speech.' And I think to myself, that man probably has children of his own now. And, maybe, *maybe* he remembers a specific point I made, or perhaps two points I made. And maybe he is passing those points on to his own son, just as I said them. And then I think" — Owens' voice dropped near a whisper now — "then I think, that's immortality. You are immortal if your ideas are being passed on from a father to a son and to his son and to his son and on and on."

The banquet following the Jaycees' Sports Spectacular in Binghamton was held at the Harpur College Union. Jesse Owens was dressed in a beige suit of modified Edwardian cut, a muted-green shirt and a loud, wide tie. He entered the banquet room by himself while several hundred guests waited in the lobby. He stood at the head table and gazed at the sea of empty tables for a moment and said, "God, I always have these damn butterflies before I talk. Wouldn't you think I'd get over it?" Soon the crowd came in and everyone ate. Then the Jaycee who was master of ceremonies said, "I give you the greatest Olympian of them all — *Jesse Owens!*"

The crowd rose as one man to give an ovation that lasted two full minutes. Jesse Owens stood easily at the rostrum and when everyone sat down, he made his speech on motivation and values.

". . . There'll be winners and there'll be losers . . . but friendships born on the field of athletic strife are the real gold of competition . . . awards become corroded, friends gather no dust . . . youth is the greatest commodity this nation has . . . honor thyself . . . honor thy God. . . ."

After yet another meal taken among strangers, Jesse Owens and the Jesse Owens image were working nicely in tandem again.

TONY TRIOLO

SLAMMING
THE DOOR ON JACK

Dan Jenkins

Jenkins, a scratch golfer and deadline writer of
enviable facility, is also author of the best-selling
Semi-Tough. Here he eases into the British Open,
Grand Slam exit for Jack Nicklaus.

He stood against one of those sand hills, one foot halfway up the rise, a gloved hand braced on his knee and his head hung downward in monumental despair. He lingered in this pose, with what seemed like all of Scotland surrounding him, with the North Sea gleaming in the background and with the quiet broken only by the awkward, silly, faraway sound of bagpipes rehearsing for the victory ceremony. This was Jack Nicklaus on the next to last hole of the British Open after another putt had refused to fall. It was Nicklaus in the moment he knew, after a furious comeback, that he had finally lost the championship and what might have been the grandest slam in golf. One more putt of any size on any of these last seven holes and Nicklaus would have completed what could seriously have been termed the most brilliant rally the game had ever known.

But one more putt did not drop for Nicklaus, and on the same hole minutes later one more chip shot *did* curl implausibly into the cup for implausible Lee Trevino. Finally, after all the shattering heroics last week at Muirfield, the whole world had a right to feel overgolfed and oversuspensed.

The honest fact is, there are two fairly incredible golfers today, Nicklaus and Trevino, and the two of them have been producing so many memorable major championships lately that it is getting hard to keep them straight. The last two U.S. Opens pretty much have been a Nicklaus-Trevino saga, and so have the last three British Opens. It may be well and good to keep talking about Nicklaus' 13 major titles, but think about this: since the 1968 U.S. Open, when he first became a winner, Super Mex has won as many big ones (four) as Nicklaus has over the same period. And, for all of that drama and suspense last week, it was still the happy Mexican who never stopped providing the comedy that the stifling pressure at Muirfield needed.

Trevino tossed out all the usual lines about God being Mexican or else Nicklaus would still be alive for the Grand Slam; about switching back and forth from the small British ball to the larger American ball and how the American ball always looked like a melon; about the castle he had rented for the week ("They got to have some kind of princess locked up in there someplace"); and about the lukewarm drinks the Scots are accustomed to ("No wonder everybody over here's so wrinkled up"). That was Trevino all week.

It probably can be said that Nicklaus waited too long to attack Muirfield, that he perished with his own conservative game plan on a course that played easier than he expected because of some unanticipated glory-be weather. When Jack finally turned aggressive for Saturday's closing 18, when he was six shots down and the lids came off his driver and three wood, he shot a 66 to tie the course record and, at one point, miraculously lead the tournament by one stroke. Jack will think long about the holes he let get away during the earlier rounds and he will dwell, too, on the six late putts that refused to disappear into the cups — a 12-footer for a birdie at the 12th, a 15-footer for a birdie at the 13th, an 18-footer for another birdie at the 14th, a 4-footer for yet another birdie at the 15th, a 3-footer for a saving par at the 16th and, the last gasp, the 20-foot birdie putt at the 17th.

Saturday, the oh-so-memorable Saturday, began with only four potential winners of this Open. Trevino held a one-stroke lead by virtue of a flood of Friday birdies. They came five in a row from the 14th through the 18th, including an astonishing hole-out of a sand shot at 16 — which even Lee admitted should have been a double bogey — and the sinking of a 30-foot chip on the last green. Next was Tony Jacklin, who was up three despite a triple bogey during the second round; and then Doug Sanders, who was only four back despite a triple bogey of his own along the way. And finally Jack Nicklaus — if he could muster an Arnold Palmer type of thing.

Jack did exactly that. Through 11 holes, as he was being cheered madly by a rousing British crowd of 20,000, he seemed to be playing, at last, the definitive round of golf. He was perfect with every club, and he had pushed to six under par. "Look at this," Trevino said to Jacklin as they went to the 9th tee. "Nicklaus has gone crazy. We're out here beating each other to death, and that son of a gun's done caught us and passed us."

Two little dramas of high order were going on at this point. Up ahead, the crowds were yelling for the Nicklaus Slam as he strode the length of the 11th fairway toward another short birdie putt. Back at the 9th, Trevino had told his caddie, "We're behind, son, Gimme that driver, we got to make something happen." Trevino absolutely killed his drive at the skinny 9th fairway. He then put a five-iron within 18 feet of the hole and made the putt for an eagle. Suddenly he was back to even par for the day, and back to six under for the tournament. And Jacklin, too, eagled the 9th, to stay within one shot of Trevino.

Nicklaus, meanwhile, tried to address the birdie putt on the 11th green that would put him in a tie with Trevino at six under. He heard the two roars for the eagles, backed away from his putt and smiled. Then he coldly made the birdie, and once more came an explosion of sound, this time from his own gallery. It was an eerie moment hearing those roars back to back to back. Trevino remembered later, "After our eagles at 9, I told Tony, 'That'll give Jack something to think about.' Then we heard his birdie roar and I said, 'I think the man just gave us something else to think about.'"

What can be said of Trevino and how he actually won? How can it be accounted for? Nicklaus worked for more than a week at Muirfield, while Trevino arrived late. Wearing a planter's hat and cracking jokes, he practiced only two days. "I brought this trophy back," he said upon arrival, "but I shouldn't have. It's just going back to El Paso."

The case certainly can be made that this was a lucky win for Trevino, unlike last year at Royal Birkdale when he destroyed the course with brilliant shotmaking. After all, he holed out four times — four — from off the greens during the course of 72 holes for his 278. And that is simply indecent.

On the second day he chipped in for a birdie 3 at the 2nd hole from 40 feet with an eight-iron. Then he holed his two ridiculous shots in the third round when he ran off from everyone but Jacklin. The first was from a terrible lie up against a bank in a bunker at the 16th. He had just dropped consecutive birdie putts of more than 20 feet at the 14th and 15th. Now he slammed his wedge into the sand. Out spurted the ball in a semi-line drive to take one harsh bounce and dive into the cup for a birdie 2. At the 18th, after two-putting for a normal birdie on the 17th, he chipped out of the weeds for a fifth straight birdie and a 66. "I think things like that happen to a man sometimes when he's trying," Lee said. "I was trying. I was aiming at the cup. I didn't come to Scotland to help Nicklaus win any Grand Slam. If I played golf with my wife, I'd try to beat the daylights out of her."

For all of this, it was one last chip shot that found its way into the hole that rescued Trevino from what looked, at the very end, like a certain victory for Tony Jacklin. Tony had won in 1969, and Tony could win again. Princess Margaret was there; wasn't this an omen?

Trevino had played the par-5 17th like a man choking on the trophy or a sausage roll or perhaps royalty. He drove into a bunker, poked it out, poked it again and then ran a short pitch over the green. Jacklin, meanwhile, was just off the green in two. He chipped on, leaving himself a good birdie chance. He was about to go to 18 with a certain one-stroke lead. Perhaps two. Possibly three.

"I think I might have given up. I felt like I had," Trevino said. "My heart wasn't really in my chip shot." Something was. It went in for a saving five. Jacklin, having watched all these crazy shots of Lee's go in for two rounds, now did what was human. He three-putted from 15 feet. And that was that. Trevino got a routine par on 18 for his second British Open to go along with the two U.S. Opens he has won in his five years as a touring pro.

"I feel sorry for Tony, who played really well. And I feel sorry for Jack. But Jack shouldn't have treated me like a butler when I had dinner with him the other night," said Trevino, still joking, still refreshingly Trevino.

In retrospect, one really has to wonder about Nicklaus' strategy, and Jack himself might well look back and question it. Maybe not, however. He is pretty stubborn about such things. He had a game plan for Muirfield and he stuck to it — at least until Saturday.

He arrived early to begin preparations for both the course and the smaller ball. There was nothing wrong with this — or else it could be said that he should not have arrived a week early at Pebble Beach for the U.S. Open. The argument that Jack was overprepared can be discarded. The final round proved as much.

There was tremendous pressure on him. The betting odds were an outlandish 2 to 1 before the championship even got under way and all of the Scottish newspapers were advertising the event as some sort of Nicklaus Extravaganza. *The Scotsman* (Edinburgh), for example, labeled its daily coverage, "The Grand Slam Open," with a portrait of Jack.

Muirfield has been called Scotland's best golf course by many authorities. This does not mean it is the toughest; that is probably Carnoustie in the wind. It means that Muirfield is the most elegant, the classiest, the most subtle, the best conditioned. It is not a long course; it has often been compared to our own Merion, given the right winds. There were one or two par 4s that Nicklaus could reach with a driver if he chose to try — and if he succeeded in hitting it straight enough. There were several others where he could reduce his second shot to a wedge if he hit with a big club off the tee. And there were par 5s he could surely reach in two blows.

Jack, having won at Muirfield in 1966 and sternly aware of the narrow fairways and numerous well-deep bunkers, had decided the only way to play the course was defensively, with caution and patience. He would one-iron it and three-iron it from the tees. On only five holes, depending on the wind, would his woods come out of the bag. "What happened, basically," he said afterward, "is that I didn't hit the other clubs straight."

It was only during Wednesday's first round that Muirfield played like a British Open course should — long, windy and rainy. Nicklaus' 70 that day was a mad scramble as he missed seven fairways on the only day his game plan made sense. When the unusually glorious weather set in on Thursday, Jack woke up and said, "Ye gods, I'll have to shoot 65 just to stay in it. The course will be a piece of cake." Muirfield was bright with sun, windless — and short. But all Jack did was go on missing fairways. Still, the field did not run away from him. And he was due a good round, wasn't he? "I haven't wasted any of my good golf yet," Nicklaus said Thursday night.

He didn't waste any on Friday either. The weather was even more wonderful, and there really weren't that many contenders for him to worry about. The first-day leader, Peter Tupling — was a Tupling worth more than a shilling? — had slipped back the way Tuplings should. A few other British surprises were still around but they wouldn't last. It was only Nicklaus against Trevino, Jacklin, Sanders and Johnny Miller, who had holed a three-wood for a double eagle, and perhaps astonishing Dave Marr, back from nowhere.

Everyone felt that Friday would be the day Nicklaus would explode. Not so. Jack was still missing fairways and was well out of it, two over par going to the 16th hole at the very time Trevino and Jacklin were at their hottest. It was only through a miracle of his very own, a chip in at the 16th, another birdie at the 17th and a struggling par at the 18th, that Nicklaus got home with a 71 and even par through 54 holes. Granted, in any other British Open that might have been fine. But Super Mex and Super Limey and the weather were seeing to it that this was no ordinary championship.

By attacking Muirfield, Tony Jacklin had met some tragedies, among them his triple bogey on the 13th hole the second day, but he had also stored up some birdies and eagles. Trevino had bounced between birdies and bogeys all along until nothing but birdies turned up late Friday in that mind-bending finish of his. And it semed clear that Nicklaus had waited too long to change his strategy. But even after he had lost, Jack disagreed, contending, "I'll always believe I played the course the right way and just didn't play well. What can I do about a guy who holes it out of bunkers and across greens?"

He can keep trying for the Grand Slam, which might only exist in a dream, after all. At least as long as Super Mex keeps popping up to interfere with history.

BEAUTY AND THE BEAST

Frank Deford

JERRY COOKE

Deford found Robyn Smith to be the most difficult subject he had ever encountered, man or woman — and the prettiest and most dedicated athlete he had ever met.

Robyn Smith, the jockey, invented herself a few years ago so that she could succeed in that role. Few athletes have forfeited more than she has to chase after a dream, to try to live out a little girl's fantasy, for she gave up a good and glamorous life in the pursuit. She changed her style and her habits, she traded in a knockout face and figure for a jockey's stark image, and she discarded her past, pretending almost that she never had one, that she just materialized, walking out of the mist at dawn one morning late in 1968 at Santa Anita. Even her closest friends have no firm idea who she is or where she came from or even, for sure, what her name is. Nor, as she protests, is any of that really important. She has constructed this whole other person, forming her out of perseverance and independence and ambition and talent — and because she likes the new person much more than whoever Robyn Smith was before.

And it has worked. There is nothing there anymore but Robyn Smith, the jockey.

Once she was good looking enough to work seriously toward a Hollywood career, but by now the transformation is so complete that Robyn Smith actually looks her prettiest in racing silks. She is 5′ 7″, standing on long, lovely legs, the kind so fine that women envy them; not just the things that men whistle at when a skirt rides high. She has dimples, chestnut hair and eyes the color of twilight that alternately doubt and challenge. Yet seldom does she flatter herself. Usually she wears pants and baggy cardigans, and after them racing silks look positively feminine on her.

She claims her natural weight is around 110, but that is preposterous. A high-fashion model of her height would hardly be that light. Probably Robyn weighed 125 before she became a jockey. She strips at no more than 105 now, is flat-chested and her riding breeches hang down, flapping, off her hips. "Her little rear end is like a couple of ham hocks," says a friend who worries about her. Her face is gaunt and drawn, and life comes to it only from the sun and the freckles on her nose.

She is still pretty, even beautiful in profile (where she does not appear so skinny), but those who knew her when she was just getting into racing shake their heads at the beauty she exchanged for stirrups. These people all say: "You should have seen her then." They all shake their heads and say that. She doesn't seem to care. Barry Ryan, a trainer she knows well, one day said something like, "Robyn, you're just looking awful," and she replied, "Great!" gaily, defiantly.

Yet she is almost paranoid on the subject of photographs she considers unflattering. Something so concrete, so conclusive as a picture perhaps forces her to remember what she was. Otherwise she has no time or inclination for that, except on rare occasions when she suddenly decides that she is giving the wrong impression, that she is sounding too mannish or neuter. Then she pauses and carefully sets the record straight. Like the thin man who is supposed to be yelping to get out of every fat man, there is still a gorgeous, alluring woman inside Robyn Smith, the jockey, and not often, but every now and then this creature tosses her head and sighs.

A newspaper reporter was trying to convince her one day that she should let him ghost her autobiography. Robyn wasn't interested. "Why don't you do one of the other women jockeys — Arline Ditmore or Donna Hillman?" she asked, putting him off.

"Donna Hillman?" he said. "You mean the pretty one?"

Robyn cocked her head and smiled at how silly a man could be. "No, I'm the pretty one," she replied, correctly.

Her retreat from glamour has been largely forced upon her, because even now that she has established herself as one of the better riders in the country, there still are whispered innuendos and snickers whenever a new trainer puts her up on a horse. And the mere threat of gossip costs her work. "This lame excuse I always hear," she says. " 'I'd like to use you, Robyn, but my wife won't let me.' And it's true — not all trainers, of course. But I have trainers' wives come up to me and say sweetly, 'Why, Robyn, we're all just so thrilled you're riding so beautifully and doing so well,' and then I'll hear that these women behind my back have said, 'That bitch better not come around my husband looking for horses.' I mean, I've actually heard these things.

"Well, the truth is, nobody at the track is impressed with my looks. I've never once had a trainer make a play for me. I've never even had one ask me out. I wouldn't go out with one even if he did ask. I just don't want to feel obligated to anyone for putting me up on a horse. Now don't get me wrong: it doesn't bother me that nobody asks. I just got over the other extreme, in Hollywood, where everyone was after my body — you know, I mean everyone was after everyone's body. So I don't mind it at all. And look, if I've got to go out with a trainer to get rides, how long would I last? *I'm legitimate.* I don't care whether anyone believes that, but that's the truth."

The record supports her. Miss Smith has ridden regularly in the big time in New York since late 1969. She lost her apprentice allowance last January, and while she had developed a grudging reputation as a pretty good "bug boy," most people expected her to fade away without the weight bonus that is granted to beginners. Besides, racing's bias against females had denied Robyn the experience that most good apprentices pick up. For example, Bobby Woodhouse, another fine young American rider, won his first race in the summer of 1969 at virtually the same time Robyn did. Yet in 1969 and 1970

Woodhouse had 1,657 mounts while Robyn had a grand total of 67. Only in the past few months has she even been able to retain an agent.

Despite this, she simply went out and forced herself to become a better rider after she lost the apprentice allowance. "She's 80% improved from last year," says Angel Cordero, one of New York's leading riders. At the spring meeting at Aqueduct this year, she finished seventh in the jockey standings although she had only 98 mounts, while all the other jockeys except one in the top 10 had at least twice as many rides. Only Cordero had a better winning percentage than Miss Smith's 20%, and it is even more impressive to note that at the top track in the country she was the leading U.S. jockey; the six riders ranked ahead of her were foreigners. By the end of that meeting it could be fairly argued that the best young American jockey was a woman.

"I never thought she would ever do anything like this," says John Rotz, who rides against her and occasionally takes her out. "And I told her so." He drew thoughtfully on his cigar. "Of course, Robyn will never listen to you when you tell her things like that."

This apparent inability to discourage easily, if at all, has been her salvation. When she first appeared in New York, nobody would give her a chance even to breeze a horse. That only encouraged her to walk around and mumble lines out of old Alan Ladd movies: "Someday, mister, you'll beg me to ride in a stakes for you." Robyn is given to stuff like that. She also says things like: "I don't need anybody at all in the world" and "I have nothing to hide."

She is attracted to melodrama, especially when it conflicts with the dull truth. The matter of how she got to New York is a small thing, for instance, but a typical example. Actually, the trip came about through the offices of a New York trainer named Buddy Jacobson, who had encountered her somewhere along the way in California, where she had been riding on the rinky-dink fair circuit. Jacobson brought her East, but he lost interest in her potential almost immediately and, as a consequence, he has been written entirely out of Robyn's script. According to her story her motivation was pretty much on the order of Saul's after what happened on the road to Damascus. " 'Dammit,' I said," she recalls vividly, " 'if I'm gonna do it, I'm gonna do it right.' " Whereupon, in her version, she then got all her money together, just ditched her car and took the next flight to the Big Apple.

Robyn is right; it is a much better story that way. But it really isn't necessary, for things were soon genuinely desperate for her in New York. Without Jacobson's help, she had to scuffle for any opportunity. She would run from barn to barn, pleading for a chance. She was getting short on money. "Time was running out," she says. "People were getting set to move south. I get very defensive when I'm down and out, so I acted like a rich girl. You know, I lied about things to build myself up. Of course, even then I thought I was a great rider. That was no front." Luckily, it rained one November morning.

"It was a cold, driving rain," says Trainer Frank Wright, a handsome Tennesseean whom Robyn came to see that dreary dawn. "I had chased her away from the barn once before, but I guess somebody sent her back because I had been one of the first to use exercise girls, and my wife is a show-ring rider. Robyn just stood there outside, with the rain falling on her, and when I looked down and saw the water running out of her boots, I said, 'Well, please come inside.' I told her, all right, I would give her a chance to gallop for me, and she just smiled and thanked me and ran right off to the next barn in the rain. Robyn always runs, even these days."

She rode her first race for Wright on Dec. 5, 1969 on a horse named Exotic Bird who was owned by a Detroit dentist. Exotic Bird's distinguishing feature was his penchant for finishing last. "What have we got to lose?" Wright asked the dentist, and Robyn just missed by a nose getting fourth money. "There's a mechanics in all sports, and a lot of people pick that up," Wright says. "But beyond that, there's a naturalness that can't be learned. In riding, when someone has that, we just say that horses run for him. You can't see it in specific style or technique. You just find it out: horses run for him. Well, horses run for Robyn, and you could sense that right away. The same horse would go in 47 for another rider, and then he'd do 46 and three for her. That was the first thing that was apparent. Trainers accepted Robyn long before owners."

Robyn had been riding for a little over a year when Wright put her up on Exotic Bird at Aqueduct. She had never seen a horse race until sometime in the spring of 1968; one day a date had just happened to take her to Santa Anita. This occurred while she was an aspiring film actress, going to acting school in Hollywood. She is not, however, "a former Hollywood starlet" as it always says in the stories about her the first time her name is mentioned.

Robyn also used to maintain that she was an English major at Stanford, class of '66, but that turns out to be a complete fabrication. Robyn says, indignantly, it is unfair to blame the Stanford hoax on her because when she was under contract to MGM the studio made up the fiction for publicity hand-outs. Unfortunately, MGM has never heard of Robyn Smith. Indeed, the studio did not have any aspiring actresses under contract at the time.

But unlike the Stanford business, which was made up out of whole cloth, the "studio" interlude has just been embellished a little. It seems that Miss Smith was enrolled at the Columbia Studio's acting workshop and had a good industry contact in Martin Ransohoff, who is the president of a large production company named Filmways. Robyn always says Ransohoff was her agent, but it turns out he really wasn't — well, let's not get bogged down in that.

Ransohoff certainly helped her, and he remembers her fondly. "There aren't many people I have enjoyed more," he says. "Robyn was the cream-and-honey outdoor type. I believe if she had stayed in Hollywood big things could have happened for her." Robyn, naturally enough, quite agrees with this assessment. "Oh, I could have made it in acting," she declares, dismissing the subject. "There's absolutely no doubt in my mind about that."

However, racing began to fascinate Robyn about this time. In Maryland a show-ring rider named Kathy Kusner was getting a lot of publicity suing for the right to ride, and it was clearly just a matter of time for the girls. That was when Robyn Smith, the jockey, was created. Her entrée at Santa Anita was a trainer named Bruce Headley, who had met her a couple of years before ("Talk about beautiful; you should have seen her then"). He let her work horses for him in the morning before she went to acting school.

"The horses weren't so scared, but boy, I was," Robyn recalls, in a most uncommon burst of self-deprecation. "Invariably, they'd run away with me, but it was dark in the morning that time of the year and Headley couldn't see. One day, when it got lighter in the morning, he said, 'Gee, you don't gallop real good, do you?' "

But Robyn was determined and, says Headley, no less proficient than any new male rider. She still was strictly a novice when an owner named Kjell Qvale, who was on the board of directors at Golden Gate Park near San Francisco, heard about the lovely exercise girl at Santa Anita. By now, March 1969, girls had won the right to ride and had become something of a fad. Everybody had to see one once, like dirty movies. Qvale gave Robyn her first mount in a race on April 5. Robyn shrugs at the whole experience. Golden Gate got publicity and she got her license.

"Everything is timing in this world," she said. She was sitting this day in some new hay in a stall at Belmont. She had on her usual costume — the pants and the dreary blouse and the cardigan — but she looked pretty, if not in any kind of starlet way. She looked like the tomboy kid sister just before they made her put on lipstick and a bra and wear the new gown with crinolines. *Wow: Is that really you, Robyn Caroline?* She was not pleased. She took off her sweater and made a muscle and a face. She made the muscle, a very nice right biceps, to prove that she is deceptively strong. She made the face because she was mad that she did not have a single mount that afternoon. Robyn is not beautiful when she is mad. She is terrifying.

"What the hell do I have to do?" she asked. "Eighteen percent I'm winning. Eighteen percent, and I don't have one ride. Ah, I should just forget about it and go shopping or something. There's jockeys who just love it when they can get a day off. But I don't have any ambition to do anything else. It's my whole life. I never knew it would be so satisfying to win. I love horses and speed, and I've always liked competition, but I never knew it would be so satisfying to win. Nothing makes me happier. I mean, some man could buy me something, anything, and it wouldn't mean as much to me as winning a race. I just love to win. It satisfies me mentally. If I don't win, I get very depressed.

"All I want to do is be happy, and racing makes me happy. It's the only thing that makes me happy."

She is obsessed with it. Nothing else interests her. Says Frank Wright, who remains a close friend: "You'd think she'd allow me 10 minutes of latitude in a conversation, but all she does is pick your brain about racing." Until the spring meeting, when she hit it big and began to show herself a little at night, Robyn was so conscientious that she almost never stayed up past nine o'clock, and she tends to torment herself any night, rerunning the day's races until she falls asleep. She lives only five minutes from Belmont in a well-carpeted apartment she shares with two pet rats, and she never strays far from that general area of Long Island. Manhattan, half an hour away, is merely another place without a racetrack that she has no reason to visit. Her social life, such as it is, revolves around the track. Her hobby is to graze horses.

"A lot of nights I come over to the stables and just walk with them," she says, "because, you know, I like them. I like to graze the horses I ride, especially the ones that win for me. It's their reward, sort of, and besides, I like to be around the animal that won for me because that means a lot to me.

"Now don't get the wrong impression. I'm not so hung up on it that I'm sick. When I do it, I just do it because that is what I feel like doing. I'm not liable to graze on a cold rainy night in February, but I have done it on a cold rainy night in February just because all of a sudden I felt like it.

"You know, not all of it is the animal. I just like to be alone. I don't think I'll ever get married. I'm just a loner. I've had friends who see me grazing, and they come over and want to talk with me. It doesn't occur to them that I might just want to be alone with a horse."

A cat came to the door of the barn. One of Robyn's stories is that she was once allergic to cats and dogs and horses and stable dust. This is why she never rode as a child. Robyn Smith, the jockey, doesn't have this allergy, although it is never clear exactly why. She took the cat in her lap and petted it devotedly and was lost, absolutely lost, for a while. Montaigne wrote, "When I play with my cat, who knows if I am not a pastime to her more than she is to me?" and one thinks that of Robyn with cats and horses alike. She has broken down and cried, hopelessly, just because a time conflict has robbed her of the chance to breeze a horse. For animals she has patience, and with them she never wears that look of suspicion she reserves for all the prying people.

One day at Aqueduct just after a trainer had lifted her up onto her mount, Robyn took the reins and broke into a huge smile. By the paddock rail a fat man, no doubt referred to as "heavyset" wherever he drinks beer, grew excited. "The bitch smiled!" he cried. "I got to bet her. I never seen her smile before." His companion, a much smaller man in a car coat who is, it seems, more of a paddock behavioral authority, was quick to rebut. "Nooo," he said. "The bitch just never smiles with the people, with the trainers and whatnot. Onna horse she smiles alla time."

"Onna horse she smiles?"

"Onna horse, yeah, regular."

Her disposition is not, for all that, so easily defined, if only because nothing about Robyn is that pat. "Now don't get the wrong impression," she declares again, with some urgency. "I'm not a recluse or anything. All those parties in Hollywood, I liked them well enough, I just had enough of that. Besides, it's just that I don't care if I'm seen. I'm not really impressed by anything. I mean that. Nothing impresses me. I guess I'm an iconoclast. I guess I'm the biggest iconoclast I know."

Alfred Gwynne Vanderbilt, who is chairman of the New York Racing Association, used Robyn as his regular rider for several months this year until they had a falling out late in June. For a while, they were good friends. Robyn confounds Vanderbilt as much as she beguiles him. "Her life is very full," he says. "She knows just what she wants to do, and she's going to do it. I asked her once what she wanted most, and she said she wanted to be the best rider in the world. In the world, just like that. I suppose she would have said the best rider in the world *ever*, but she just didn't think of that at the moment."

The fact is, though, that obscured by all the forced *National Velvet* business, in barely four years this young woman has risen from learning how to stay on a horse to a position among the elite in a very hard, dangerous profession. That she has managed this ascent despite the strong bias against women in her field makes the success story all the more remarkable. Miss Smith is no *National Velvet;* she is pure and simple Horatio Alger, an old-fashioned all-American melting-pot hero who just happens to be a heroine. Her natural instincts and a large talent were requisite, but what kept her afloat were the corny storybook values: determination, confidence, stick-to-itiveness, sacrifice and all the rest. She has never let up. "You've got to remember," says Frank Wright, "that Robyn had to be at her very best every morning. Every morning. Because every morning there was someone around just waiting for her to slip up so he could say, see, I told you so."

Miss Smith's big break came when Allen Jerkens of Hobeau Farm gave her a chance and, significantly, he took her on largely for reasons of spirit. "I liked her interest," he explains in his soft, measured way. "She has a lot of desire and as much determination as anyone I've ever seen." Around the track Jerkens commands respect. "The fact that he put her on live horses — that was like the *Good Housekeeping* seal," Wright says.

Jerkens liked the way horses ran for Robyn. She was always strong out of the gate — even Bruce Headley, her first tutor, remembers that distinctly — but Jerkens noticed that she could rate her mounts well, too. "She gives a horse a chance," he says. He considers Robyn a weak finisher, though. Women riders as a group have suffered this criticism because the stretch drive is where a jockey's strength tells. So it is especially meaningful when a rider such as Cordero now testifies: "Robyn is saving more ground and she is keeping her cool at the end." Presumably, even though the notion infuriates her, Robyn is just never going to be able to regularly out-muscle male riders down the stretch, so she is going to have to depend on these other assets.

She has some advantages. Her general style, notably her seat, is copied from Eddie Arcaro; she read his book and follows it faithfully. Perhaps more important, she brings a clever mind to her business. Vanderbilt says that aside from Eric Guerin, who rode Native Dancer for him, he never had a jockey who could size up a horse so well.

Robyn is bound to improve simply by getting more chances to ride. Like many other inexperienced jockeys, she cannot yet, for instance, switch the whip from one hand to another without first lodging it in her mouth, and her left-hand whipping is atrocious. She also has a tendency to lose her concentration and treat a horse like a car in traffic, stop and go, or to let a race get away from her, if only for a couple of moments. "It usually happens about the quarter pole," Jerkens says. "I'll tell her — well, you took your little nap again — and she'll get furious. But I don't see her blowing races that I think she should win."

Says Vanderbilt, "Even before Robyn rode for me, I wanted to see her make it. She deserves to make it. She's just plain good, and she cares. Horses run freely for Robyn. She has no fear out on the track; she's a fighter. As far as I know, this is the only girl in any sport who has ever competed with men on equal terms."

Robyn has reached this unique estate because she is a natural athlete and because she has always competed with men as a matter of course, if not at such a high level. Since the word "Jockette" was removed from the ladies' locker room at Aqueduct, her only real complaint about the facilities is that she cannot go into the men's quarters and play pool with them — despite her assurances that "I won't look."

As a kid she played boys' games, and certainly jockeys don't intimidate her because she is, after all, taller than everybody she rides against. "The men jockeys have treated me terrific," she says, "but then, all my friends have always been men. I resented being called a tomboy, though, because I wouldn't want to be a man. I like them too much. I just get along with them, period. Women resent this for some reason. My mother used to resent this. Like when she and my father would have people over, I'd hang around with the men." Robyn always addresses married couples as "you guys."

She exercises every morning, runs religiously, and indulges herself only in a little wine and brandy. She is a fine golfer, long off the tee, and picks up any sporting activity easily. Ransohoff, the film producer, took her deep-sea fishing. "We hit a school of albacore," he says, "and I mean they were rolling. Robyn hung more albacore in that hour than any man on board."

"I'm thin, but I'm strong," Robyn explains clinically, getting set to flex again. "I always had good muscles. I'm a rare physical individual — and I'm not trying to be narcissistic about it. It's just that I'm very unusual in that way."

Yet Robyn has taken off so much weight that she appears to have no emotional reservoir to sustain her. Her system is littered with the residual effects of weight pills, water pills, hormone pills, big pills, little pills, pill pills that she gobbles indiscriminately. Even when she was a world-beater at the spring meeting, she was constantly at a temperamental flood tide. She breaks into tears regularly, not only over losing a race but, say, while watching some banal TV drama. The least aggravation unnerves her. People fall out of her favor upon the smallest alleged slight, only to return just as whimsically to her good graces. Her fetish for freedom borders now on mania; it is easier to schedule an appointment with the Dalai Lama than Robyn Smith. She has become less receptive to criticism, and woe to the most well-intentioned inno-cent who forgets and idly tells her the same thing twice.

Indeed, in the last couple of months, she has contrived to bring such disaster down around her pretty head that at times she seems bent on self-destruction, her own worst enemy. When she was riding so high several weeks ago Barry Ryan was moved, in a moment of sad prescience, to say: "I don't want people to get mad at Robyn because now that she has made it to the top, I'm afraid of what she might do to herself if she starts to go down. Someday soon we're going to find out whether Robyn Smith is a big girl."

Sadly, she sometimes is a horrid little one. One day, for instance, she canceled her mounts at the last minute, saying she was sick. She was not too ill, however, to pop over to Belmont that afternoon and take a good Jerkens horse she rides, Mighty Lak A Rose, out to graze. Shortly thereafter Miss Smith was set down for 10 days for careless riding (she bore out on the turn, and in the ensuing jam another jockey fell), and perhaps she fumed even more over a Dutch Uncle warning she received from one of the stewards, who cautioned her that her reputation was being made vulnerable by her new habit of hanging out at a particular restaurant.

Systematically, it seems, she has set out in recent weeks to heap vitriol on those who have helped her the most. Among the more important people she has cut down are her agent, George DeJesus, and Alfred Vanderbilt. Robyn maintains that Vanderbilt was "too demanding to work for" and that she stopped riding for him of her own accord. He says that his patience was exhausted and he terminated the arrangement. Whichever the reason, she made a scene at the time, cussing him out in public.

Of course, that sort of thing can be expected of Miss Smith. She is consistent in the sense that she has always been given to temperamental excess, in good times and bad. "I make my own conflicts," she says evenly. Two years ago she flew completely off the handle and lashed a Jerkens stable foreman across the face with a shank. There has been nothing as intemperate as that recently, but Robyn continues to have a bad reputation with service employees — attendants, clerks, guards. They forgive her her ambition, reasoning that a woman could not have made it without uncommon drive, but they find her brusque, cavalier and often, to their mind, thoughtless.

Robyn protests that her singular status encourages people to judge her critically, and certainly, where female horse people are concerned, she suffers the whip of jealousy. She is, after all, living out the impossible dream of a lot of small girls who grew up to find the dream suddenly possible, but still beyond their capabilities.

"I know," Robyn says. "All my life people have said I'm not very friendly. But listen, I'm friendly with some people. I have real friends. I'm moody, but if I'm bitchy, I get it right out of my system." Indeed, she is quite as tactless with friends as with strangers, although she can be extraordinarily generous with people she cares for.

Miss Smith's disposition may be affected by the fact that she is probably very hungry almost all of the time. She nearly starves herself except for periodic eating bouts when she simply goes berserk over food — "like six ravenous wolves," according to one startled witness. Recently, for example, she devoured at a single sitting two shrimp cocktails, two orders of prime ribs and another large one of ground sirloin. On the side, she put away three-quarters of a bowl of Caesar salad. When she goes on this kind of dinner binge, she will wash it down, alternately, with white wine and Tab. The next day she dutifully returns to her starvation-pill diet.

A couple of additional pressures weigh heavily on Miss Smith. One is the press, including articles such as this one, which she abhors. Part of the problem is caused by her rather misguided interpretation of the First Amendment. This is tied, part and parcel, to her conviction that anyone inquiring "How are you?" is prying. In support of this attitude, she believes in a policy of mystery and circumlocution which results in exactly the inverse of what she intends. That is: almost everybody who knows her is mad with curiosity about her past.

In Miss Smith's behalf it should be stated that she has not been treated with much sensitivity by the press, which invariably has dismissed her as a cliché:

FORMER HOLLYWOOD STARLET MAKES GOOD AS HARDBOOT.

In almost every story about her, the most meaningful inquiries have dealt with how much profanity the male jockeys employ in her presence. Has the Washington press regularly asked Margaret Chase Smith if the guys tone it down on her behalf in the cloakroom? Otherwise, it has all been straight out of the Tupperware school: Yes, girls, jockettes put their pantie hose on one leg at a time, too. "I just hate it," Robyn says, with considerable justification.

She can be taken pretty much at face value when she says that she does not want publicity. She has turned down endorsement offers primarily because she doesn't give a hoot. "I'm going to be highly successful," she declares, with all the emotion one would employ in ordering at McDonald's, "so there'll be a much more interesting life for them to write about 10 years from now. But the main thing is I just don't want to do it, so I'm not going to. I just want to ride."

Unfortunately for Robyn, besides the professional prying she has also attracted rumor and gossip on an amateur basis. In an unwelcome tribute to her special celebrity status, the track abounds with Robyn stories which are labeled just that, as in: "Want to hear a new Robyn story?" She is never Miss Smith or Smith in the track vernacular; always Robyn or Robynsmith, run together, and occasionally The Bitch. The latter title is not pejorative, only vulgar recognition of the fact that she is the one member of her gender regularly around. (If somebody says "that bitch," however, well, that is a horse of another color.)

Not only are there Robyn stories, but there are Robyn jokes, which are less malicious, if not more amusing. Sample: Did you hear Robyn took off her bikini top at the pool and was arrested for indecent exposure? No, what happened? They dismissed the case because of insufficient evidence.

When Alfred Vanderbilt began to be seen regularly in her company, the Robyn stories really began to run away with themselves. Vanderbilt, 58, a member of The Jockey Club, on a third marriage, was as easy a target for innuendo as his rider. No one could resist at least some maiden-aunt snickering about the patrician millionaire owner and his beautiful mystery woman jockey.

In truth, there was much less there than met the eye. Vanderbilt may have acted a little teen-age silly about Robyn, but even with all the gossip that she was going to cost him his job as head of the NYRA, he was sincerely devoted to her best interests. Robyn used to get peeved at Vanderbilt sometimes because she thought he was snooping — she thinks everybody is snooping — but she certainly appeared to appreciate Vanderbilt's efforts on her behalf.

"Yeah, I know what they're all saying," she said firmly when the rumors about her and her boss were everywhere. "I'm used to it. It's just a, well, more of a daughter thing. I mean, there's no romance. Look, I'm a whole lot closer to Mrs. Vanderbilt than I am to Mr. Vanderbilt. You ever heard that? No, because nobody wants to hear that. But I think Mr. Vanderbilt is a wonderful man. There's no one nicer!" It was but a few weeks later, after he took her off his horses, that she was loudly ranting at Vanderbilt in a well-populated Aqueduct corridor.

Thus, while the criticism of Robyn is often cruel and unfounded, she hurts her reputation with her temper and her vague, devious, even fictional responses. Particularly, after both the Stanford and MGM claims turned out to be so much poppycock, Miss Smith became fair game for closer scrutiny. The bald facts are that there is no record of any Robyn Caroline Smith (or anyone like that) born in San Francisco when she claims — Aug. 14, 1944, nor for several years on either side of that date. Nor does any person with that name seem to have attended school in Hawaii, where Robyn says she grew up. Clearly, either the rest of her authorized life history is as bogus as the college-Hollywood malarkey, or she has adopted a new name.

The irony in all this mystery is that no one who knows Robyn well thinks she is hiding anything deep and dark in her past. The feeling is that she probably is just making a harmless retreat from a life that was sad or drab or both. *There will be a much more interesting life for them to write about 10 years from now.* Some friends suspect that she came from a broken home or possibly was an orphan. Others think she may have endured a bad marriage during that blank period when she was supposed to have been an English major at Palo Alto. Robyn says she has no living relatives. By her spare account, her parents both died of natural causes a couple of years ago.

Nonetheless, the one constant, if vague, reference point in her allusions to her childhood is a strong, magnanimous father whom Robyn reluctantly identifies (this time) as a wealthy lumberman. Robyn's father pops up in her rare off-guard recollections only to give her things or to take her places, such as on hunting trips or on wonderful boats. Sometimes the father is referred to as a stepfather or uncle. He never has a name.

Asked about the "y" in her name, she declares without equivocation that it is "the girl's way" of spelling Robin. Oh. The birth date on her jockey's license makes her 28 in two weeks, though it is possible that she cheated a little when she first applied for a license, claiming her age was 24. Vanity aside, there could be a good reason for that, since no one over 25 can ride as an apprentice. Anything is possible. Maybe she is 16. Maybe she is Anastasia. Who really knows anything about Robyn Caroline Smith's past except that somehow it pains her?

Despite all her historical camouflage, Robyn is usually the very model of candor. She is bold and straightforward in expressing her views and unafraid to stand by herself. She is the classic example of what a modern woman who so desires can be — free and competitive. One major contradiction of the feminist movement is that the women in its forefront seek a society based on merit, where sex is no factor, but they have become professional females themselves. Gloria Steinem is much more defined by her sex than all the Fab housewives she is fighting to save. By contrast, and without surrendering any of her femininity except perhaps a couple of unimportant inches off her bust line, Robyn Smith is the true brave new woman.

"I never think of myself as making progress on behalf of anybody but myself," she says. "I have no interest whatever in the women's movement except in the sense that I believe everybody should have the right to do what they want to do. I don't want to invade a man's world. I just want to ride horses. I'm not out to prove anything."

Yet Robyn's uncommon success has made her a symbol, whether she likes it or not. Among other things, it has caused a great many knowledgeable people in racing to speculate about a time, say within a generation or so, when a substantial minority, or even a majority, of race riders in America will be female. This theory has a persuasive socioeconomic base to it. The success and proliferation in the U.S. of Latin American riders — usually referred to around the track as "the Spanish boys" — has come about because most American men have grown too large for riding and too soft to put up with the grueling 19th-century apprenticeship which is based on the postulate that to be a good rider a boy first must become proficient in mucking out stalls. Inherent in the hypothesis that women will dominate the jockey ranks is the suggestion that American women are really a breed apart from American men — a smaller, disadvantaged race, just like the Spanish boys.

It is a very neat, plausible forecast; Robyn thinks the whole thing is so much bunk. "I don't want to talk against women," she says, "but most just cannot ride a racehorse. There's something lacking, and as far as I can tell it's a combination of both the mental and the physical thing. Mostly it's a lack of coordination, I guess. From the time I was a little teeny girl, I could always throw a baseball like a boy." To leave no room for doubt, she pantomimed at smooth overhand delivery. "But you know how most women throw." She acted out a jerky pitch. "I don't know why that is. It's the same way with riding a horse, though. Most women can't do it right.

"The trouble is that the women who generally would be best at riding are the big heavy broads who could never make the weight." She paused and thought about this for a moment. "You're just not going to find a lot of women like me," Robyn said.

You should see her now.

A SANCTUARY VIOLATED

Jerry Kirshenbaum

Arab terrorism in Munich aroused worldwide speculation as to whether the Olympics could, or should,
continue in their present form. As the gunfire
quieted, the author cabled this report from a city
in mourning.

JAMES DRAKE

The outrage could scarcely have been greater or the grief deeper, which only partially suggests the sway the Olympic Games hold on men's minds. Certainly, the awful events cast their shadow across sport. Even as rabbis within Munich's high-walled Jewish cemetery prepared the bodies of the 11 fallen Israelis for the journey home, the Olympics were resuming after a 24-hour interruption. One of the first competitions following the delay matched Rumania against Hungary in team handball, which, like murder, was new at these Games. The Rumanians won 20–14, but Nicolae Nedef, their coach, could not rejoice. "The game doesn't seem to matter so much," he said.

Similar sentiments were voiced often as the Games of the XXth Olympiad wound to their melancholy conclusion. Five years of elaborate planning by the West German people had been undone, and from this bitter irony flowed others. The Games were meant to erase memories of German militarism, yet the Olympic site was suddenly aswarm with armored cars and, surrealistically, *Polizei* in sweat suits carrying submachine guns. As in a nightmare, Jewish blood was spilled again on German soil, although this time the Germans were cast as would-be rescuers. And, in the end, a $650 million stage built for sport became instead a platform for calamity.

Calamity struck because there was no way of controlling which madmen or jesters might choose to strut out from the wings. A youth in a flowing white robe stood outside the tent-roofed Olympic Stadium holding a sign —

NO NATIONS, MANY CULTURES

— yet his brotherly message had been mocked even before the Games began when the threat of boycott by African and U.S. blacks led the International Olympic Committee to expel Rhodesia. Later, demonstrators, wielding iron bars, battled police for three days outside Munich's massive, sooty Palace of Justice in what Bavarian officials called a leftist plot to disrupt the Olympics. Finally, providing what alone would have been controversy enough at a less troubled Games, the IOC drummed Vince Matthews and Wayne Collett out of future competition — meaning the 1,600-meter relay — after they chatted and were otherwise disrespectful while *The Star-Spangled Banner* played following their one-two finish in the 400 meters on Thursday.

The IOC found the behavior of the American runners "disgusting," possibly because of the immediacy of the horror that began when Arab terrorists scaled the eight-foot fence surrounding the Olympic Village shortly before dawn the previous Tuesday. For 20 hours attention had focused on the three-story building at 31 Connollystrasse, a street named for a Connolly other than Hal or Olga — one James B., a triple jumper who in 1896 won the U.S.'s first Olympic gold medal. As cameras zeroed in on the hangmanlike visage of a terrorist moving about a balcony in a stocking mask, the idea took hold that it was not only the lives of the Israelis but somehow also the very future of the Olympics that was at stake.

Except for the grim faces of reporters and the curious who collected on the grassy slopes surrounding the village, the scene could have passed for one more well-attended Olympic event. Instead of timing races, spectators consulted their watches to keep track of each deadline extension — there were four in all — the terrorists granted. Even after news of the attack was made known, the Olympics, astonishingly, had gone on, and the organizers did not call a halt to competition until 4 p.m., almost 12 hours after the first two Olympians had been murdered.

Despite the efforts at business as usual, it was glaringly clear that sport was not immune to violence. Even such an apolitical performer as Mark Spitz suddenly was vulnerable. As a Jew and the athletic hero of the Olympics, Spitz seemed an inviting target for terrorists, a thought that occurred to U.S. Olympic officials rather late in the chronology of events. Spitz and his coaches had been permitted to leave their Olympic Village quarters unguarded and ignorant of the attack at 9 a.m. Tuesday, four hours after the guerrillas struck. Only when the Americans arrived at a press conference elsewhere on the Olympic grounds did they learn of the tragedy. "They'd just take me hostage — they wouldn't kill me, would they?" Spitz asked worriedly. Eventually, five guards were posted at Spitz' room, and he left Munich 24 hours ahead of schedule.

On Wednesday morning, when athletes were to have begun the decathlon, 80,000 people filled the stadium for a memorial service. Olympians from the U.S. and other lands, including surviving Israelis in *yarmulkes* bearing the Olympic symbol, massed on the infield. The solemn occasion was marred by the absence of Soviet athletes and by the bumbling speech of 84-year-old Avery Brundage, who was in his last days as IOC president. "The Games must go on," he thundered to great applause, and he called the murder of the Israelis one of "two savage attacks" on the Olympics, the other being the black African pressure that resulted in Rhodesia's expulsion. His coupling of the two events aroused criticism, and he later had to issue an apology, regretting "any misinterpretation" of his words. Not Brundage but the reaction of the crowd bothered Asher Lubelski, a spectator and one of Germany's remaining 32,000 Jews. "The people came not in memory of the Israelis," he said. "They came to see if the Olympics would go on."

The Israelis put their dead aboard an El Al jet which took them home on the eve of Rosh Hashanah, the Jewish New Year, but not before Joseph

Inbar, president of the Israeli Olympic Committee, said, "Enough blood has flowed to end the Games." Egypt, Kuwait and Syria, apparently fearing reprisals, dropped out, and some Norwegian and Dutch athletes left in protest. But most agreed with the Soviet long jumper, Igor Ter Ovanesian, who said, "It is terrible what happened. I don't feel like competing now. But it is good the Games continue. Terrorists should not be able to disrupt the Olympics."

The life-goes-on attitude was at once comforting and unsettling. The Olympics were canceled during both World Wars, but the Games were held despite Korea in 1952 and Hungary and Suez in 1956. In Mexico City the Games began only a few days after at least 50 students — other reports put the toll closer to 300 — were killed by government bullets during a massive political demonstration. German and IOC concern over the fate of the Israeli athletes was unquestionably genuine, but it was obvious that that worry was coupled with an almost equal concern for the fate of the Games.

In carrying on, the men who ran the Games doubtlessly feared that to do otherwise might doom the Olympic movement. As Munich wearily prepared for the closing ceremonies, a pageant in which a military band was scheduled to serenade Brundage with "For He's a Jolly Good Fellow," the 1976 Games must suddenly have seemed a dubious prize to Montreal, where one can almost imagine an Olympic Village surrounded by barbed wire and armed sentries to guard against firebombing Quebec nationalists. On the other hand, it was possible to hope that the violence in Munich was an aberration and to seek comfort in the fact that until the attack occurred, Israeli and Arab athletes had competed and lived virtually side by side.

By the weekend the Israeli quarters had become a shrine of sorts, and West German President Gustav Heinemann was among those who placed a wreath at the door. A block away dwelt the Lebanese, one Arab group that stayed on after the tragedy, a decision that Assistant Delegation Chief Emile Nassar discussed one afternoon. "We contacted the Prime Minister," said Nassar. "He advised us to do whatever the spirit of sport told us to do." Never has that spirit been more difficult to define than it was last week in Munich.

THERE HAVE BEEN SHOOTINGS IN THE NIGHT

Kenny Moore

HANS-GEORG RAUCH

**As a member of the U.S. Olympic track team,
Marathoner Kenny Moore was a near neighbor of tragic events.
This brief report of the mood in Olympic Village
was more evocative than most stories ten times its length.**

I was torpid, just out of bed, ready to jog on a humid, glaring day. The Olympic Village gate was locked. A guard, dressed in silly turquoise, said, "There have been shootings in the night. You cannot leave."

I started back to my room. On the way I met my teammate, hammer thrower George Frenn, whose parents were born in Lebanon. He told me Arab terrorists had broken into the Israeli quarters, shot two people and taken others hostage. George was seething. "I hate lunatics," he said.

I lived in an apartment on the fifth floor of the U.S. building with Frank Shorter, Steve Savage, Jon Anderson and Dave Wottle, all middle- or long-distance runners. Frank was on our terrace, staring at police lines, ambulances and newsmen assembled under cover near the Israeli dorm, 150 yards away.

"I haven't felt this way since Kennedy was killed," he said. "Imagine those poor guys over there. Every five minutes a psycho with a machine gun says, 'Let's kill 'em now,' and someone else says, 'No, let's wait a while.' How long could you stand that?"

We took turns on the terrace, plucking seeds from a fennel plant there and grinding them into our palms. Below, people played chess or Ping-Pong. The trading of Olympic pins continued. Athletes sunbathed by the reflecting pool. It seemed inappropriate, but what was one supposed to do? The scratchy, singsong notes of European police sirens sounded incessantly. Rumors leaped and died. There were 26 hostages. There were seven. The terrorists were killing a man every two hours. They were on the verge of surrender.

At 3:30 p.m. I phoned a friend in the press village.

"Have you heard?" he asked. "The Games are stopped."

"Stopped?" You mean postponed or canceled?"

"Postponed for now. But they say it may be impossible to start them again."

I went back to the room, where my wife Bobbie was waiting, and I wept. I experienced level after level of grief: for my own event, the marathon, those years of preparation now useless; for the dead and doomed Israelis; and for the violated sanctuary of the Games.

In Mexico and here the village had been a refuge, admittedly imperfect, from a larger, seedier world in which individuals and governments refused to adhere to any humane code. For two weeks every four years we direct our kind of fanaticism into the essentially absurd activities of running and swimming and being beautiful on a balance beam. Yet even in the rage of competition we keep from hurting each other, and thereby demonstrate the meaning of civilization. I shook and cried as that illusion, the strongest of my life, was shattered.

In the evening Bobbie and I walked around. We met Ron Hill, the British marathoner. Ron was agitated. "Why should this stop the Games? It's all political, isn't it? Let the police seal the thing off. The rest of the town isn't affected. I want that marathon to stay on Saturday."

"They're talking about a one-day postponement," I said. "Surely one day shouldn't matter."

"It does to me," he said.

Tom Dooley, one of our walkers, responded, "All political? Those people are just politically dead?"

Hailu Ebba, the Ethiopian, 1,500-meter runner, said, "I have led a calm life. I can't believe those people are in that building and could get killed. They could shut this whole place down. Running is not that important."

At 10 p.m. Bobbie and I decided to spend the night away from the village. On our way to the front gate, the only one where exit or entry was permitted, we met John Carlos. John, often strident, now was muted, thoughtful. He shook his head. "People were upset over what I did in 1968," he said, "but I just expressed my feelings. I didn't hurt anybody. Now what are they going to say? Can they tell the difference?"

At the gate, the guards were now admitting no one, nor permitting anyone to leave. Hoover Wright, one of our assistant coaches, and his wife were also trying to get out. We looked at each other in confusion. Someone who knew him shouted from the crowd: "Hoover, there's going to be shooting! There's going to be shooting!"

We turned to check other exits and met Lee Evans, who said it was impossible. We went back, through the rising furor, to the room.

After a few minutes Dave Wottle came in from, to our amazement, a run. "I went out the back gate," he said. He had covered a three-mile loop and returned to the rear of the village, where he found his way barred by ropes. He jumped the ropes and then the fence. "I heard some guards yelling 'halt!' but I just waved without looking. After 50 yards I came to another group of guards. One recognized me. He said, 'It's Wottle,' and they laughed." When Dave looked back, he saw five guards returning guns to their holsters. "If I had known they were so jumpy, I'd have walked around out there all night."

Then it seemed over. Anderson and Savage, who had been kept outside the main gate for an hour, came in and told how helicopters had taken terrorists and hostages to an airport. The late news said the Israelis had been rescued. We went to bed, shaken by the prolonged anxiety but relieved.

We awoke to the final horror. The first newspapers said, "Sixteen Dead."

I walked to the memorial service. Russian soccer players were practicing on a field beside the stadium. Concession stands were open, smelling of sauerkraut. The program was long-winded in four languages. The crowd applauded when Brundage said the Games would go on.

"The Games *should* go on," said Tom Dooley, "and they will. But for the wrong reasons. The Germans don't want any hitches in their organization. There are the financial considerations. Those people who applauded just want to see who will win the 5,000 and the hell with the rest."

"What are the right reasons?" I asked.

"Just one. To stay together. Who wins or loses now is ridiculously unimportant, considered against these men's deaths. But we have to stay together."

"Can we go to future Olympics, knowing this might happen again?"

He was quiet for a moment. "I don't know. Maybe Olympians will have to be like the early Christians now. We'll have to conduct our events in catacombs, in quiet forests."